A Musical Affair

A Musical Affair
A Novel

A novel about divorce, deception, love affairs, expensive secrets,
long overdue forgiveness, the power of beautiful music,
and just how Celeste, with a little help from her friends,
manages to raise over $200,000 to fund her festival.

by
Carrie Jane Knowles

Owl Canyon Press

First Edition, 2021
All Rights Reserved
Library of Congress Cataloging-in-Publication Data

Knowles, Carrie Jane
A Musical Affair —1st ed.
p. cm.

ISBN: 978-1-952085-10-9
Library of Congress Control Number: 2021933135

Owl Canyon Press
Boulder, Colorado

OTHER BOOKS BY
CARRIE JANE KNOWLES

The Last Childhood:
A Family Story of Alzheimer's
Lillian's Garden
Ashoan's Rug
A Garden Wall in Provence
Black Tie Optional:
17 Stories
A Self-guided Workbook
and Gentle Tour on How to Write
Stories From Start to Finish
The Inevitable Past

COLUMNIST
Psychology Today: Shifting Forward
psychologytoday.com/shifting-forward

2014 NORTH CAROLINA
PIEDMONT LAUREATE IN SHORT FICTION

cjanework.com

DEDICATION

To our son, Neil Barr Leiter,
who asked me to help him build a music festival,
and believed we could do it together.

To my husband, Jeff Leiter,
who never doubted for a minute
that we could make it happen.

And to Hedy and Cole,
who have never hesitated to stand and applaud
all the crazy dreams and adventures
+we've had together as a family.

"Music gives a soul to the universe, wings to the mind,
flight to the imagination and life to everything."
Plato

"That is the way with music.
It is beautiful, and then it ends until it begins again."
Franco, Director of the Tuscan
Chamber Orchestra

PART ONE
THE MONEY

Chapter One

⌘

CELESTE

The last thing Celeste had wanted to do today was to sit through yet another concert pretending she was something she was not. Nothing in her life had turned out the way she had hoped or dreamed it would.

Truth be told, what she wanted more than anything right now was to wallow in her failures, get a good night's sleep, fly back to Raleigh empty handed, and turn in her resignation as the director of the newly formed Chamber Society.

She wanted to forget about her recent divorce and this stupid job her ex-husband's lawyer, Charles Mooreton, had tricked her into taking.

She was, however, not working on her tan or packing to leave. Instead, she was sitting on a folding chair in the front row as the honored guest of someone named Franco, waiting for the music to begin.

The outdoor Piazza del Duomo adjacent to the 13th Century Duomo di San Martino in Pietrasanta began to come to life right as the last wisp of warm Tuscan sun swept across the ancient courtyard. Instead of settling in for a quiet night of drinks and dinner, the people of the town began bustling with excitement and activity. Waiters and shop owners on either side of the imposing white marble façade of the stately Romanesque Duomo left their usual workstations and flooded the piazza.

The cooks and waiters chatted and laughed as they began unloading chairs from a small flatbed truck. One by one the chairs were lined up in neat rows across the width of the piazza, facing a raised stage at the foot of the tall stone retaining wall at the end.

A stage, a few folding chairs, and suddenly a magnificent concert hall emerged where moments before there had been shops and cobblestones. As soon as the last chair was unfolded, the early evening stars began peeking through the coming dusk to provide the stage lighting.

At the top of the tall stone retaining wall, that served as the backdrop for the makeshift stage, Celeste could hear the sounds of children playing soccer.

As the newly created concert hall took shape, everyone at the bars and coffee shops hurried to finish their drinks and appetizers. When checks were paid, they left the restaurants and move out into the piazza in order to claim their seats.

The waiters, who were setting up, graciously offered a seat in the front row to Celeste. The old women of the town with their black shawls and shopping bags joined her. Then a rumble of small children pushed and tugged on each other in order to secure their rightful spots, sitting cross-legged on the ground in front of their grandmothers.

Except for the squirm and excitement of the children, the crowd whispered quietly amongst themselves and waited patiently for the musicians to arrive. Once all the seats were filled, the remaining people who had come to hear the Tuscan Chamber Orchestra took chairs outside from one of the nearby bars, found a wall to lean against, or sat under the trees lining the piazza near the stage.

The whole town was abuzz with anticipation. There had been the usual assortment of quartets and trios during the annual weeklong music festival, but this year, the final concert was presented by a young chamber orchestra that dared play without a conductor.

An orchestra without a conductor? Who had ever heard of such a thing? How was it possible?

Tickets to the final concert were the most coveted of all the festival tickets because the best group was always saved for last. However, no one now sitting in the courtyard had been able to buy tickets for the final concert. It had been a private affair for the big donors and local politicians. The handful of back row tickets that had been available to smaller donors had cost one hundred Euros each, much more than a waiter, a shopkeeper, or even Celeste could afford.

The night before, Celeste had sat at a bar with the other tourists drinking Campari and soda, watching as the piazza filled with shiny, black, chauffeured cars. Dozens of deeply tanned women, wearing jewels and swirling silk dresses, emerged from the cars and swept into the courtyard like ballerinas, while the swaggering men who accompanied them, their tailored linen jackets slung casually over their shoulders, walked in noisy clusters behind.

The expensive final event had caused quite a scandal. The Mayor and his wife arrived late for the concert and, like royalty, brazenly strutted up the stairs and down the middle aisle of the cathedral to their front row seats. Rumor had it that the orchestra had waited half an hour for them to arrive and had just started playing when the huge wooden doors of the Duomo flew open.

One of the festival organizers, a young woman, who was the daughter of the owner of the Duomo Café, told her father that Franco, the principal cellist and founder of the Tuscan Chamber Orchestra, had sworn loudly under his breath as the latecomers strode up the aisle. However, when Franco saw who it was, he stopped the orchestra and had them wait until the Mayor and his wife sat down. Once comfortably seated, the Mayor nodded his head to Franco, and the orchestra started the concert all over again.

"Disrespectful," everyone hissed when they heard the story repeated.

The general opinion of the citizens of Pietrasanta, even before the incident at the concert, was that the Mayor and his wife, his third, and twenty years younger than either of the first two, were arrogant at best.

As if the incident of the late entrance wasn't enough, when the concert was over, the rich patrons applauded politely and promptly left the Piazza in order to attend a catered reception at the Mayor's home at the top of the hill. The musicians left with them as well.

None of the rich patrons or members of the orchestra had stayed around to eat dinner or have drinks as had been anticipated by the restaurant owners and the waiters. All the cafes closed early, and everyone left feeling empty that the festival, the event they looked forward to all year, was over.

Before the bakers could open their shops the next morning and the cafes could brew their first bitter cups of espresso, a rumor had caught fire.

Franco, who, along with the other members of the orchestra, was staying at the Hotel Palagi, told the concierge that he found the pretension of the final concert and the infernal echo in the old Romanesque Duomo equally annoying. However, when he discovered that the American woman, who was whispered to be attending the festival in order to hire an ensemble to play in the United States, had not been among the invited guests, he got angry.

After the concierge finished apologizing for the bad behavior of the festival organizers, he stepped closer to Franco and told him, sotto voce, that the festival usually provided a special concert in the Piazza for the people of Pietrasanta who couldn't afford the more expensive festival tickets. But no such concert had been scheduled for this year.

Without hesitation, Franco announced that the orchestra would gladly play one more concert in the warm summer evening air for the workers in the restaurants, the people who lived in the town, and the tourists who ate their picnics of bread and cheese at the beach and who slept in the cheap hotels.

It would be a free concert for everyone who loved music: a gift from the Tuscan Chamber Orchestra. He would be especially grateful, he told the concierge, if the woman from the United States would attend.

The concierge smiled, thanked Franco, and immediately notified the other concierges as well as all the local shopkeepers, of Franco's declaration.

Within an hour everything had been arranged.

That morning, Celeste had begun to doubt her rather hasty decision to pack her bags and fly to Italy to attend the Pietrasanta Music Festival. She had come to the festival believing she could find a string quartet in order to jumpstart the now defunct Chamber Society and make her life a success.

But so far, she had not found one she loved.

When she came down for breakfast, ready to do nothing but sit in the hotel garden and enjoy the warmth of the morning sun on her face, the concierge tried to push yet another concert flyer into her hands.

"Franco told me to give this to you and to invite you to come to his concert," the concierge had announced proudly.

"Who is Franco?" Celeste asked.

"He is the leader of the brilliant new Tuscan Chamber Orchestra! They are playing another concert tonight. He wants you to be his special guest!"

"Where is this concert?"

"In the Piazza del Duomo! It will be a most spectacular concert just for you and the good people of Pietrasanta," he said proudly. "And it is free."

"I have plans," Celeste protested.

At precisely that moment, she knew without hesitation that she hated Charles Mooreton and her ex-husband, David, in equal proportions. She hated David because he had cheated on her and made her life miserable. She hated Charles because, as David's lawyer, he had managed to maneuver things in court in such a way as to leave her in rather pitiful financial straits. When the two of them had finished with her, all she had left was a slightly shopworn, older version of her plain but pretty brown haired, blue-eyed self. She was older, probably not wiser, but she still had good legs.

At the not so forgiving age of forty-two, she not only had to take a job for the first time in her life, but also had to move out of her fancy house in the tony Five Points neighborhood and move in with her mother on the less prestigious south side of town.

She needed this last day in Pietrasanta in order to relax and pull herself together, not to attend another concert, or to pretend to be the newly appointed director of the Chamber Society.

She was thinking she might indulge in an afternoon at the Alchimia della Bellezza to get a haircut and a massage, then afterwards do a little shopping and take herself out for a nice dinner. She still had some of Charles's money in her pocket. She figured he owed her something.

"No thanks," Celeste had said again, trying to move past the concierge so she could go outside to sit in the sunshine and start her day alone with a thick, dark espresso.

"It's a gift," the concierge pleaded, trying to push the flyer into Celeste's less than willing hands. "A gift for you and the people of Pietrasanta from the wonderful Tuscan Chamber Orchestra. The musicians are all young and in love with the music. You love classical music, yes? That is why you came to Pietrasanta, yes?"

"Sort of, yes, of course," Celeste responded.

"This will not be just any concert. This will be magical," the concierge announced.

"I don't believe in magic."

"Franco has asked me to invite you. You must go," the concierge urged. "You must hear the very best musicians in all of Europe! The stars will shine. Young people, old people, all the people of Pietrasanta will be crowded into the square. The moon will come out and kiss the musicians. They will play from their hearts. It will not be like the concert last night with the pompous rich people and their polite applause. You will hear laughter. You will see tears. The music will break your heart."

"I cannot live through another broken heart," Celeste protested.

"This will be the most magnificent concert of the whole festival. It is a gift to everyone who loves beautiful music. It is bad luck in Italy to turn down a gift."

Celeste wondered if there was anyone left in the world who truly loved classical music. Did anyone even care? Celeste had fallen in love with classical music when she took music appreciation in college, which was why she had even entertained Charles's unexpected offer to become the executive director of the new Chamber Society. It had all sounded so exciting the way Charles had explained it, that she would have a chance to write a new chapter in her life and make a name for herself other than Mrs. David Anderson.

"You'll go?" the concierge asked once again.

"If it's a gift," Celeste said, taking the flyer from his hand, "then I might as well go."

As the sun began to set, the orchestra members talked and laughed together as they strolled into the Piazza. The night was warm and the air sweet and heavy with the smell of summer and suntan lotion.

"No coats tonight," Franco called out to his fellow musicians.

Tuxedo jackets were quickly shed and thrown over their shoulders. The young men in the orchestra began to strut arrogantly down the center of the Piazza del Duomo imitating the Mayor who had come late to their concert the night before.

"And no starting over for the Mayor or anyone else," Franco shouted. The crowd stomped its feet and applauded.

Instrument cases were opened, white tuxedo shirtsleeves rolled back, and some of the musicians paused for a moment to fan themselves with their music. The bright Tuscan sun took its cue from the orchestra and obediently began to set, becoming a thin golden line across the red tiled roofs of the surrounding buildings.

"No ties either," Franco said, giving his black bowtie a gentle tug, pulling the soft worn silk from around his neck and stuffing it into his pants pocket.

The crowd began to build, pouring from the shops as doors were locked and businesses shuttered for the night. The noisy children, who had been playing soccer, left their game and were now leaning over the wall above the stage, their thin tan arms thrown over the cool ledge of the ancient wall. The smallest and youngest of them rested their chins on the smooth worn stones, hoping to be able to catch a glimpse of the musicians below.

Chapter Two
⌘
FRANCO

Shortly after the orchestra had packed up and the crowd left, Franco grabbed Celeste's hand and steered her through the back alleyways to a tiny, hole-in-the-wall Chinese restaurant. They were alone. The whole evening had been like a wonderful dream: Celeste sitting among the honored grandmothers, the star kissed sky, the Piazza filled with people, and the music…oh, the music!

The music had filled Celeste and left her feeling daring and more beautiful than she could ever remember feeling before, or at least more beautiful and worthy than her eighteen years of living with David had made her feel. She wanted to go dancing. She wanted to watch the moon grow heavy with the anticipation of morning. She wanted to show David and Charles and all the other people she once thought were her friends that she was someone: not just a has been, done nothing, ex-wife.

From the moment the last note of the night was sounded in the hushed square and the audience jumped to their feet in applause and appreciation, she knew she had to bring the Tuscan Chamber Orchestra to Raleigh in order to light a fire that would become the newly reborn Chamber Society. She was ready to change her life.

She wanted to make people sit up and take notice. She wanted them to fall in love with the music. She also wanted a little revenge.

The cool night air was still sweet with the taste of summer. Celeste was surprised she was eating Chinese food under the enchanting Tuscan moonlight and shamelessly flirting with a beautiful Italian man who most likely was someone else's husband. She had never cheated on David and this little bit of flirtation felt deliciously dangerous.

When she crushed open her fortune cookie, she laughed. The message inside was written in English.

"What's so funny?" Franco demanded in his slow, lilting English tinged with the singing rise and fall of his native Italian. He brushed his thick black hair from his face and shook his head a little. With his hair pushed back, Celeste could see that Franco's eyes were so dark brown they were devoid of iris or pupil, just brown, like a fresh drop of ink. Definitely sexy.

"It's in English," she said, waving the little piece of paper in the air like a flag.

"So read it," Franco said, nudging her a bit as though her fortune were all that mattered.

"It says my lucky number is three."

"What else?" he asked, grabbing at the strip of paper.

Celeste pulled her hand back in a tease, going along with the ruse that he might be interested in her, not in what she might be able to do for him. She smiled coyly, twisting the little strip of paper in her fingers again before un-rolling it as though she was pulling at a fine silk thread that would eventually unravel her clothing and reveal everything.

"It says, 'Beautiful music often rings with discord.'"

"Hindemith," Franco said, smiling.

"Who wants to listen to discord?" Celeste asked.

"Ah, but with Hindemith, there is also power, beauty and grace. Plus, a little discord."

"My audience probably prefers Bach," Celeste said.

"What about you?" Franco asked.

"Bartok. Maybe the wonderful Divertimento for String Orchestra you played this evening. The adagio was magnificent."

Franco's cell phone rang. He took it out of his jacket pocket, looked at it once, turned it over on the table and pushed it aside. Celeste guessed it was his wife, or perhaps his mistress.

"So, what's your decision?" Franco asked, taking her hand.

Franco had just proposed she hire his orchestra and bring them to the United States.

"Hmmm," Celeste teased. "Let me think."

Celeste knew, without question that Franco and his little orchestra were exactly what she needed in order to turn both the Chamber Society and her life around. Even though she'd never done anything like hiring a chamber orchestra to come to the United States to play, she had already begun to realize there were going to be problems with the logistics of hiring a whole orchestra, even if it was a small orchestra. There would be the cost of the visas, plus the expense of hiring twelve musicians, renting a concert hall, pay-ing for food and lodging, not to mention, printing, advertising and whatever a gala would cost. Good music aside, like so many other things in life, the deciding factor would inevitably be the money.

She liked Franco. He was easy to be with and not so hard to imagine sleeping with, wife or not. Still, she really didn't need a whole orchestra, not even a small chamber orchestra, nor could she probably afford one. She and Charles had not really talked about money yet.

What Charles had told her to do when he handed her a ticket and the money to go to Italy was to find a nice Italian quartet with two men, two women, the kind of group that would make everyone in the audience happy and excited.

She had taken the job along with the ticket and the money because she had wanted to feel excited again about something…anything. Her divorce had been deadening.

Franco's group was more than sexy enough to turn things around for the Chamber Society, as well as for her life. If she could convince Charles and the Board to pay the money to bring the orchestra to Raleigh, perhaps she could convince the Board to take advantage of what she'd found and do something really big: maybe a hot summer festival rather than a dragged out, same-old chamber music season.

Hell, a little music festival centered on a hot new orchestra was exactly what was needed to turn the lackluster Chamber Society into something people could get excited about. She'd show that little jerk of an ex-husband she could be someone other than his cheated on, dumped ex-wife.

"Hmmm, Celeste?" Franco cooed, stroking the back of her hand.

"I don't know," Celeste said, struggling to remember his question.

"What's to know? Don't you want to spend a little more time with me?" Franco cajoled.

With that, he swept his phone off of the table and deftly dropped it into his inside jacket pocket. With the phone gone, he turned his full attention to Celeste and let his long-tapered fingers dance across the tops of her hands until she softened, smiled, and turned her hands so their palms touched. Trouble.

"How much would the orchestra cost?" she asked.

"Not so much for you. For someone else, perhaps yes. For you and the chance to play in America? We would do it for love."

After dinner and many drinks, Franco hailed a cab for the two of them. When they got to her hotel a few minutes after midnight, he paid the driver and sent him on his way. Once in the lobby, Franco kissed Celeste gently on each cheek then turned to leave. As she watched him swing through the revolving hotel door, Celeste noticed he took the phone out of his pocket and made a call.

She wasn't sure if she was relieved Franco didn't ask to come up to her room or if she was annoyed that her one chance at an Italian fling had vanished.

Celeste had tried to talk to Franco about what it would cost to bring his orchestra to Raleigh for a week of concerts, rather than only one concert. She had tried, but he put off talking about money, saying he'd be back by ten the next morning to have coffee with her before his rehearsal. After the rehearsal, they could continue talking while he drove her to the airport.

"Business," he insisted, "is not something one should discuss late at night with a beautiful woman."

Music, however, was business, and in the case of hiring a chamber orchestra, expensive business. Very expensive.

Celeste needed to talk to Charles before Franco reappeared at ten.

Chapter Three
⌘
CHARLES

It was five o'clock in the afternoon in Raleigh, and Charles Mooreton was sitting on the edge of Jessica's bed. He picked up his silver cufflinks from the bedside table and slipped them into the French cuffs of his stiffly starched white shirt, tugging at the sleeves as he did.

"Your phone rang," Jessica said. It was not a question, but a statement.

"Sorry," Charles said.

"You didn't answer it."

"Later," he said.

"Her?" Jessica asked.

"You mean my wife, Lou Anne? It's five o'clock. She knows I'm working."

"Then why'd she call?"

"She didn't."

Jessica shook her long blond hair and got a pouty look on her face.

"Trust me, she doesn't know about you," Charles said.

Jessica rolled to his side of the bed in order to take the other cufflink out of Charles's hand and thread it through the cuff of his shirt, letting the sheet slip off her long slender body as she did so.

"Would she be angry?"

It was a ridiculous question, one that made Charles wonder why the hell he had ever hired Jessica to run his office.

"If she knew, she'd first call the newspaper in order to make sure it got ugly. I'm pretty sure she would want the whole world to know I'd screwed up. Then she'd call her daddy. Angry doesn't begin to cover what would happen next."

Jessica giggled.

Charles stood up, slapped Jessica's naked butt, and left.

Jessica hated it when he acted like he owned her.

Charles walked the six blocks back to his office, stopping by Café de los Muertos for a double espresso. Since Jessica moved to the condo, he had made it a point to walk from the courthouse downtown to his office on Glenwood, stopping at Café de los Muertos on Hargett along the way. The walk helped him clear his head. More importantly, his stop for coffee gave Jessica time to get back to the office before he did, which Charles thought made things look less suspicious. Plus, making a stop at Café de los Muertos was a surefire way to build a credible alibi as to why it always took so long for him to go from the courtroom to his office. Habits were often the best alibis.

"Hell of a case," he said to Michael as he stepped up to the counter to order.

Michael took his time tamping down the coffee grounds before he clicked the basket into the machine to run the drip.

"Who'd you get this time?" Michael asked.

Charles often came by Café de los Muertos late in the afternoon in order to brag about the settlements he'd won in court that day. Michael knew half the reason he got good tips from Charles and his other regular customers was because he took extra care with the way they liked their coffee. The other half was that he was always willing to listen to their bullshit.

"Some smartass surgeon who deserved what he got. He was banging the neighbor while his wife was out tutoring kids in a reading program at the elementary school. She tutored every Wednesday morning. And like clockwork, he visited the neighbor every Wednesday morning. I guess some doctors don't golf on their days off. That's funny, isn't it?"

"They really take Wednesdays off?" Michael asked, smiling, waiting for the coffee to finish. "I always thought that was some kind of urban legend."

Charles went on with his story. He needed to make sure Michael remembered he was there today, just in case he ever needed him as a witness in court. Besides, he wanted to finish his story: it was a good one.

"So, one day, the electricity goes out in the school and the kids get sent home early. That's when the wife comes home to find her husband's car in her neighbor's driveway. She's thinking something is wrong, so she goes over. No one answers the door, so she walks in…bingo!"

"And where's the other woman's husband?" Michael asked.

"Playing golf."

"That's funny," Michael said, handing Charles his espresso.

"I hate these guys," Charles said, easing into a seat at the counter. "They've got to be stupid cheating on their wives. You should see this surgeon's wife. A real fox, a Prada bag full of daddy's money, and smart. No way anyone in his right mind would ever cheat on her. Tall, brunette, with legs from somewhere near her tits, non-stop all the way to the floor. If you saw her, you'd never believe she'd had three kids."

"What'd she get him for?" Michael rang up the coffee and picked up the five-dollar bill Charles had slapped on the counter. The bill for his espresso was $3.75. Charles picked up his change and flipped it into the tip jar.

"Everything," Charles said chuckling. "Ought to be my middle name, don't you think? Charles Everything Mooreton. Has a nice ring to it."

"Yeah," Michael said, grabbing a rag to wipe the counter clean of coffee grounds. "Sounds like money."

As soon as Charles got back to his office, he returned Celeste's call.

"What'd you find?" Charles asked, skipping over hello.

"I know we had discussed a quartet. But we really hadn't talked about the money. There would be visas to pay for, of course, and expenses and airfare, food, lodging, plus money to pay the musicians, and other things," Celeste said.

Charles was doodling while he listened to her talk. He had never believed Celeste would actually find a quartet in Italy, but now that she had, maybe he could play the big shot and underwrite the opening concert featuring the quartet. He thought Lou Anne would love it, plus it would throw her off the scent of Jessica's new condo.

Charles began to play with some figures while Celeste waited for his response.

"Four musicians, visas, plane tickets, food and all that, along with money for the musicians, we're maybe looking at something in the budget of, let's say, $14,000 to $18,000. Twenty at the most. You agree?" He asked.

"If we brought a quartet," Celeste said.

Charles was pretty sure he was good for eighteen. Even twenty was cheaper than running an ad in the newspaper every week for his law firm, and definitely classier than late night cable TV commercials, although you could catch a lot of business that way. But he didn't want to be known as a late-night cable TV kind of divorce evangelist. He wanted to be high profile. Handle only the interesting cases: messy ones, guaranteed to get his name in the papers from time to time.

His dream divorce was representing some big shot politician. A governor would be nice, or maybe a state senator. A prominent politician was one hundred percent guaranteed frontpage news. A case like that could be dragged through the courts and the papers for days, maybe even weeks. It was advertising of the kind you couldn't buy at any price.

Celeste broke his fast rolling train of thought.

"What would you think of a really good small chamber orchestra? Young, and talented. And instead of presenting a series of concerts over the year like the Society has done in the past, we could change things up, really do something unique, in fact, out of the box big, like build a summer festival around the orchestra," Celeste paused.

"A festival?"

"Since the bulk of the cost is in the plane tickets and visas, why not take advantage of having the orchestra in town? Instead of having them do one concert to open the season, we could have them here for a week, and they could play four, maybe five concerts. Build a real summer festival around them. Do a fancy gala and a sneak preview open rehearsal. A summer festival could put the Chamber Society back on the map."

Charles liked the idea of being on the map.

"How much?" Charles asked.

"More than fourteen or even eighteen or twenty."

"How much more?" He was playing out some figures on his desk blotter. He'd had two or three good divorces lately. Hell, Celeste's divorce with David, plus the money he was paid under the table for hiding David's occasional infidelities and financial secrets was a windfall, and the one this afternoon was going to net him another tidy sum in fees plus the cash he'd make on the side for keeping a few secrets for his client. A chamber music festival could get him some great exposure. Classical music had its appeal to the money crowd.

"Well, for a weeklong festival, we'd have to pay the musicians at least $2,000 each. There are twelve musicians, so that's $24,000 just to cover their fees."

"Two thousand each? Are they all Italian?"

Charles had liked the idea of bringing a group from Italy. His wife, Lou Anne, was hot about Italy right now. Some book she'd read. All she seemed to want to talk about at home lately was going to Italy. He'd figured if they could find an Italian quartet for her to brag about, they could forgo the Italian vacation.

He didn't like taking time away from Jessica.

"They're from all over."

"Like where?" Charles asked. All over could be good. Raleigh was getting to be an international city. Not such a bad idea to look like you embraced diversity.

"Italy, of course, along with France, Spain, maybe Germany, and one of the musicians is from Brussels," Celeste answered.

France was good. Charles didn't speak French, but he knew his wines.

Lou Anne could pull out the stops at home and make a French meal for a small private affair before one of the concerts. She liked doing stuff like that, using the good china, entertaining her girlfriends. Italy would make his wife happy and everyone loved Spain. Germany always felt a little creepy to him. And Brussels? He didn't know a soul from Brussels and had never heard about their food and sure as hell had never drunk any of their wine.

"What's with this Brussels thing?"

"What thing?" Celeste asked.

"I mean, who cares about Brussels. What's there?"

"Good beer and great chocolate."

"Okay." Beer was good. But chocolate was definitely classier. Maybe instead of a sit-down dinner, Lou Anne would want to host an after-concert champagne and chocolate reception for some of his clients, their significant others, and a few close friends. He'd have Jessica print up some classy invitations and arrange to have real French champagne and Belgian chocolates flown in. Lou Anne would be in her element.

"So, you think this is a good idea? I've got your go ahead?"

"What's the bottom line?" Charles asked.

Celeste had been doing some doodling of her own. The figure she'd come up with was more like $100,000, or tops, $150,000.

"Could be as much as a hundred grand, maybe a few thousand more, which would include naming rights for you, of course. We'd make a big splash with radio, newspaper ads, flyers, posters, a nice mailing to the right people. We might even be able to do some private concert at your home if the musicians are up for it. Invite the mayor and some of the legislators. What do you think?"

He wrote the figure down then circled it with a flourish. The doodling started again: Charles Mooreton, attorney at law, Charles Mooreton, Philanthropist and Arts Advocate, Charles Mooreton, Your Advocate in Court and Raleigh's Advocate for the Arts. The Mooreton Music Festival.

"I like it," he said. "Let's go with it."

Chapter Four
⌘
JESSICA

Jessica wasn't in love with Charles, but sleeping with him had its financial perks, along with a certain amount of job security. Their little affair, of course, was a secret, and secrets, she'd learned, from being Charles's office manager, were powerful motivators.

Even after some dirt digging by a good divorce lawyer, a careful investigation by a private detective, and a court ordered full financial disclosure, most wronged wives still had *no* idea how much cash flowed through the river of their lives to their husbands' lovers. There were some secrets that were best kept, and kept tightly, and Charles was one of the best secret keepers in the business.

Charles was twenty years older than Jessica. Which made him old enough to want someone twenty years younger than he was to keep him feeling successful. He was a good investment. Jessica had carefully selected him. She knew what Charles was worth before she ever applied for the job as his office manager.

In addition to having a whispered reputation as someone who knew how to take care of things, he made money, lots of money.

More than making a lot of money, Charles wanted to be a respected pillar of the community. However, he wasn't exactly from the right family, and he wasn't polished by old money, so he decided to remedy the situation by marrying old money. He thought that Lou Anne's old money would make him old money.

But it didn't.

That whole better than thou old money thing drove him crazy.

His wife's family was a charter member of the Old Raleigh set, and no matter how much money Charles made, his money would always be new. But that didn't stop him. He drove himself to make more, have more, and be better known than his father-in-law. Jessica liked that in a man.

Lou Anne's daddy had been better than rich, and Charles knew it down to his bones. Charles's father-in-law, Buddy Chester, had been the driving force behind almost everything in town: the symphony, the art museum, the Board of Governors of the University of North Carolina, and even the Masons. Everyone loved Buddy. To top it off, Lou Anne never tired of telling Charles about her daddy and how much he loved UNC.

For his part, the greatest sin Charles had ever committed in Buddy's eyes, of course, was the fact that he graduated from Campbell Law School rather than UNC. Ever the pragmatic NC State University frat boy, Charles felt lucky he'd been accepted to Campbell at all and took the UNC slight and constant public needling from his father-in-law as permission to cheat on the old man's daughter.

Charles's own father was a retired NC State professor in the Ag School. He was a bit of a drinker and had been known on more than one occasion to drink too much at faculty parties and stand on the second-floor balcony of his faux-Colonial Cameron Park home to piss out into the night onto their front lawn.

Jessica didn't kid herself that she was Charles's first transgression. She didn't keep score, and those kinds of details didn't bother her. But she did take pride in knowing she might be his most expensive.

There were the usual gifts: a pair of sapphire earrings, a lovely turquoise necklace from their trip to Arizona for the Trial Lawyers' Convention, and a rather wonderful string of black pearls he'd picked out for her when they met that time in Hawaii. But the real prize was her most recent acquisition: the condo.

She had gone to Wake Tech Community College for an associate degree in business and knew a thing or two about investing in real estate. When she discovered one of Charles's recent clients had this tidy condo love nest he wanted to unload way below market value (and preferably for cash just like he had bought it) before his soon to be ex-wife found out about it and sued that particular girlfriend for alienation of affection, Jessica jumped on it.

Actually, she had Charles jump on it.

What she asked for one day, while Charles was lying naked in her bed preparing for court, was for him to buy the condo for her. Buying her the condo, she quietly noted, would not only help out his client, but at the same time do something nice for her. When he balked, she coolly pointed out that purchasing the condo and giving it to her would also help him.

Ever since they started sleeping together, Charles insisted she get rid of her roommates. Then he moved her into a one-bedroom apartment of her own in Cameron Village where he paid the rent. He didn't want any room-mates around. Blackmail, and how to avoid it, was forever on Charles's legal mind.

Jessica deftly argued that the condo should be in her name, not his. A steady monthly trickle of cash tied to either a one-bedroom apartment in Cameron Village, or a downtown condo, was too easy to trace and hence a bit risky. If Lou Anne ever did look into Charles's accounts, or suspect he was seeing someone, that little river of cash would be the first thing she'd wade into.

If, however, Charles took the condo off of his client's hands as part of his payment for the divorce, there would be no cash to trace. Not for the client nor for Charles. Both parties would benefit. Plus, if he put her name on the deed rather than his, no one would ever have to know or suspect anything. If Lou Anne ever had questions about Jessica owning the condo, it would be perfectly believable that she could have bought it. A well-paid office manager such as Jessica could easily afford the address.

Charles was hesitant to roll over on such a gift. Pearls were one thing, property another. But the more he thought about the condo and the compromised situation his client was in, the more he agreed. If he was no longer paying Jessica's rent, and if she owned the condo free and clear, there could be no suspicions from Lou Anne about his relationship with Jessica. Also, on the plus side, the condo was in an ideal location. If he were ever seen coming or going from her place, it would be easy to explain he was either dropping off something or picking up something on his way to or from the courtroom.

As to why he might have to drop by Jessica's place on his way to the courtroom, Charles concocted the perfect alibi. He made Jessica promise, if he arranged with his client for her to get the condo, that she would go home every day for lunch. This frugal move could easily be explained as both a way to save money and a newly found healthy eating habit.

Habits, he impressed upon Jessica, were the best alibis in the world. Plus, her healthy lunch habit guaranteed a quick afternoon pick-me-up for Charles on his way to and from the courtroom any day of the week.

Once the deed was signed and tucked away into her safe deposit box, Jessica knew she had Charles right where she wanted him. She not only had a condo, but also the perfect secret about both him and his client that would keep her gainfully employed for a long, long time.

She had never cared that much about lunch anyway.

Chapter Five
⌘
FRANCO

It was one o'clock in the morning. He came bearing gifts: a bottle of Danielle's favorite Merlot.

Franco took his time pouring a glass of wine for her.

"A beautiful color, this Merlot, no?"

"Yes, yes, a beautiful color," Danielle said impatiently. "So?"

"So, I thought we should have a taste."

"And?"

"Talk about music," Franco announced.

"Franco, it is late, and unless you have something exciting to tell me, I am going back to sleep."

"You are exciting," he said, slipping his free hand under the covers to stroke her leg.

She pushed his hand away.

"Are you going to tell me or torture me?" Danielle asked.

"Tell you what, my lovely wife?"

He handed her a hefty glass of Merlot and waited.

"To America!" Franco said, looking into her eyes and smiling.

"Yes?" Danielle shouted.

"Yes, I am almost sure."

"Almost?" Danielle asked.

"I'm thinking we should play the Vivaldi *Four Seasons*, with you as the soloist. Really blow them out of the waters. Isn't that what they say in the U.S.?"

"Almost?" Danielle asked again.

"Tomorrow morning, I know for sure, but I am pretty sure," Franco answered. "The American woman and I will meet again tomorrow morning to talk about money."

"I should come along," Danielle offered.

"After the deal is sealed."

"Franco," Danielle glared at him, half in a tease, half angry.

"There was nothing," Franco said, crossing his heart with his empty hand and kissing it. "I swear. Nothing. Just business. You can believe me this time."

Celeste had been up half the night working the numbers. She was pretty sure she had Charles on board. Given she was now talking about a festival rather than a boring music series, she thought it would be easy to get additional money to beef up the advertising from a couple corporate sponsorships. She was pretty sure, sure enough sure. But not so sure about everything that she had slept well.

Franco's call from the desk came right at ten, as he had promised. She took one last look in the bathroom mirror, checked her lipstick and worried a moment about the strapless sundress she'd chosen. She didn't look bad for her age or the little sleep she'd had during the night after her call to Charles. Her cheeks were flushed with excitement. Before leaving the room, she grabbed a sweater and threw it over her shoulders.

Franco was waiting in the lobby. He kissed her lightly on each cheek.

"Coffee?" Celeste asked.

"There's a café here in the hotel or we could go across the street and sit outside," Franco said.

"It is such a beautiful day. Let's sit outside."

Franco offered his arm and Celeste took it, crossing the busy street with him and dodging traffic as he lifted his hand like a conductor, directing pedestrians, and stopping cars.

"Madame," he said, pulling out a chair for her. Celeste smiled and took her seat. Before she could say anything, Franco raised his hand and the waiter appeared with two steaming espressos, each with a single biscuit balanced on the saucer.

"So," she said, taking a careful sip of the hot beverage.

"So?"

"So, how much does your orchestra cost?" Celeste wanted to get down to business.

Franco and Danielle had talked about it most of the night while they drank their way through the bottle of Merlot and planned what they would play.

Life would be easier for them if they had an agent, but they didn't have an agent. They ran the orchestra as a collective.

Danielle had argued that they needed to call a meeting with the other members before they could commit. Franco said they didn't have time for a meeting. Besides, to play in the United States was worth more than money for them.

"How much do you think we should cost?" he said, picking up his cup to take a sip.

Celeste had thought about it. She'd never hired an orchestra before. She'd also never paid to fly an orchestra from Europe to the States. She didn't know what she was doing but she was feeling bold and wanted to close this deal before she headed back to Raleigh.

"There are expenses involved. For instance, the plane fares," Celeste explained.

"You will pay the plane fare, yes?"

"Of course."

"And the cost of the visas?"

"Of course," she said, unwrapping the biscuit that came with her coffee. She had no idea how much the visas would be. She would check on the cost of the flights as soon as she got back.

"Good," Franco smiled. Danielle would be pleased with him that he had managed to get both the cost of the plane fares and the visas covered for all the players.

"Then, of course, there are meals and housing. I was figuring that instead of coming to play one concert, you would come for a week, play maybe four or five concerts. We could do a gala event and have an open rehearsal the afternoon before the first big concert where special guests could watch you work. The gala and the rehearsal would be a sneak preview where people could meet you. Get folks excited about the festival," Celeste explained.

"A sneak preview, an open rehearsal?" Franco was not sure what she meant.

"The sneak preview would be a special gift for all the donors. They could hear you, see you work, tell their neighbors. It would be a chance for them to meet the orchestra and then spread the word. The gala would be a fancy evening affair with drinks and hors d'oeuvres for the big donors. Our goal with the gala would be to get them personally involved and ready to write checks for another festival next year."

"Four or five concerts, a sneak peek and an open rehearsal?"

"So how much money are we talking about here for the week with your orchestra?" Celeste asked.

"What do you think?" Franco tried to dodge the question. He was still thinking about what the orchestra would say regarding an open rehearsal where people could hear them before things were perfect. Danielle had this funny thing about perfect. Plus, getting to perfect often involved an argument or two among the players. Franco wasn't sure the open rehearsal idea would fly with Danielle or any of the other orchestra members. And the gala…well, that would be open for negotiation.

"We're covering the flights, the visas, housing and meals and we're talking about having you in Raleigh for a week for four or five concerts, a gala and an open rehearsal. I could maybe pay $2,000 to each of the players."

"Two thousand each for the week, for this festival of yours?" Franco asked.

"Yes, two thousand," Celeste agreed.

"U.S.?" Franco asked hesitantly.

Celeste had forgotten the dollar was weak right now and that 1,000 Euros was, at best, $900. Maybe $2,000 wasn't enough. In the meantime, she was beginning to worry about the cost of getting the visas.

"Two thousand American dollars for each musician," Celeste said confidently.

"Four, not five concerts and the open rehearsal?" Franco asked.

"Four concerts, some music at the gala for the big donors, and an open rehearsal."

"Four concerts, the gala, plus the open rehearsal," Franco said.

"Do we have a deal?" Celeste asked.

Franco looked at his cell in order to check the time: 10:30. He had told Danielle to call the orchestra, get them together for a rehearsal. That he'd be back at two to talk with them. Celeste had an urge to snatch Franco's phone out of his hand and toss it into the street.

"Do we have a deal?" Celeste asked again.

"A deal. Yes. We have a deal," Franco said. "Sorry, I have to go to prepare for the rehearsal. I must practice, but I will pick you up this afternoon to take you to the airport, and we can talk more about it then."

With that, Franco tucked the money for the two espressos under his saucer and left.

Chapter Six
⌘
DANIELLE

Franco pulled up in front of the airport drop-off, jumped out of his car, ran around to the other side and opened Celeste's door.

"We are good?" he asked, as he helped her out of the car and pulled her carry-on luggage from the backseat of his old Peugeot.

"I need to talk with my Board," Celeste said.

"About?"

"The money, the festival, just a whole lot of things."

"And this Board will say yes?" Franco smiled as he took her hand and gave it a gentle squeeze.

"Yes, I'm sure…or at least pretty sure, but I have some work to do," Celeste warned him.

"Of course."

"They've never hired an orchestra before."

"You don't think they will like us?"

"I think they will love you. It's the money I'm worried about."

"You should not worry so much about the money. We will worry about the music. The festival is about the music!"

"Yes, but sometimes it's about the money." Celeste replied.

Franco kissed Celeste on the cheek, hopped in his car and drove away. Celeste picked up her suitcase and walked into the terminal.

She had told Franco the Board had never hired an orchestra before, but the truth was, she was the one who had never hired an orchestra before. As she made her way to her gate, she took a deep breath, crossed her fingers, and hoped she could count on Charles to come through with the money.

The traffic getting back into town was bad. Franco was almost half an hour late getting to the rehearsal.

"She's gone?" Danielle asked, putting her violin down in order to stop the rehearsal.

"Celeste?"

"Is there someone else you were needing to drive to the airport?" Danielle snipped.

Franco unfastened his case and pulled out his cello. He took out his bow and began to tighten the bow hair. He was stalling for time.

"Is there someone else?" Danielle asked.

The other members of the orchestra looked away and began tuning. They had another concert to prepare for in a neighboring town that evening, and they were anxious to get on with it.

"Not now," Franco said, forcing a smile.

Everything with Franco was not now, not later, not ever. Danielle kept quiet.

"Shall we work on the Vivaldi?" Franco said, as he shuffled through his music.

The orchestra looked at Danielle. Danielle had told them all about the conversation she and Franco had had about playing *The Four Seasons* if they went to America.

"It's for sure? We have a contract?" Danielle asked.

"Yes," Franco lied. "Why do you think it took me so long?"

Danielle had met Franco when they were students together in the Conservatoire de Paris. Danielle had not intended to fall in love with Franco. In fact, she wasn't sure she had ever intended to fall in love with anyone. Since the moment she won her first violin competition at age 12, she had only thought about having a solo career.

To top it off, she had always made it a practice not to go out with other musicians. There was enough competition in her life without adding to it by having a love affair with another musician.

But Franco was different. For one, he was a cellist. For another, he was a dreamer, and what he dreamed about was building a chamber orchestra of virtuoso players who would make music without a conductor getting in their way.

Danielle had been the star of the Conservatoire and was being groomed for a big solo career. That was, until the afternoon when Franco stopped her in the hallway right after her practice session and asked if she would consider being the concertmaster for his orchestra.

She thought it was a joke. In fact, a rather presumptuous one. Why would she want to play in his orchestra? She said no.

She said no again when he asked her the next day. And no again when he asked her the next week. And no again when he presented her with a beautiful bouquet of white roses after her next solo recital and begged her to reconsider.

She continued to say no, and Franco continued to persist in asking. Eventually, she agreed to come to one rehearsal with the hope he would stop bothering her.

"One rehearsal," she explained, "and nothing else. I will play one rehearsal with your orchestra so you can see for yourself that I am a soloist, not a concertmaster. Then I hope you will quit bugging me."

She had no intention of playing in Franco's orchestra or, for that matter, any orchestra. She had her sights set on a solo career.

That was, of course, until she attended that first rehearsal and not only fell in love with Franco, but with his chamber orchestra.

Philippe, one of the other stars of the conservatory, who Danielle had always thought was also headed for a solo career, was assistant concertmaster. Michele and Alain, both from Paris, finished out the first violins. Sophie, an extraordinary violinist from Brussels with whom Danielle had played duets during her first year at the conservatoire, was principal second. Ingrid, from Germany, and Miguel, a first-year student from Spain, finished up the seconds. Gabriella, a cellist from Avignon, shared the stand with Franco.

Manuel and Carmen, two very tall, passionate musicians from Italy made up their powerful viola section, and another Italian, Guido, a gregarious and talented musician, was their bass player.

It was an impressive lineup. Danielle had not quite imagined such a group. When she sat down and they read through Dvorak's *Serenade for Strings in E major*, she felt like she'd been hit by a tsunami of music and was drowning in the beauty of it.

Franco stopped the orchestra when they finished the Tempo de Valse and tapped his bow against his stand.

"Let's try the Valse standing up," he said.

The cellos remained seated, and the rest of the orchestra stood. On Franco's nod, the Tempo de Valse began again, and this time it was not only music, it was a dance, a waltz, with musicians and instruments swaying together to the crescendos, dancing to the warm tumble of notes.

Danielle closed her eyes as she played, riding the swell and the waves of the music as it twisted and pulsed through the room. For the first time, she felt as though she had at last arrived in the place she had been practicing for her whole life.

She could not only feel the music through her skin, down through her bones and into her soul. She could taste it.

It was sweet. It was good, and she knew she would never again find playing solo as satisfying as playing with Franco's orchestra.

The rehearsal was going well. They played through all four concerti of *The Four Seasons*. Danielle loved the piece and, more than that, loved playing the solo part with her friends supporting her. It was a great rehearsal, one full of promise.

"How many concerts will we play?" Danielle asked Franco as the orchestra packed up for the day.

"Four," he answered.

"Four? With three or four pieces for each concert!" Danielle wailed.

"We will use the concerts in America to prepare for our next season. It will be perfect."

"When did you say we would do this?"

"Next summer," Franco said.

"When next summer? June? July?" Danielle pressed.

"Let's all go out for a drink to celebrate!" Franco called out to the group.

Gabriella slipped the straps of her cello case over her shoulders and linked her arm through Franco's for a brief moment.

"I've always dreamed of playing in America!" Gabriella sang out, "Let's celebrate!"

"Let's!" Franco agreed giving a sweeping motion to the group to join them.

Danielle glared at the two of them and followed behind.

Chapter Seven

⌘

GABRIELLA

Gabriella had a secret. Normally, she had trouble keeping secrets, but this one was a good one. Plus, keeping this secret gave her a certain amount of power as well as pleasure.

Danielle might be married to Franco, but she was his lover.

Chapter Eight

⌘

MILLIE

It was impossible for Celeste to sleep on airplanes. Sleeping meant closing her eyes. When she was seven, her father had tried to teach her to swim. She really didn't want to learn to swim because she was afraid of putting her head under water. Over and over again, her father told her if she only kept her eyes open, she'd be safe.

Unfortunately, that same summer, her father ran off with another woman in the middle of the night. She never saw him again. All of which seemed to increase her fear of drowning and, to make matters worse, made her a terrible sleeper as a child and an insomniac as an adult. Her fear of sleeping was intensified by stressful situations.

Flying was stressful. Hurtling through the air over a vast body of extremely deep and probably very cold water in a crummy aluminum tube not only made no sense to Celeste, but it was about as far from any concept of safe as she could ever imagine. She hated flying even more than she hated swimming.

Her fear of flying, however, had recently been eclipsed by her fear of driving with her mother.

As the plane touched down and proceeded to bump gingerly across the tarmac to the gate, Celeste, like all the other passengers around her, turned on her cell phone. There was one voice mail.

"It's your mother," Millie's voice yelled out through the message on her phone. "I'm circling now. Pick you up at the door. Hurry up. I'm almost out of gas."

Celeste grabbed her carry-on bag from the overhead compartment and ran as fast as she could through the terminal. She was glad she had traveled light and hadn't checked any luggage. If her mother said she was almost out of gas, she was probably coasting along on fumes and would sputter to a halt at the side of the road any minute. Millie was not one to pay much attention to things like speed limits, gas gauges or warning lights.

Right when Celeste stepped out onto the sidewalk, she saw her mother come spinning around the corner. The car looked more like it was out of control than out of gas.

"Jump in," Millie yelled at Celeste as the front-right tire of her car bumped over the edge of the curb and jerked to a temporary resting place. With her left foot on the brake, Millie revved the motor with her right, grabbed her favorite Steiner 12X40 Big Horn Binoculars hanging around her neck and took a good look at Celeste as she struggled to pull the passenger seat forward in order to jam her bulging carry-on bag into the back seat of Millie's old VW beetle.

"You told me you were going to see the eye doctor about glasses while I was gone."

"Don't need glasses. I've got these if I need to see anything that's far away. These Big Horns are better than glasses, and besides, they cost me almost $300 and they work just fine. Why should I spend money for glasses?"

"It isn't safe for you to be driving around reading street signs with those hunting binoculars."

"Can you read that sign over there?" Millie pointed to a small sign about a hundred yards down the walkway at the last gate exit. The sign was far enough away that whatever was written on it looked suspiciously like the fine print on a medicine bottle.

"Of course, I can't."

"It says one dollar a bag for curb service. I rest my case. Get in."

Celeste clicked the front seat back into place and slid in. The car smelled of rotting onions and cigarettes.

"I thought you quit," Celeste said.

"I thought about quitting, did quit for one afternoon while you were gone, then I got to thinking about the fact that next month is my eighty-second birthday. I decided that at the sterling age of eighty-two I ought to be old enough to do anything I want, and what I wanted to do right then was to have a cigarette, so I did. And if I want to have another, I will. Buckle up, young lady. It's the law."

Millie jerked the steering wheel to the left and hit the gas pedal hard, cutting into the traffic like a jacked-up racecar driver.

Celeste closed her eyes and prayed.

"When we stop to get gas, how about I drive?" Celeste said as lightly and kindly as she could.

"Don't need gas," Millie announced.

"You called me and left a message saying you were running on empty."

"I exaggerated."

Celeste leaned over to check the gauge.

"It's full," said Celeste.

"Filled it up yesterday."

"Then why did you say I needed to hurry because you were running out of gas?"

"Judge Judy comes on at four. I don't want to miss it."

Celeste let it roll.

"Your car smells like cigarettes and rotting onions."

"Rotting onions, rotting onions. Let me think for a minute. Aw jeepers, that was what happened to those onions! Picked them up after I dropped you at the airport when you left town last week. I'd seen this recipe in the newspaper about onion soup. Sounded good and I wanted to try it, so I stopped at the Food Lion, the one on Lake Wheeler Road, and I guess I forgot to take them out of the car. Don't think I ever made the onion soup. I guess the onions must still be in the car. They're probably in the backseat somewhere. That's where I usually put the groceries. Damn trunk is stuck again."

"It's been stuck for years."

"That's what I said, the damn trunk is stuck, so I have to put everything in the backseat. Hope you didn't throw your luggage on top of that bag of onions."

Celeste whipped her head around to look.

Chapter Nine

⌘

CHARLES

Charles decided to drop by Jessica's condo for a quickie on his way home from the courthouse. It had been a late afternoon trial and another home run for his team. With a touch of wizardly legal skill, he had managed to make one of Lou Anne's friends, Binky Covington, the very wealthy ex-wife of Mr. Thaddeus Covington.

It was a fairly high-profile divorce and far from pretty. Charles had to work overtime to keep the whole mess out of the paper.

From the first accusations and the first retainer check to the final proceedings of this particularly nasty divorce took a little over two years of hard work. But the two years paid off with one of those rare triple-crown wins where he made the ex-wife happy, made his own wife happy, and also made a butt load of money, which always made him happy. To top it off, he really didn't like Thad Covington, the newly minted ex-husband in question. Thad was another one of those obnoxious Carolina fans and Charles was happy to see him sweat.

Thad's father was an old golfing buddy of Lou Anne's father. Consequently, Charles had been forced to spend far too many evenings listening to Thad, Thad's father, and his father-in-law, crow about the glories of being a Carolina Blue Tarheel. God, he hated it when UNC won anything.

Truth be told, he'd had a fine time this afternoon taking Thaddeus Covington to the cleaners.

Charles loved it when he won, especially when great bundles of money were involved for both him and his client. Binky's divorce was exactly the kind he treasured: messy, with heaps of denial regarding philandering on the part of the husband, lengthy settlement negotiations (which included a house in town plus one on Bald Head Island), and a truly harrowing bloodletting of a financial disclosure.

Until Charles became a divorce lawyer, he had never really had a clear notion of exactly how big and powerful big money could be.

His first ever divorce case involved a man and a woman who were both cheating and hiding assets. Better than that, each was not only willing, but also eager, to go to court to ruin the other. Fortunately, there were no children from their particular union. Unfortunately, however, there were three children from past marriages: two boys from a previous marriage of the husband and a girl from the wife's previous marriage. And, as luck would have it, the children were old enough and bold enough to think they had a stake in who got what and weren't afraid to say so.

There were also some rather ugly allegations on the daughter's part (child of the woman) that the husband in question and, perhaps his sons as well, had made some rather improper advances. Given the circumstances, the daughter was asking for financial compensation in addition to what her mother was asking for in the settlement.

Charles was hired to represent the mother and her daughter. The daughter wanted a ticket out of Raleigh and a full ride on the soon-to-be-ex's checkbook to New York University ($60,000 a year tuition plus another $20,000 for housing and food). She wanted to study acting.

The mother wanted everything, including revenge. The husband had cheated on her for years, and her response to his cheating was to find someone for herself. It was a true catfight and his legal baptism by fire.

It was his first big win.

It was also the first time he was asked to keep secrets.

That particular trial taught him everything law school had failed to even mention. There didn't seem to be a textbook or a seminar in law school on how to keep secrets and hide assets.

Though there might not have been a textbook on questionable legal practices, Charles had the forethought to keep a personal account of things on his first divorce case and all subsequent proceedings. He called it his black book of best kept secrets, and he filled in the pages as various opportunities came along. He kept the book safely locked in the top drawer of his desk in his office.

Over the years he used the book to document who was hiding what from whom along with how much they paid him in cash to keep those secrets. It was quite a collection of indiscretions and no doubt would come in handy someday. In fact, it had already proven rather useful. Like tattoos, people who got one divorce often came back for another. And, as Charles had discovered early on, it is not uncommon for individuals involved in a divorce to have skeletons they are willing to pay any price to keep buried.

Binky's messy divorce from Thaddeus Covington was a first divorce for both of them and a crushing success for Charles. Under his excellent representation, Binky received an initial tidy buyout lump sum of $100,000 so she could have a few months to reorganize her life. She also got the house in town, the beach house on Bald Head Island, a healthy alimony settlement for the next twenty years, one year of alimony for each year they had been married regardless of whether she remarried or not during that time, and of course, full custody, child support and college tuition for their only child, Emily.

In all, it was a most satisfying day and more than likely, a good one for the music festival. Charles was pretty sure after today's success in court, Binky was going to step up to be a major festival patron.

Like all nasty divorces, this one had its secrets, and it was his job as the lawyer to keep those secrets hidden. Silence, as both Charles and his clients always understood and quickly agreed, had its price.

Binky's divorce held a dandy of a secret, the disclosure of which could possibly ruin Binky if it were to get out. More than likely, if Thad found out about the secret, it would ruin Binky's chance of a favorable financial settlement, as well as custody of Emily.

Binky's secret was a clear deal breaker, which made keeping her secret and this particular win quite satisfying, as well as lucrative, for Charles.

About two months into the preliminary divorce proceedings and the inevitable mud-slinging and bare-knuckle accusations, Binky made an appointment to talk to Charles. It was time to make her confession. Like all confessions, this one started with a quietly closed door and a quick glance down the hallway to be sure no one was lurking outside who might overhear what she was about to disclose.

Guessing what might be coming next, he smiled and offered Binky a chair. Out of courtesy and curiosity, he buzzed Jessica and told her to hold all calls, which Jessica understood to mean she was not only to hold his calls, but to make sure no one bothered him or came into his office, including her.

Binky was not bad looking for a woman in her mid-forties who had put on a pound or two since leaving college. She was wearing an impeccably tailored, designer-label little black dress and a single strand of luminescent eggshell white pearls. It was the kind of carefully chosen outfit one might wear to Christ Episcopal Church on Easter Sunday morning.

The pearls were good ones, Charles was certain of it. Binky's fingernails had been recently manicured and were polished in a rather demure understated pink blush rather than her usual vampire red. The whole effect was one of chaste purity. The confession, Charles was sure, was going to be worthy of his attention.

Binky graciously cut to the chase. Before she met and married Thad Covington, chair of the Wake County Republican Party and a major spokesperson and financial backer of the Right to Life movement, Binky had had an abortion. Charles folded his hands on his desk in a thoughtful gesture, waiting for the punch line.

"I had wanted to keep the baby," Binky added.

"And?" he asked, knowing there was more to the story than just a small mistake on Binky's part.

"It was complicated."

"It generally is," Charles agreed.

"I was a student at UNC at the time. The father was a Morehead Scholar, from one of those families that bleed Carolina Blue."

"My least favorite color of blue," Charles noted.

"We were in love," Binky said.

"That's nice."

"You're not making this any easier, Charles."

"I'm just sitting here listening," he responded.

Binky unsnapped her grey patent leather Prada handbag. He pushed a box of Kleenex across his desk. Binky pulled two tissues, glared for a moment at Charles, and dabbed her eyes.

"As I was saying, I had wanted to keep the baby," Binky continued.

"And?"

"His family didn't want a baby mucking up either their son's reputation, his Morehead Scholarship, or his future."

"Your family?"

"Knew nothing about it."

"Do they know now?" Charles asked.

"No."

"Who else knows?"

"No one except him, his mother and father, me and now you."

"That's it? You've told no one else?"

"Shortly after the abortion, I started dating Thad. Given his political leanings, I decided to keep the whole mess a secret. I'm sure you can understand why."

"And you're telling me because?"

"There was some money involved," Binky explained.

"From?"

"His family. They not only paid for the abortion, they paid me off to keep the whole thing a secret."

"And his family is?"

"That's part of the secret."

"And I can't know, because?" Charles asked.

"It doesn't really matter who the family is, and it's probably better for both of us if you don't know. It was a long time ago."

"So, the issue at hand is the money they paid you to keep these secrets."

"You could say that. That, and the abortion. Abortion and most other forms of women's liberation are still an issue with Thad. If he knew, I would probably lose Emily. He would be more than happy to paint me an unfit mother. He already thinks I'm the underlying cause of all of Emily's problems."

"Where's the money now?" Charles asked, taking notes.

"It's hidden."

"And you want to keep the abortion as well as the money hidden from Thad for obvious reasons."

"Obviously," answered Binky.

"Can I ask how much?"

"It's in a Swiss account. I used some of the money to take a trip to New York for the abortion. It was spring break. I told my parents I was going to fly out of New York to Switzerland to travel with a sorority sister. After the procedure, I flew to Zurich to deposit the rest of the money in one of those hidden Swiss bank accounts. Then I flew back to school and that was that. The money felt dirty. I haven't touched it," Binky explained.

"That's more than twenty years ago. Long enough so it has grown and is probably big enough today to cause quite a stir in the financial disclosure of the divorce. In addition, the abortion could also raise some issues for Thad. Obviously, I don't want anything to jeopardize my chances of not only getting, but also keeping full custody of Emily. I have to have full custody of our daughter. Thad may be Mr. Chamber of Commerce and Mr. GOP, but he's a real prick of a husband and father."

"I'll need to know everything," Charles announced. "Or at least enough to help you keep both the abortion and the money secret. If I go through with this, I need some kind of reassurance from you that the money will stay hidden for several more years. You won't be able to touch it until the dust has settled."

"And the dust settles when?" Binky asked.

"Depends on how long it takes for Thad to remarry and have other children. Do you anticipate needing this money anytime soon?"

Binky smiled.

"That depends, Charles, on how good a divorce lawyer you really are, doesn't it?"

"Here's the deal," he said, beginning to doodle on his calendar, a bad habit of his, but one that always got his creative juices flowing. "If we try to rush things through in order to give Thad less time to find out about all this, Thad and his lawyer would most likely become suspicious and start sniffing around for some reason to look into your private affairs."

"What happens if we give him too much time to dig around? The Morehead Scholar in question was one of his fraternity brothers," Binky explained.

Charles let the new information sink in a moment.

"A close friend?" he asked.

"Usual frat brother crap. Christmas cards, reunions at the homecoming game, that kind of stuff. I wouldn't call them best friends. They don't play golf together, if that's what you're asking. They don't really have much in common."

"Politics?"

Binky hesitated. "I wouldn't say so."

Charles made some notes. The secret man was shaping up to be someone who was rich, liberal and probably prominent in politics on the other side of the fence from Thad. If he was still around, he could cause trouble.

"We're going to have to let things simmer. Drag it out a bit while we fight over all the details of your husband's philandering. We need to make this look like your standard run of the mill divorce where the aggrieved wife is only looking for a way to put her life back together after enduring twenty years of a bad marriage with a philandering husband who happens to be rich. Unfortunately, this gives Thad and his lawyer a bit more time to dig around, which means you're going to have to be a model wife for at least as long as it takes us to get to court."

"What do you mean by a model wife?" Binky asked, fingering her pearls nervously.

"If you've got something going on the side," Charles said, looking up from his notepad. "You need to get rid of him or her and do it quickly."

Now that the ink was dried on the divorce papers and Thad's lawyer had not uncovered either the abortion or the Swiss bank account, and Binky's secret-keeping cash was locked in his safe, Charles didn't care when, where or who Binky screwed.

Chapter Ten
⌘
MILLIE

Charles called Lou Anne from the courthouse with Binky's good news and let Lou Anne know he had quite a bit of paperwork to finish and file on the divorce before coming home. He told her to get takeout for the children and hire a sitter so the two of them could go out to celebrate. He had made reservations for eight o'clock at Bloomsbury Bistro, her favorite. He hinted he had a surprise for her.

Charles had been worried about how much money Celeste said they would need to hire this orchestra, but with Binky's divorce settled and a fresh flow of money coming in, as well as a tidy sum of cash for keeping Binky's secret, he was pretty sure the money for the festival was there.

He hadn't really expected Celeste to find anything interesting in Italy to salvage the lagging Chamber Society. However, a festival of the kind Celeste had proposed with this hot young chamber orchestra was turning out to be precisely what Charles needed right now. The festival was the perfect thing to distract Lou Anne from letting her suspicious mind glide over his ever-increasing late hours at work. Jessica was wonderful. Too wonderful. And Charles found himself wanting to see more of her.

Up until this point, his sweet arrangement with Jessica and their love nest had been a perfectly kept secret. Charles, however, was well aware Raleigh was a small town and not the easiest place to keep a secret from Lou Anne for long.

His latest arrangement with Jessica made him feel secure, if not a little careless at times. Jessica was not at all part of Lou Anne's circle. Jessica worked for a living and didn't do lunch. She was also too young to hang out with any of Lou Anne's crowd, so it felt fairly safe and easy to keep Jessica, if not a secret, at least in the shadows and out of the way of suspicion. Lou Anne, however, could get pretty prickly from time to time and Charles knew she periodically checked his cell phone for messages and kept a close watch on their bank and credit card accounts.

Phone calls and money were easy to hide. His many philandering divorce clients had provided him with invaluable insights over the years regarding the art of keeping affairs secret.

Charles learned quickly from his client's mistakes. He kept a separate credit card in his locked desk drawer for the sole purpose of special travel arrangements and presents for Jessica. He also gave Jessica cash on the first of each month to pay for utilities and such, so there wouldn't be a paper trail that led back to his pocket.

In addition, in order to keep Lou Anne in the dark about his present indiscretion, he called Jessica only from the office phone. If he ever needed to contact her when he was out, he tried to find a pay phone. He never used his cell to call her.

Pay phones were few and far between in Raleigh. There was, however, one conveniently located in the courthouse. It was a kind of throwback to the "right to one phone call" and all that legal stuff. In desperation, he had once used the clerk's phone in the county jail, telling the officer in charge some story about his cell phone battery dying.

Lou Anne had caught him cheating once. But it wasn't with Jessica. It was with a hot female lawyer he knew from law school. It was early in their marriage, and Lou Anne dragged Charles to a marriage counselor rather than to court, so he was spared a divorce that time. The incident, however, served as a cautionary tale for Charles and forced him to be considerably more careful.

Just as Charles was rounding the corner to Jessica's condo, Millie, Celeste's mother, stopped at the traffic light. She watched as he, looking cautiously over his shoulder, made his way to the side entrance.

Millie was curious as to why he looked over his shoulder as he approached the building. She did not like Charles. She hated the way he had treated Celeste during the divorce proceedings and was deeply suspicious about this whole Chamber Society job thing.

Millie swung her car to the curb, rolled her window down so she could get a closer look, and peered through her binoculars, catching him right before he stepped through the side entrance. She looked at her watch.

"Why would Charles Mooreton go into Park Devereux's side entrance at 4:35 in the afternoon?" she wondered out loud.

Millie pulled out a ratty Moleskin diary from her purse. Keeping notes on everything she did, or saw, was a lifelong habit of hers.

She drew a line under the last entry she had made a couple days ago: *Picked up Celeste at the airport at 3:30 pm. Made it home in time for Judge Judy.*

Under that line, she noted what she had just witnessed: *saw Charles Moore-*

ton enter Park Devereux at 4:35 on Wednesday afternoon. He was alone and looked suspicious.

"Something funny is going on," she said to herself. She picked up her binoculars in order to scan the balconies facing Dawson. She saw the curtains in a second floor end unit being drawn shut.

End unit, second floor. Curtains drawn at... She looked at her watch again. *Curtains drawn at exactly four thirty-seven.*

Millie rummaged in her handbag until she found her cell phone.

"Celeste," she yelled. She didn't trust the tiny phone. She was pretty sure it wasn't big enough to pick up the sound of her voice. Besides, there didn't look to be any kind of receiver in it. It just seemed to be all buttons and noise. Damned if she could figure out how it worked.

"Yes," Celeste said, patiently. Her mother didn't sound hurt or hurried, just loud, as usual.

"I saw that scumbag lawyer, Charles Mooreton, going into Park Devereux."

"He's the president of the Board of the fine organization for which I now work. He's my employer, not a scumbag."

"Wasn't he David's lawyer?" her mother challenged.

"Yes. He's a lawyer, and he was David's lawyer."

"Then he's a scumbag, and the fact that I caught him going into Park Devereux at precisely 4:35 in the afternoon, looking over his shoulder, I might add, as though he's up to no good, proves it."

"And you're calling me because?" Celeste asked.

"Because I'm your mother, and I thought it was important to tell you what I saw. Charles Mooreton is up to no good."

"Are you looking through your binoculars?"

"Not now. I'm calling you. Can't talk on the phone and look through the binoculars at the same time. You should know that," Millie explained.

"Are you in your car, driving?"

"I am in my car, but I'm not driving. I pulled over. Don't you know it's not safe to talk on the phone while you're driving? You don't talk on your cell phone while you're driving do you, Celeste?"

"No, Mother, I don't. Now I want you to hang up the phone right now and drive away from wherever it is you're pulled over before you get arrested."

"Arrested for what?" Millie asked.

"For spying on innocent people."

"I'm not spying, and he's not innocent. I can smell trouble. You know I can."

"Mother…"

"I'm not so sure about this chamber music thing. A chamber is a bed-room. Did you know that? Why would anyone make a society about bed-room music, classical or not? Sounds suspicious to me."

"Go home," Celeste commanded.

"I'm going," Millie said, and with that, she snapped her flip phone shut, rolled up her window and eased her old VW down the road to Earp's Sea-food to get some fresh fish heads for her cats.

Chapter Eleven
⌘
LOU ANNE

Lou Anne rummaged through her purse, found her buzzing phone, and checked the caller ID. She let it ring a couple more times before she decided to take the call. She was having lunch with Roger Matthews and didn't want to be rude, but she took the call anyway.

"Charles?" Roger asked when Lou Anne finished talking and finally hung up.

"Charles has made reservations for dinner tonight at Bloomsbury Bistro. Says he has a surprise for me," Lou Anne said.

"What kind of surprise?" Roger teased, running his hand along the side of her thigh underneath the table. Lou Anne still looked as trim and fit as she had when she was at Carolina. The only thing that told her age were the small lines at the corners of her eyes and the few threads of grey you could see in her hair when the sunlight caught it just right. She not only looked good for a forty-year-old woman; she was classy. Definitely classy.

"Not here," Lou Anne said, pushing away his hand.

Roger and Lou Anne were having lunch at Iris, the restaurant in the NC Museum of Art. It was only lunch. Nothing more. Lou Anne had been careful to tell Charles not once, but twice, that she and Roger were having lunch together in order to discuss the upcoming fundraising campaign for the Museum. She wanted everything strictly on the up and up. There was nothing to it. They were two old college buddies, who were now both members of the Museum Board of Directors, meeting about the upcoming annual Art of the Auction fundraiser.

Roger was co-chair of the event and had called Lou Anne earlier in the week to ask her to join him for lunch at the Museum. He said he was hoping to woo her into agreeing to head up the effort to find corporate sponsors for the event. Lou Anne quickly agreed, thinking it might be nice, for a change, to do something other than chauffeur her two children around.

"If not here, then where? If not now, then when?" Roger asked as he let his fingers trail away from her thigh. He couldn't believe how beautiful she was still. Lou Anne, perfect Lou Anne with her strawberry blond hair and her long dancing legs. What in the world was a fox like Lou Anne doing with a short, balding guy like Charles? Nothing about her had faded over the years.

"I thought this meeting was about helping you find corporate sponsors," Lou Anne said, straightening her napkin as though it could protect her from another one of Roger's advances.

"Not sex?" Roger teased.

"No, money."

"You drive me crazy when you talk dirty," Roger whispered.

Lou Anne once again smoothed the napkin on her lap, brushing his hand away.

"You're not making this easy for me," she said.

"Why should I make it easy?" he asked.

"Because we grew up in the same neighborhood, went to high school and college together. Our parents know each other," Lou Anne said.

"Just the other day your father told my father that he thinks your husband is a..."

"Don't go there," Lou Anne warned.

"I was going to say lawyer. Your father thinks your husband is a lawyer."

"Liar," Lou Anne said.

"So, why didn't you go out with me when we were at Carolina? Was I such a loser?"

"You dumped my best friend, Binky, remember?" Lou Anne reminded him.

"You didn't go out with me because you were being loyal to Binky?" Roger asked.

"I've always thought friendship was stronger than a one-night stand."

"Who was talking about a one-night stand?"

"There were rumors," Lou Anne said.

"What about the rumors about Charles?" Roger asked.

"Charles and I have two children and are happily married."

"Which is why you said you'd meet me for lunch, right?"

"I agreed to meet you because you said you'd like to talk to me about helping you with the fundraising event," explained Lou Anne.

"Thought it might make it easier for the two of us to see each other more often. Get to know each other better, and all that."

"Because your wife wouldn't mind if we worked together, right?"

"My wife wouldn't mind if I took a trip to the moon with a harem of blond teenage girls. Well, maybe she might mind the blond girl thing. She left me. How do I say it delicately? For another woman."

"I hadn't heard," Lou Anne said.

"The rumor mill has gotten that rusty? I thought for sure Binky might be the first to hear and blast it all over Raleigh."

"She's been busy with her divorce from Thaddeus. Besides, you hurt Binky."

"There were circumstances," Roger said, picking up his glass of Bordeaux and taking a big swig.

"That's what men always say when they dump some woman," Lou Anne said.

"Binky and Thad are getting divorced?"

"Got," Lou Anne corrected. "Charles was her lawyer. It went through this afternoon."

"Bet that was ugly."

"Charles and I never discuss his clients. Raleigh is a pretty small town. Another reason to keep this meeting strictly business."

"Strictly business?" Roger pressed his hand against the side of her leg.

"I agreed to have lunch because I am interested in your offer to head up the corporate gifts part of the fundraiser," Lou Anne said.

"I had hoped you would be intrigued," Roger said. "But, please understand, bottom line is that I'm interested in an affair, not a fundraiser."

Lou Anne thought it best to say nothing and keep her options with Roger open.

Chapter Twelve
⌘
JESSICA

Charles called from the courthouse to let Jessica know she needed to get the paperwork ready to close the Covington case.

"A good day?" Jessica asked.

"Amazing," Charles responded. "Thaddeus actually broke out in a sweat when it was all over. I loved it."

"You're the best," Jessica said, opening his right-hand desk drawer and fishing for the envelope that held Charles's desk key.

"Love it when you talk dirty!" Charles crowed. "Got some loose ends to tie up at the courthouse. What say I come by for a visit on my way back to the office before I go home?"

"Almost done here. I can be at my condo in fifteen." Jessica said.

When she hung up, Jessica unlocked Charles's top desk drawer. Now that the divorce between Binky and Thaddeus Covington was finalized, it was time for Jessica to check the black book for secrets. Charles had long ago forgotten he had once indulged in a drunken bragging session about his secret keeping business. He had no idea that Jessica knew where he kept his black book or the key to his top drawer.

She never looked in the book before a divorce was finalized. She felt that kind of snooping was bad luck as well as bad manners.

It didn't take her long to find Binky's entry. It was the last one in the book.

Jessica turned on the copy machine and began printing some additional pages for her own little file of secrets.

Chapter Thirteen
⌘
CELESTE

Celeste was hunched over her desk idly doodling on a scrap of paper. Math was not her strong point. Neither was following directions. She had been trying all day to puzzle through the confounded City of Raleigh Arts Commission grant application. The only section she'd completely understood and had been able to fill in so far was the place where she wrote that she needed the money to bring an orchestra from Europe in order to create a summer music festival. Beyond that one bold statement, she didn't have a clue about what else she was supposed to say or needed to do in order to fill out the application and get the money she needed. It was a mystery to her.

Franco had verbally agreed that the orchestra was coming. She didn't have a signed contract, a venue, or know how to build an audience or an artistic direction for the Chamber Society.

Unfortunately, she wasn't even sure how much the whole damn thing was going to cost.

As the day and the task dragged on, it was slowly dawning on Celeste that, beyond dressing up and writing checks for charity fundraisers, she really didn't have any idea how to run a music festival or a non-profit. She had always been a worker bee before. She had never had the confidence to be queen.

She had this nagging suspicion that Charles was fairly certain she didn't have the skills to be the director of anything. She was also fairly sure that he had hired her in order to keep her from digging back into the lousy divorce settlement she had gotten.

Why else would Charles have insisted she be hired? Surely not guilt. She sincerely doubted he had ever felt a flicker of guilt for anything he had done either in or out of court.

Whatever David and Charles were up to, she wasn't about to let them win this round and make her look like a fool. She picked up the application and read through it once again, searching for any place where she knew the answer or at least knew enough to make it up.

Unfortunately, all that wonderful dreaming she had done in Italy about how she was going to show David and Charles exactly what she was made of, had been shaken out of her this morning when she had gotten up early, got dressed and went downtown for the mandatory 8 am meeting of potential grantees with the City of Raleigh Arts Commission. Morning was not her glory.

"Shit!" Celeste banged her hand on the table.

"Watch your mouth young lady," Millie shouted from the kitchen.

"You say shit all the time, Mother. Just the other day I heard you say 'Shit,' no—shout 'Shit,' at the top of your lungs. You were outside on the sidewalk, and I was sitting right here working, and I heard you say 'Shit.' I'm sure the neighbors heard it as well."

"Of course, I said shit. I had accidently jammed my house key into the door lock on my car and it got stuck," explained Millie.

"You need to get glasses."

"Got my binoculars."

"A lot of good binoculars are going to do you when you're trying to fig-ure out which key is your car key, and which one is your house key."

"Since you don't have anything nice to say to me, and you seem to be oth-erwise occupied with shouting profanity and banging your hand on the table, I think I'll go out and buy some more fish heads for the cats."

"Please go. I have work to do," said Celeste.

"I thought you wanted this job."

"I didn't want this job or any job for that matter. I was perfectly happy being married and going out to lunch, remember?"

"David was an asshole," Millie added.

"Can't argue with that. However, that doesn't change the fact that I was perfectly happy being married, I didn't say being married to David, but being married, writing checks to charities, eating lunch with friends. I was good at that."

"Not to mention living in that big hideous house of bad taste."

"That house of bad taste as you call it, was most recently redone by one of the finest interior designers in the state. Lorenzo Montrose had a two-page spread in Architectural Digest featuring our living room."

"That wasn't all he spread," commented Millie.

"It's such a pleasure living with you, Mother."

"I hate it when you call me Mother."

"Would you prefer I call you Millie?"

"'Her Majesty' will be fine for the moment."

Chapter Fourteen
⌘
CHARLES AND LOU ANNE

"So, what's the surprise?"

Lou Anne took a small sip of her wine. They'd finished their soup and were waiting for the main course to arrive.

"How about a music festival?" Charles offered.

"The Aspen Music Festival? You know how much I've been wanting to go!"

"Guess again," he said.

"Tanglewood?"

"Closer to home."

"Spoleto?"

"Closer."

"Where?" Lou Anne asked.

"Here."

"What on earth are you talking about?"

"I'm not going to take you to a music festival. I'm going to GIVE you one. It's my gift to you for being such a wonderful wife," he explained.

"People don't give other people music festivals. They take them to music festivals. What are you thinking of?"

"I was thinking this has been a good year for me, I mean, for us. Plus, I've had a couple of really lucrative divorce cases recently."

"Binky called me this afternoon. Sounded like she'd been celebrating ever since she stepped out of the courtroom, like she got what she wanted and some things she didn't even realize she wanted."

"It was a good day," Charles said, inhaling a rather large mouthful of his bourbon. "A very good day. Good enough with what I've made from some other cases this year to buy my own, I mean our own, music festival. You like classical music, don't you?"

"How much?" Lou Anne asked.

"How much what?"

"How much money are we talking about here?"

It always surprised Charles how old money never talked about their own money but felt like they had some God given right to ask anyone and everyone else about theirs.

"Enough," he replied coolly.

"Ten grand? Twenty?" Lou Anne prodded.

"Enough to hire a hot new orchestra from Europe," Charles replied, tapping his middle finger on the rim of his glass.

"A hot new orchestra?" Lou Anne laughed.

"Chamber orchestra. The Tuscan Chamber Orchestra. Tuscan, referring to Tuscany, Italy."

"I know where Tuscany is," Lou Anne snapped.

"Aren't you impressed?" Charles asked.

"Where, exactly, did you find this orchestra? And, please don't tell me they are only going to cost ten grand. I'm not that stupid."

Lou Anne pulled the paper cocktail napkin out from under her wine glass and began rummaging in her purse looking for a ballpoint pen and a pair of reading glasses.

"Celeste found them."

"Where in h-e-double-l did Celeste find them, and why in the world do you believe they are any good, or that you, Charles Mooreton, could build a music festival?"

"I'm not building the music festival. Celeste is. It was her idea. She found them in Italy. I thought you liked Italy. Haven't you been reading some book or the other about going to Italy?"

"The name of the book is *Eat, Pray, Love,* and it's not about going to Italy so much as it is about finding yourself. Which has nothing to do with anything we are talking about. By the way, how much are we talking about? And why would you believe anything that Celeste has to say?" Lou Anne was peering over her reading glasses with pen in hand, ready to start making calculations.

"Celeste is the new executive director of the Chamber Society. She's going to bring it back to life. I'm sure I told you and pretty sure Binky and the rest of your girlfriends have discussed it at length over lunch."

"I believe you represented her ex, not her, and she didn't get much of anything in her divorce and, therefore, had to move in with her mother and find a job to support herself, poor thing," Lou Anne said.

"Celeste is hardly a poor thing, and I think she's quite happy to have the chance to do something exciting with her life, like create a festival. I think it's rather innovative of her, to tell you the truth. Right after we hired her, we sent her to Italy to look for some fresh new talent for the upcoming season of the newly formed Chamber Society. That's where she found this orchestra," Charles explained.

"People don't find orchestras, Charles."

"Celeste *found* this orchestra at a music festival in Pietrasanta. We were really looking for a quartet, but this orchestra was so good Celeste thought we could cover the cost of bringing the musicians here if we had them for a week, instead of only one concert. She came up with this brilliant idea to build a festival around them. Celeste is really quite good at what she's doing, and I'm happy to have an executive director on board who can get excited about rebooting the Chamber Society. There's a lot of untapped potential for mounting a summer festival rather than just restarting the same old thing. Celeste is quite the visionary."

"How much are we talking about? Thirty? Forty thousand?"

"I'm not fronting all of it. Celeste thought…"

"How much did Celeste think?" Lou Anne asked.

"Ninety, maybe a hundred, but, like I said, there's some real potential here, and we ought to take advantage of it."

"Celeste's asking for a hundred thousand for a festival with some orchestra she heard once in Italy. Is that what you're telling me?"

Charles motioned for the waiter to bring him another bourbon. Lou Anne covered his glass with her hand, looked at the waiter and shook her head no. The waiter stepped away from the bar and walked into the kitchen to get their food.

"I'll drink what I want when I want it," Charles snapped.

"Oh, look," Lou Anne said, changing the subject. "Here's our food. I'm hungry, aren't you, Charles?"

"Thanks," Charles said as the waiter put his plate in front of him.

"You were talking about a music festival," Lou Anne said, cutting a small bite of her lamb chop.

"Celeste thought a summer festival, rather than a boring series of concerts that dragged through the year, would be a great way to revive the Chamber Society," he said.

"Since the Chamber Society has been dead for two years, it could use some new life, that's for sure. But an orchestra?" Lou Anne asked, smiling.

"The Tuscan Chamber Orchestra."

"Right, from Tuscany, in Italy, I believe you said."

Charles detested it when Lou Anne was smug and repetitive and in control.

"I have the money, and I plan to spend it on the festival. A festival is a much better advertising investment than late night television ads," he added.

"You're planning to put your name on it?"

"I'd thought about it," he said, coyly.

"I'm so glad you had a good day in court today with Binky and all. It's really wonderful news. I had lunch this afternoon with Roger."

"Roger?" Charles had let his mind drift to Jessica's bed, and he couldn't for the life of him remember anyone named Roger.

"Roger, Roger Matthews. We're on the fundraising committee for the NCMA. Remember?"

"Of course, Roger Matthews, how could I forget all those perfect teeth? UNC, right?"

Lou Anne ignored the UNC thing.

"Roger and I agreed that I should take on the task of finding corporate sponsors, and he'll handle the rest."

"You'd be good at that," Charles said, chewing on a fatty piece of steak, thinking about ordering a bottle of red wine to go with the meal. "Should we order a bottle of Shiraz?"

Lou Anne drained her last bit of Chardonnay. She preferred white to red, but she needed to make peace.

"I do believe Shiraz would be perfect with my lamb," she said.

He nodded to the waiter and ordered the wine. While the waiter poured a taste so Charles could approve the wine, Lou Anne charged on.

"Like I was saying, Roger and I decided I would handle the corporate fundraising, and he'd do the private big donor stuff," Lou Anne explained.

Charles took one sip, nodded his head, then held his glass steady so the waiter could fill it to the top.

"Corporate fundraising?" Charles asked.

"Like I did for the Junior League Fling a couple of years ago."

He swallowed hard, remembering how that particular project of Lou Anne's had cost him about ten thousand.

"A toast," Lou Anne said, "to Binky's divorce."

Charles didn't like how this conversation had taken such a sudden left turn to Binky's divorce. He was scrambling to keep up.

"To Binky," he said.

"And to Charles," she added.

"That's kind of you," he said quietly, waiting for the other shoe drop.

"No need for modesty. Binky said you did a spectacular job. Must have been some settlement. Binky can be pretty high maintenance. How's your meal?" she asked.

Charles took another bite of steak, chewed quickly, and washed it down with his wine.

"Good enough," he said, smiling.

"You know how this corporate thing works," Lou Anne said, cutting her lamb chop into bite-size pieces. "It's a little like rolling a snowball down a hill. Got to scoop up that first donor to get things rolling. And, the bigger the first donor, the bigger the ball is going to be when it gets to the bottom of the hill. Money begets money. Right, Charles?"

Charles refilled his wine glass.

"I was thinking it would be really wonderful if you could start that ball rolling for me. You and Binky that is," Lou Anne said, taking another nibble of her lamb. "How's your steak?"

"How much?" Charles asked.

"How much were you planning to spend on your festival?" asked Lou Anne.

"Our festival," he corrected.

"Yours, ours, whatever. How much?"

"I don't know for sure yet," he said weakly.

"Well, let's talk about it. I'm thinking that instead of spending all that money on your festival, you should give half of that money to me for my fundraiser. Fifty-fifty seems fair. What do you think?"

"Ten," Charles offered.

Lou Anne shook her head and took another bite of her lamb.

"I'm thinking you would write a check to me for something more like forty," she said.

"No way," Charles spit, almost choking on his wine.

"Didn't you say something about eighty thousand? Maybe even a hundred? I thought I was being generous with an offer of forty as my part of the split."

"That's what the festival will cost, not what I'm planning to pay," Charles corrected.

"Bottom line," Lou Anne said.

Charles knew if he told her he was going to put up sixty, she'd want thirty. It would make him crazy to give Lou Anne thirty thousand dollars.

"Fifty-fifty?" Charles asked.

"Fifty-fifty."

"I was thinking of putting up forty. So, if we're playing 50-50, you get twenty, and the festival gets twenty."

"To Binky," Lou Anne said, again. "Dessert?"

Chapter Fifteen
⌘
CHARLES AND CELESTE

Charles begged off after dinner, telling Lou Anne he needed to swing by the office in order to finish up a few things. For once it was the truth. He needed to call Celeste.

Celeste picked up on the first ring.

"How's it going?" she asked, as though she knew all about Binky's trial and had been sitting around waiting for Charles to call, which she did and had been. Even though she was out of the loop with Binky and her crowd since her own divorce, the grapevine was both fierce and reliable. An old acquaintance had called her with the news. Binky's settlement was the buzz of the afternoon, and Celeste had been waiting to hear how the festival might benefit.

"I'm calling about the money for the festival," Charles said. Tell the truth and tell it fast was his motto. He needed to get this out and move on.

"How much?" she asked, hoping he had a nice round figure. Something she could plug into one of the budget lines on the grant request in order to make sense of what to do next, and how much to ask for from the Arts Commission.

"Should have a check to you by the end of the week," Charles said.

"Great!" Celeste walked to the kitchen table, picked up a pencil and pushed the grant application aside. Maybe she wouldn't even have to write a grant. Maybe Charles was going to offer to write a check for the whole thing. She held her breath.

"Lou Anne and I are delighted to be able to kick in $20,000 to start the ball rolling for the festival."

"Rolling?" she blurted.

"That's how this kind of things works. Hook that first big donor, get that snowball rolling down the hill, and other donors will jump on board."

"But I thought…" Celeste started.

"That's why we hired you. Knew you were good at this kind of thing.

Know you won't let us down. Jessica will have the check ready for you by Friday."

With that, Charles hung up. He was anxious to get to Jessica's where he could at last unwind and relax.

Chapter Sixteen
⌘
FRANCO AND GABRIELLA

When he left the house after dinner, Franco told Danielle he had a freelance recording job and wouldn't be back until after midnight. Telling the truth was easy. He did have a recording job, but the session didn't start until nine. There was plenty of time.

He rang Gabriella's buzzer.

"Ola!" she sang out over the intercom as she let him in.

"Hey," he said as he slipped in the door and grabbed a soft handful of her bare ass. Gabriella eased the straps of his cello case off his shoulders and nudged his instrument into the corner in the hallway.

"Coffee?" she asked, her hands sassy on her hips.

"Coffee *after* would be great," he said, shrugging off his coat. "Some caffeine could help get me up for the session."

"So, let's get it up," she teased.

Sex with Gabriella was uncomplicated. Franco loved it.

He loved Danielle, but she was complicated. She was driven. She was also a better musician than he was. In fact, she was a better musician than anyone else in the Tuscan Chamber Orchestra. There was no question about it. Danielle could have easily had a solo career but chose, instead, to be his concertmaster and his wife. With Danielle as concertmaster, he had big dreams for the Tuscan Chamber Orchestra.

However, if Danielle knew he was fooling around again, she might threaten to leave him as well as the orchestra. It would be the worst possible outcome for both of his worlds.

Things were tense at home. Danielle was starting to make new demands on him. She wanted him to promise he'd never cheat on her again. She wanted children.

He was happy being married, but children were another matter. Children would definitely complicate his life.

He didn't think Danielle knew about Gabriella. He also didn't think he needed to mention to Danielle that Gabriella would be at the recording session with him today.

Gabriella pulled Franco's sweater up over his head and started unbuttoning his shirt. She leaned over and blew a kiss in his ear.

"You think too much Franco. Relax," she whispered.

He laughed, pushing her hands away so he could take off his shirt. Right now, he didn't want to think about anything, and he didn't want to talk about Danielle.

Before he managed to slip off his pants, Franco's phone buzzed.

Chapter Seventeen
⌘
CELESTE

Even though she had eaten only three donuts and drunk five very bad cups of lukewarm black coffee during the grants conference in the morning and nothing else the rest of the day, Celeste had started some serious drinking the moment she'd hung up with Charles.

Twenty thousand. She'd written the number down on a blank piece of paper. Once she had started working on the grant proposal and had added up the various items they had asked her to account for, she realized she needed at least $200,000 to build the festival. Charles's twenty thousand wasn't even enough to cover her salary for the year.

She stared at the unfinished paperwork on her desk. She seriously doubted the Arts Commission was going to roll over and give her $180,000 to cover the rest of the expenses for the festival. She vaguely remembered something they had said in the meeting about the grants only covering, at most, twenty percent of the operating budget of an ongoing, well established organization or event. Twenty percent of $200,000 was $40,000. That plus Charles's $20,000 made $60,000, leaving her $120,000 short.

When Celeste asked about the festival's chance of getting the full twenty percent, the Arts director kindly pointed out that the newly resurrected Chamber Society, as Celeste had envisioned it as a festival rather than a concert season, was no longer an old established organization that could use the past to predict the future. Instead, it was something new and bold that, unfortunately, did not qualify for the twenty percent.

The festival, however, was eligible for some seed grant money.

Celeste had no idea what seed money was and didn't have the courage to ask how big the seed might be. She suspected, since seeds were small, that seed grant money wasn't much.

She was doomed.

The grant application budget page was daunting. She had never before had to make a budget for anything. When she was married to David, there was always enough money for whatever she wanted.

She decided she had to break down the budget before she could build it up, so she began drinking and working in earnest in order to figure out exactly how much this damn festival was going to cost. After she poured herself a third stiff gin and tonic, she made a list.

She would tackle the big-ticket items first.

Twelve musicians at $2,000 each equaled $24,000. The math was simple. Next big item: the plane tickets.

She would have to buy twelve round trip tickets. When she wrote down the dates of the festival, the first real moment of reckoning hit. Franco had proposed they do the festival in July. Celeste had agreed. When they set the date, July sounded far away and doable. At that far away moment, Celeste had not even considered the fact that July would be the height of the tourist season, and therefore, the most expensive time for her to fly an orchestra from Italy to Raleigh, North Carolina.

After half an hour of looking for plane fares on the Internet, it became all too apparent that tickets in February between Italy and Raleigh would be much cheaper than the same tickets the first week of July.

Why did she think a festival in July was the right idea? Why not February? She took a long pull on her gin and tonic. She was determined to move on and try to work with what she had.

Once she plugged in times, dates and such on Travelocity, she found the cheapest plane tickets available were $1,760.91 per person. She couldn't believe it, and furthermore, couldn't believe she didn't even think about the cost of the plane tickets and checking with Travelocity when she first approached Franco and Charles and proposed this crazy festival.

There had to be something cheaper. Maybe with twelve tickets she could get some kind of a group discount? She called American Airlines.

When she finally got through to the woman in charge of group sales, Celeste told her she would need twelve round trip tickets from Tuscany to Raleigh during the first week in July. Twelve people. Four first violins, three second violins, two violas, two cellos, and one bass. The agent found the same price she had found through Travelocity and told her what she already knew: twelve tickets at $1,760.91 each would cost her $21,130.92. She informed Celeste that a group was defined as twenty or more.

When Celeste whined about the price, the agent calmly informed her that July was the height of the tourist season and that $1,760.91 wasn't such a bad deal. Celeste finished what was left in her glass and mixed another drink while she was still on the phone. The plane tickets alone were going to cost her more than the $20,000 Charles was willing to pay. Right when she was starting to hang up, the ticketing agent stopped her.

"I believe you'll need fifteen tickets, not twelve," the agent informed her.

"I can do the math," Celeste said, "if I have twelve musicians to fly from Italy to North Carolina, I believe I will need twelve tickets."

"Count again," the ticketing agent said. "You have twelve musicians, including two cellos and a bass. Correct?"

"So?"

"Twelve musicians plus seats for three large instruments makes 15 tickets."

Celeste wanted to throw her phone on the floor and stomp it to death. Fifteen roundtrip tickets at $1,760.91 a ticket was going to cost her $26,413.65!

Before the plane even took off, Celeste would have spent Charles's $20,000 and was already $6,413.65 in the hole.

Celeste thanked the agent for the information regarding the additional tickets, hung up and began working on the list for the grant. In addition to the plane tickets, she needed to pay for meals, housing, ground transportation, visas, concert hall rental, advertising, postcards, postage, posters, and programs, not to mention money to pay the musicians as well as her own salary. Maybe she wouldn't take a salary. She was sure there were other things to pay for that she either hadn't thought of or couldn't even imagine. So far, the business of running a non-profit had been quite an eye opener and she hadn't even gotten to the point of selling the first concert ticket or taking the first curtain call.

Celeste wondered if Franco and the other musicians would be willing to accept $1,000 to play a festival in the United States rather than $2,000. Didn't he say that they were so excited to play a festival in the U.S. that they would do it for love?

She didn't have any idea how in the world she was going to raise the rest of the money.

She needed to talk to Franco.

"Excuse me," Franco said to Gabriella, pulling his sweater back over his head and slipping his arms into the sleeves before taking his phone from his pocket. Gabriella hooked her fingers into his belt loops and started to follow him as he answered the call. When Franco looked at his phone and realized it was Celeste who had called him, he pushed Gabriella's hands away and opened her balcony door. A chilly wind blew through the apartment.

Gabriella feigned a pout, then went into her bedroom to throw on a robe. She sat on the edge of the bed waiting.

"Hello," Franco said.

"Hope I'm not interrupting anything," Celeste said.

"No, no not at all," Franco reassured her.

"Are we wedded to a July festival? Or could we move it to, let's say, October? Or, maybe February?"

"There is a problem?" Franco asked.

"No, no problem, I was just thinking..."

"But you said July," Franco reminded her.

"Yes, of course, July."

"We are all ready for July. July is good for us."

"Good. And, if we needed to move it to October?"

"No good," Franco said, getting worried.

"February?"

"We have contracts. Concerts we've promised to do. Plus, you want us for a week. That is a long time."

"Yes, a week is a long time," Celeste agreed.

"So, we need to come in July. July is perfect."

"Perfect," Celeste echoed.

"So, it's July? Like you promised?"

Celeste hadn't remembered exactly what she had promised or if she had really promised anything. Nothing, so far, was in writing.

"July it is," Celeste said.

"And we have the $2,000 for each of the musicians?"

"Yes, $2,000 for each musician."

"It is exciting, coming to America to play for you," Franco said.

"Yes, very exciting," echoed Celeste.

Chapter Eighteen
⌘
MILLIE

When Millie got home later that evening to feed the cats, Celeste was gone. She had left a note saying she needed to go out and would be home late. There was an empty gin bottle in the recycling bin.

The three cats were mewing, howling and circling Millie's legs as she struggled to get the fish heads unwrapped and into the cat's bowls.

Millie had to lock Matilda into the bathroom in order to feed her. Given the option, Matilda would happily eat every morsel of food Millie put out for all three of her cats. Eleanor and Sebastian would starve if Millie didn't feed them separately. Fortunately, the other two cats were relatively well behaved and were fully capable of sharing a bowl without a fight.

"Patience, my dear Matilda, is a virtue. You could use a little virtue, not to mention a diet. Getting a bit plump there, my girl," Millie said as she pulled the fish heads free of their wrapping.

Matilda leaned against Millie's legs and let out a howl, nearly knocking the fish heads out of her hands and onto the floor.

"One for you and two for the others. You'll get yours as soon as I can put it into the bowl. Now, go into bathroom if you want to eat."

Matilda plopped down on top of Millie's feet, refusing to budge.

"Now, Matilda," Millie said, wiggling her feet free of the cat, "you know you can't eat out here with the others. You eat in the bathroom by yourself. Remember?"

Matilda, reluctantly but obediently, followed Millie into the bathroom.

"Remember to eat slowly," Millie admonished Matilda as she shut the door and turned her attention to Sebastian and Eleanor.

"Here you go, my dears," she said, putting their communal bowl on the floor in the kitchen. The two cats moved together to the bowl, purring as they started eating.

"I remember something," Millie muttered to herself. "Something funny about Park Devereux."

She wadded up the paper the fish heads had been wrapped in, stuffed it in the trash and grabbed her tattered Moleskin notebook out of her purse.

"Where is it?" Millie asked herself.

She couldn't find what she was looking for, so she started going through the pages slowly, from back to front, one at a time, trying to remember what it was that she had forgotten.

"Where is it?" she shouted.

Sebastian and Eleanor looked up from their shared bowl. Eleanor walked over to Millie and started to rub against her legs.

"I'm okay," she said, comforting the cat. "But I've forgotten what it was, what I saw, a couple of months ago, no, maybe last year."

She kept flipping through her notebook, front to back, back to front. Then at last, at the very beginning of the book, she found what she had forgotten: *Tuesday. 3pm. Saw David walking into the Park Devereux.*

The problem was, she couldn't remember exactly when she had seen David go into the Devereux. Since it was at the front of the book, it was probably a long time ago.

Unfortunately, she hadn't written down the date.

Chapter Nineteen
⌘
BINKY

Even though they lived less than a mile away from St. Mary's High School, Raleigh's expensive, Episcopal college-prep boarding and day school, when Emily enrolled, Binky thought it was best for all involved that Emily live on campus.

Her start at St. Mary's came at the height of Binky's fighting with Thad. The domestic scene was rough. To top it off, Emily was in the midst of her own troubles with her father, and it was a rare day at home when someone wasn't shouting, acting out, or slamming doors. Binky loved her daughter dearly, but Emily was a handful, and life with Thad was a tiny bit calmer with Emily out of the house.

Binky blamed Thad for Emily's difficult disposition. It had been an all-out war between the two of them from the time Emily could walk and talk. Emily was headstrong and smart. Unfortunately, Thad was equally head-strong and smart and had made it clear from day one that he expected his darling daughter to be perfect in all things. Especially perfectly well behaved. Emily not only failed to comply, she managed to turn failing to meet Thad's demands of perfection into a kind of blood sport.

It was Emily's personal mission in life to show her father every day, in every way, exactly how loud, wild and imperfect she could be. Binky, for her part, failed to intervene. She had a deep respect for Emily's gift for gall.

Binky didn't, however, appreciate some of Emily's recent antics. The divorce had sent Emily into a tailspin of negative activity. Binky had thought the divorce would have released Emily from her mission to wreak havoc on their lives and would have turned things around for her daughter.

She was wrong.

The letter from St. Mary's was open on the kitchen counter:

> *Dear Mrs. Covington:*
> *It has come to our attention that you and your hus-*

band have recently divorced. You daughter, Emily, shared this information with us when she was removed from her English classroom again last week for some rather inappropriate behavior.

We understand what a stressful time this has been for you, your husband, and Emily. During her most recent counseling session, Emily mentioned that since the divorce, you now have full custody of her and that, when not at school, she will be living with you.

We think it best, given the recent upset of the divorce, that Emily withdraw from St. Mary's for the remainder of this semester, and perhaps next semester as well, in order to move back home and have some time to make a good adjustment and prepare herself for the transition from high school to college.

Given her recent difficulties in English and her other core classes, we think it is not advisable for her to enroll in another high school, but rather, to be homeschooled. We have some excellent resources we can offer you for finding appropriate tutors and can provide guidance on how Emily can best continue to follow our curriculum from home as well as take the required standardized tests at the end of the year.

As a senior, Emily has a great deal on her plate and needs to have the best environment possible to help her concentrate and succeed. Because we want to see her succeed and reach her full potential, we will also be happy to continue to offer her help with choosing the appropriate college placement.

In preparation for this move, Emily has been excused from the rest of her classes this week in order to pack up her room to prepare to come home. Please make plans to help Emily move out by Friday.

If there is anything we can do to help during this difficult time, please let us know.

Sincerely,
Marjorie Duncan
Dean of Students, St. Mary's

Binky could not quite imagine what else Emily could have possibly done in English, besides fail. It seemed Emily was particularly proud of failing English. She knew it drove her father crazy. By failing English, there was no way she was going to graduate. Graduating was the bottom line for Thad. That is, graduating from high school and getting accepted into UNC. But that was not happening. Emily had made sure of that. The last time she took the SAT, she had filled out the bubble sheet in such a manner as to spell out the words: MY FATHER IS A BASTARD.

Surprisingly, the pattern she created by using the bubbles in the test to spell out the word FATHER had not garnered many correct answers, but BASTARD had managed to get her into the 60th percentile. Emily loved the irony of it all.

Unfortunately, the divorce had left Binky with a bit of a hangover and the wild taste of freedom in her mouth. She was neither eager nor prepared for the prospect of having Emily home 24/7. She couldn't quite wrap her head around the idea of homeschooling.

She was going to need some help.

Chapter Twenty
⌘
CELESTE

"I forgot to tell you!" Millie shouted. She was standing in the open doorway of Celeste's bathroom. Celeste was in the shower, working on sobering up after yesterday's unsuccessful grant writing gin and tonic therapy session.

"I can't hear you," Celeste called out, careful not to move. She was braced in the shower, hands against the wall, in order to keep from throwing up while the warm water poured over her. She had, in her enthusiasm for just how much she was over her head with the festival, drunk probably three drinks too many in a long day and night of drinking too many. The taste of gin was sour in her mouth. As the first edge of sober began to creep into her body, she felt lucky, no, damn lucky, that she had managed to drive home last night without wrecking the car or getting stopped for drunken driving.

"I said," Millie raised her voice yet another decibel, "that I forgot to tell you something."

"Can it wait? Like maybe until next year?" Celeste asked.

Millie ignored her.

"It's important. Something you need to know about."

"Okay, tell me."

"I saw David going into Park Devereux," Millie shouted.

"Like I care."

"At 3 o'clock in the afternoon, on a Tuesday!" she added with emphasis.

"When?"

That was the problem. Millie wasn't sure what day she saw him, that is, what month and date, other than it was a Tuesday. She always wrote down the name of the day and the time, but she wasn't so good at writing down the dates of things or checks she had written. She liked recording what she saw and liked knowing what day of the week something happened. It gave her a sense of purpose and mystery to her life. Details like the date or the month and recording checks in her check ledger didn't grab her.

"I told you, Tuesday," Millie answered, hoping that was good enough.

"Last Tuesday?" Celeste asked.

"Tuesday a while back," offered Millie.

Celeste eased one hand off the wall and grabbed the bottle of shampoo. She flipped up the cap with her thumb and gave a good solid squeeze, put the bottle back, and began to gingerly rub the shampoo through her hair. She closed her eyes and let the suds roll down the front of her face. If she tried to lift her head, the room spun.

"How long ago?" Celeste asked.

"Long."

"Like a month?"

"Maybe longer than that." Millie confessed.

"So?" Celeste managed to say without getting too much soap in her mouth.

"Pretty suspicious, don't you think?"

"Sure." Celeste's head was beginning to throb. She didn't want to think about David, not then, not now.

"Remember I told you I saw that scum bag lawyer walking downtown the other day?"

The suds from the shampoo were mostly gone, and now there was only water cascading down her face. Celeste tried her best to stand up straight, take her hands off the wall and turn around in order for the hot water to pour down her back. Hot water running down her back might feel good. Turning around, moving at all, felt bad. She wondered how long she was going to have to stand in the shower until her mother left the room.

"You mean Charles Mooreton, my boss?" Celeste said, hoping her mother would shut up and leave.

"Saw him go into Park Devereux."

"So?" Celeste tried to interject a note of sarcasm in her voice. She gripped the shower head in order to steady herself.

"Charles Mooreton was David's lawyer," Millie said.

"You're suggesting that perhaps Charles and David are having an affair?"

"I'm saying, Miss Smarty Pants, that I have personally seen first David and now his lawyer, who happens to be your new boss, go into the Park Devereux in the middle of the afternoon. I think something rotten is going on and that you had better keep an eye on Charles Mooreton, along with that ex-husband of yours while you're at it, because there's something suspicious about all of it. If you want to ignore all that, then go right ahead."

With that, Millie left the bathroom and slammed the door.

Celeste reached out and grabbed a dry towel off the rack, turned off the water and stood there wondering what it was she was supposed to do, and moreover, what she would do or could do if her mother was right.

She was too hung over to puzzle through whether or not what Millie had uncovered had anything to do with her, or if she even cared.

Chapter Twenty-One
⌘
BINKY

Binky's roots were showing.

"Hey, girl," Steven said, parting her hair with the sharp tip of his comb. "Been a while."

"Too long," Binky replied, happy that Steven owned the shop and had his own room. No one else needed to know her secrets.

"I'm thinking about adding some highlights. Make your face sparkle and shine!"

"It's final," Binky said, turning her head to the right in order to catch her profile in the mirror, trying to imagine what a few highlights might do to lift her spirits and perhaps her sagging chin.

"We're talking single?" Steven asked.

"Single and laughing all the way to the bank."

"You go, girl." Steven said, beginning to mix the potion that would do away with Binky's troublesome roots.

"Now, if I can only get my daughter sorted out."

"What's happening?" Steven said, dabbing chemicals onto her roots, sectioning, dabbing, then sectioning again.

"Emily has managed to get herself booted out of St. Mary's." Binky tipped her head towards Steven's open door. Steven took one quick step to the left and flipped the door closed with his foot.

"Why did she do that?" he asked, continuing his magician-like work across Binky's dark roots, sectioning and dabbing.

"Don't know exactly *why* she did it, but let's just say she did a real good job with it this time. I'm sure it has something to do with the divorce."

"It's been hard on both of you," Steven said.

"Sometimes I don't know what is going on with Emily."

"It's not easy being a teenager these days," Steven said, twisting a lock of Binky's hair, trying to figure out the best places for some highlights. What he had in mind was to play up Binky's bright blue eyes with a splash of light like a halo around her face.

"Emily has been a handful from day one. Truth be told, I'm not sure I was the right mother for her."

"Listen, Binky, every mother that comes in here thinks the same thing from time to time. It'll pass. Emily's lucky she's got you," Steven offered.

"They're suggesting homeschooling. Said they don't think St. Mary's is the best environment for Emily right now."

Steven didn't say anything. He kept picking up locks of hair and laying them out around Binky's face while deciding what to say about Emily.

"How do you feel about that?" he asked.

"Maybe school isn't her thing. Maybe she should get a job, I'm thinking she needs more structure. It's time for both of us to get our lives in order. I'm thinking it might be good if she got out into the real world a little. Do something for someone else, and afterwards, if she wants to go back to school, she can go to the community college, get her GED. Lots of people drop out and become successful. Look at Steve Jobs. Emily's smart. Should be getting straight A's. She doesn't apply herself, never has."

"Smart and pretty, for sure," Steven said. "Takes after her mother."

"You know of any part-time jobs?" Binky said, hoping Steven might hire Emily to be a receptionist.

"How about an internship?"

Binky began to fidget.

Steven plowed ahead. "Like you said, sometimes people need to go out and do something for someone else before they can get it straight about who they are and what they want. I think an internship might be just the ticket. Find something where she could volunteer, learn some skills. Stuff school can't teach you."

"Don't know how Thad will take Emily dropping out of school," Binky said as much to herself as to Steven.

"If it's an internship, she doesn't have to drop out. The internship could be part of her new homeschooling program. Never say she's dropped out. Oh, no, no, no…" Steven said, placing the sheets of foil under the various locks of hair he'd sectioned off so he could brush on some highlights and give Binky's hair a lift.

"You're a genius, Steven," Binky said, smiling at her tin foiled image in the mirror. "A fucking genius."

"Thanks," Steven said, wondering exactly how light he could go with Binky's highlights before she would look trashy.

"An internship. That's the ticket. I could help her with history and English, pay a tutor to get her through the math and science bits, then add an internship for the afternoon. Get her out of the house. Give her focus."

"Get her out of your hair?" Steven said, jokingly.

"Precisely," Binky said, anxious to get done with her hair and out to lunch with Lou Anne Mooreton.

"Kicked out?" Lou Anne said, picking through her salad to find all the mushrooms and onions in order to deposit them on the edge of her plate. The mushrooms didn't look fresh. She didn't like mushrooms anyway. As for the onions, she was meeting with Roger again later in the afternoon in order to iron out more details about the fundraising and to let him know she'd gotten her first big check, from Charles, to get the ball rolling.

"Not exactly kicked out," Binky said, backtracking a bit. "The divorce has been tough on Emily. Tough on both of us, and the school thought it would be best if Emily came home and finished the year by homeschooling."

"Last week, Rachel asked if she could be homeschooled, and I looked at her and said, 'Honey, you've got the wrong mother,'" Lou Anne said, spearing a chunk of lettuce and carefully dunking the tiniest edge of it into her low-fat raspberry vinaigrette dressing.

"Homeschooling isn't for everyone. But Emily and I have always been close, and I kind of like the idea of having her home again. I probably won't see her much once she goes off to college next year."

"How's she going to do that?" Lou Anne asked.

"Do what?" Binky asked.

"Go off to college if she doesn't complete her senior year."

"Who said anything about Emily not completing her senior year?"

"You said she got kicked out of St. Mary's and was coming home, and you were thinking of homeschooling her. Sounds to me like she's not going to finish. Besides, what is some college going to think about her leaving school in the middle of her senior year? From what you've told me before, Emily hasn't exactly been a straight A student. Where does she think she's going to go? UNC?"

Binky drove a big fat French fry into the puddle of ketchup she'd squirted onto the middle of her plate. Even though Lou Anne was her best friend, she could be a tad too blunt sometimes. Plus, Lou Anne had the same "Carolina" thing that Thad had, and it about pushed her to the point of crazy, like Carolina was the only school in the world. She had graduated from UNC too, but had refused to drink the Kool-Aid.

"Carolina isn't the only school in the world, you know," Binky said, working her fry deeper into the ketchup. "Besides, I didn't say she *wanted* to go to Carolina. I only said that, for right now, coming home is the right thing for her. If you think about it, being homeschooled might work to her advantage, could even give her a leg up on the other college applicants. She can do all her required courses in the morning and have her afternoons free to do an internship. Emily is dying to have some meaningful work. She's hoping to find something that really excites her and also contributes to the community. Seems to me that experience beats straight A's in a dog fight."

Binky smiled, ate her ketchup drenched fry in two bites.

"What kind of internship?" Lou Anne asked.

"Thought you might have some ideas. Emily has always been interested in the arts. You know she used to sing in the chorus at Wiley Elementary. Had that beautiful solo in third grade that everyone raved about. She has a nice voice. Even took a dance class at Arts Together when she was five. Know of any arts organization looking for a good intern?"

Lou Anne speared another chunk of salad and trailed it through her dressing, taking the time to think about what to say or offer to do. She was less sure of Emily's desire to contribute to society than Binky seemed to be.

"Look, I don't know if this will be of any help, but Charles and I are making a significant contribution to the upcoming festival of the newly restarted Chamber Society."

"Festival?" Binky asked.

"You remember Celeste?" Lou Anne went on.

"I heard she moved in with her mother after her divorce."

"Charles was batting for the other side on that one, and it seems he got a better deal for her ex than he got for Celeste. The poor thing had to get a job."

"Doing what?" asked Binky.

"Charles hired her as the new director of the Society. I think he was trying to make up for what he did to her in court. He was feeling so guilty, he sent Celeste to Italy to look for a group for the upcoming season. That's when she got this idea to create a summer festival rather than have a series of Sunday concerts like they always used to do."

"A summer festival? What does Celeste know about running a festival?" asked Binky.

"Who knows and who cares? Like I said, Charles and I are making a significant contribution to get the ball rolling and make this thing happen."

"Emily really loves music. Sounds big, like Celeste might need some help," Binky said waving another ketchup drenched French fry in the air.

"You're right about that," Lou Anne said, smiling. "Seems she and Charles have big ideas. They are planning on bringing some orchestra in from Italy. It's shaping up to be quite the musical affair."

"Do you think I should call Celeste?" Binky asked.

"Sure. Tell Celeste that Charles and I thought she might need some help. That we think Emily might be the perfect intern for her."

"I will!"

"Do you think Charles is sleeping with his office manager, Jessica?" Lou Anne asked.

"Jessica's a stone-cold fox. If you were Jessica, would you sleep with Charles?"

"I sleep with Charles," Lou Anne said.

"Anything happen to make you think Charles is sleeping with Jessica?" Binky asked.

"I was just wondering."

"He might be sleeping with someone, but I doubt he's sleeping with Jessica."

"That's what I thought."

Chapter Twenty-Two
⌘
EMILY

Emily was in her room rolling a slender cigarette with a pinch of marijuana in it when her mother came busting in.

"What have you done to your hair?" Emily said, casually licking the cigarette paper in order to seal her careful work.

"Steven gave it some highlights," Binky said.

"You look like a whore."

"Nice," Binky said, snatching the freshly rolled cigarette out of Emily's hands.

"Hey, what do you think you're doing?"

"No smoking. Not at school, not at home. Not anywhere. Do you understand?" Binky said.

"Yes, mother dearest. Now give me back my little roll," Emily said, thrusting her hand out towards Binky.

"I said, no smoking and no drugs."

"Who said I was going to smoke it? If I wanted to get high, I wouldn't bother with something as weak as this shit. I sell them," Emily said, opening the small wooden jewelry box on her desk. The box was full of tightly rolled cigarettes. "I get two bucks a piece for them. Call them my party perks. A touch of nicotine and a pinch of weed. A little smoke to take the edge off before exams or a date. The girls at St. Mary's love them. Word has gotten around that I'm bounced, so demand is running high right now. Someone started a rumor that you were going to send me away to boarding school, maybe even military school. Do they have military schools for girls? Given my recent dismissal, I could probably get three bucks for each of these. Maybe I should offer a discount since I won't be on campus anymore: two for five."

"Bounced?"

"Isn't that what happened? Or, didn't they tell you? Or, maybe you were too busy busting Dad's chops in court to pay attention. Let me go over the details with you once again. I got kicked out for dealing, for skipping classes, for a whole long list of bad things."

"Let's get this straight," Binky said, snapping the lid of Emily's jewelry box shut. "You haven't been kicked out. The school and I have decided that you need a break and believe that homeschooling will allow you a chance to focus on your work and also give you time to pursue an internship in the arts."

"You're joking, right?"

"I'm not," said Binky.

"What internship are you talking about?" Emily asked.

"With a new music festival."

"What kind of music?"

"Chamber music. Classical," Binky answered.

"Think again."

"I'll be calling the director of the Chamber Society this morning. I'm hoping to get an interview scheduled for you tomorrow."

"No way," Emily said, pulling out another cigarette paper and taking a pinch of tobacco and a pinch of weed.

"Put that away and get dressed. You're getting a haircut and those eyebrows tweezed. Afterwards, we're doing some shopping. You'll need something other than sweatpants that say St. Mary's across the ass if you're going to be the new intern for the Chamber Society Festival."

Chapter Twenty-Three

⌘

CELESTE

"Celeste, how are you?" Binky bellowed.

Getting a call from Binky took Celeste by surprise. Since the divorce and moving out of the big house in Five Points, she hadn't heard a peep from either Binky or anyone else for that matter. Binky, however, rarely called just to say hello. In fact, she had quite the reputation of only calling or going to lunch with you when she wanted something.

"Nice to hear from you," Celeste said, trying to get her bearings. She felt she should be careful not to say too much to Binky about either the festival or how she was doing personally these days. Binky was one of those people who seemed to know everything about everyone and was happy to dish the dirt.

"I was having lunch with Lou Anne Mooreton this afternoon, and she happened to mention you're now the director of the Chamber Society. Congratulations!" Binky exclaimed.

"Thanks," Celeste said.

"Heard about your divorce. Rotten, really rotten. Men suck, if you know what I mean. I just divorced Thad."

"Wasn't Charles your lawyer?" Celeste asked

"Yeah, took Thad to the cleaners. Brilliant, really."

"He represented my ex," Celeste said.

"Heard you're living with your mother."

"She needed some help," Celeste lied.

"She's lucky to have you living with her," Binky responded.

"So, how can I help you?" Celeste asked.

"Like I said, Lou Anne and I were having lunch today, and we were talking about you. You should really join us sometime. We miss seeing you. Anyway, she was telling me about this new festival she and Charles are funding, and it sounded so fascinating. I can't imagine taking on the responsibility of creating a festival all by myself. Heaven knows I couldn't do it. Have you ever done a festival before?"

Celeste really didn't have the time today to get insulted by Binky or drawn into doing something for Binky.

"I've worked on lots of committees, some big events, that sort of thing," Celeste replied. "You and I actually worked together on a couple of projects. Remember that fundraiser for literacy?"

"That was only a fundraiser. This is a music festival. Heard you're thinking about bringing an orchestra from Europe," Binky said.

"A small chamber orchestra, from Italy, actually. They're spectacular."

"Lou Anne was saying it was really wonderful that you have such vision and drive and that you were making big plans about doing something new and exciting with whatever is left of the Society since it died out a couple years ago. It could sure use some spark, if you know what I mean," Binky said.

"Lou Anne and Charles wrote a rather large check to help fund the festival," Celeste offered, hoping Binky had some extra money herself these days to throw around. "The orchestra we've hired is really special. I think you'll like them. They're young, from all over the world. I plan to build a summer music festival around them, something new and different from what the Society has done in the past. It'll take some money and quite a bit of work, but it will be worth it. Definitely worth it."

"I agree," Binky offered.

"So, you're willing to write a check?" Celeste asked.

"A check?"

"To match what Lou Anne and Charles have written. Get your name up there with the big donors," Celeste felt she had managed to turn this conversation around to suit her needs for once, rather than Binky's.

"Of course, I'll make a contribution," Binky replied.

"Given your recent divorce," Celeste added, "getting involved in the festival will be a great way for you to reestablish yourself in the community."

Binky bristled.

"Happy to be involved, to reestablish myself in the community like you said. You know, it's things like the Chamber Society that make this a real community. And, of course, I'd like to be part of that. So would Emily."

"Emily?" Celeste asked.

"My daughter. I think you've met her. She's decided to spend this last year of high school at home. Homeschooling. She wanted some time to really get focused on her schoolwork in order to get ready for college. She's quite eager to do something important with this time. Make a contribution to the community before she graduates and goes off to college. She's looking to get some direction and real-life experience. Maybe have an internship somewhere."

"Wasn't she with you that night when we were working on the literacy campaign?" Celeste asked.

"She was such a help at that fundraiser! I don't know what we would have done without her."

If Celeste remembered correctly, Emily hadn't been any help at all. Instead she spent the whole night off in a corner talking on her cell phone.

"Emily loves the arts, particularly music. Like I said, she is hoping to get an internship. She's been talking about how she might want to be the director of a community arts program one day. I was thinking that this festival you're planning is a rather big job, and that maybe Emily could be a great help getting things organized. She's a real genius when it comes to organization. Plus, you'd be such a wonderful role model for her!"

"I'm really not the role model type," Celeste said.

"When Lou Anne told me about the festival, the first thing I said to her was how happy I am to be in such a good financial situation with the divorce and all and how wonderful it would be to help you build this festival by writing a check, and, in return, maybe you could help Emily. Give her an internship, teach her the ropes, let her get involved. She needs something to write about for her college essay."

"I'm not sure," Celeste hesitated.

"How about I bring Emily by to meet you tomorrow when I drop off my check. You could show her around the office and give her some idea of what she'll be doing. We were thinking she could start on Monday. You know, begin the week fresh with something new on her plate. She'll have her schoolwork in the morning, of course, eat lunch with me and be ready to work at, let's say 1pm? We figured she could work every day from 1-5pm, unless, of course, she has a hair appointment or something like that."

"I don't know what I'd do with an intern," Celeste said.

"Should I write out the check to the Chamber Society or to the festival?"

"The Chamber Society," Celeste offered.

"Perfect! We'll see you tomorrow, at your office. How about noon?"

"Noon would be good."

Celeste hung up and looked around her tiny office space. She barely had room to sit down. She had no idea where she could or would put an intern. Right before Celeste left for Italy, Charles had moved all the files and junk from the old Chamber Society from his office to hers. There were cardboard boxes full of stuff stacked everywhere.

The office was really more of a closet than a room. It was in an old building in downtown Raleigh where half a dozen other arts organizations had their offices. As dreary as it was, it was the only space she had where she could escape from Millie when she needed to, and this morning, with the headache she had from drinking too much last night, she needed to have some peace and quiet.

Her office had a beat-up reclaimed wooden teacher's desk, a chair, two grey metal filing cabinets and a wobbly portable worktable overflowing with old mailings, programs and posters Charles had dumped on her. She couldn't believe she told Binky that she and her daughter could come to the office to meet her.

She had been so swept away with her divorce, the move to her mother's home, Charles's offer to hire her to resurrect the old Chamber Society, her trip to Italy, and now the daunting prospect of raising the money she needed in order to actually have a festival, that she hadn't spent much time in the office.

She picked up her cell phone and dialed Millie.

"Any chance you're going to the liquor store this afternoon?" Celeste asked.

"You out of gin already?" Millie shouted.

"No need to shout, the phone works perfectly well if you hold it up to your ear and talk normally. By the way, I'm not out of gin. Only had a couple drinks last night."

"Don't put your phone near your face! Could scramble your brains! Just last week there was this story on WRAL about these phones being bad for children. Said they had lithium or some other bad thing in them. If I were you, I wouldn't take any chances," Millie shouted.

"I need boxes," Celeste shouted back to be sure her mother heard her and understood what she needed.

"You moving out?"

"Cleaning up my office," Celeste said.

"You planning on living there?" Millie shouted.

"I'm getting an intern!"

"An intern?"

"To help with the festival."

"You paying them?" Millie asked.

"You don't pay interns," Celeste shouted back.

"What fool would work for free?"

"Binky's daughter Emily needs a role model."

"I'm not surprised," Millie said.

Chapter Twenty-Four
⌘
ROGER

Roger Matthews studied his reflection in the bathroom mirror at the museum. He looked good, relaxed. Not bad, in fact. Perfect for another encounter with Lou Anne Mooreton. He had chosen his outfit carefully. Crisp gray gabardine slacks, black cashmere blazer with monogrammed silver buttons, black Italian loafers with charcoal grey socks, a pale yellow button-down shirt, no tie. It was the look his ex-wife used to call moneyed casual.

His ex-wife. After the divorce he had made it a point never to use her name again, only her title: ex-wife. He still had trouble believing she had left him for another woman. It was the kind of thing that, as his mother blurted out the other day, had never happened in their family before. As though there was shame in it, and it was somehow his fault.

How could it be his fault that his ex-wife woke up one morning and discovered that she preferred women to men? Maybe she always knew she preferred women to men but was afraid to come out. Perhaps she had married him, believing that if she tried being heterosexual, the desire to be with a woman would go away. But it didn't.

Certainly, he didn't do anything that made her hate men. In fact, she had made it quite clear, when she told him she was leaving him, that she didn't hate him. She just preferred having a relationship with another woman rather than having a relationship with him or any other man. It was not his fault. There was no fault to it.

It made him crazy that people didn't or couldn't understand that sexual identity wasn't exactly a preference. It was not a choice. It just was.

He deeply regretted that he and his ex-wife had never had children. Perhaps if there had been children, his mother would not have seen the whole sordid affair of his divorce as something shameful for their family. Perhaps she would see it wasn't him but his ex-wife who was at fault, that is, if there was a fault.

"There's no fault in any of it," he said into the mirror. He had all his hair, and it had only a touch of grey. The boyish frat boy look had disappeared with the advent of the flecks of grey hair at his temples. His face had definitely matured. Even in the end, his ex-wife said he was handsome and if she were attracted to men, she'd be attracted to him. He liked her for that.

He had wanted children. They had tried early on in their marriage. When they weren't able to have children, his ex-wife always swore it was because she didn't want children, and her body knew it.

It had nothing to do with him. There was nothing wrong with him. He had already proven that to himself with Binky. That was a secret he'd kept hidden from everyone, even his ex-wife. It was a secret that had some comfort attached to it when he and his ex-wife couldn't conceive.

With Thad out of the picture, it was a secret that worried him a little. What if Binky needed money now that she was divorced from her big money source and decided to make their sordid affair public after all these years?

What if?

He squared his shoulders and looked straight into the mirror.

"There's no fault in any of it," he said again.

He liked what he saw in the mirror and was feeling pretty good about himself and his future.

He had never liked Charles Mooreton. Charles was short, pudgy and full of ego. Lou Anne deserved better.

Lou Anne stepped into the Ladies Room in order to take one last look at her makeup before going into the museum lounge area to have a late afternoon drink and meet with Roger. She had been in a rush and had tried to put on her lipstick at the traffic light on Hillsborough before making the turn up Blue Ridge to the museum.

She'd made a mess of it. There was a small smudge of lipstick on the edge of her front teeth and the curve of her upper lip looked sharper than she usually liked. She pulled a fresh tissue from her purse and rubbed at the smudge on her teeth. She found her lipstick, redrew the lines on her lips, blotted, and checked her watch. She had plenty of time.

She was five minutes late for their meeting. Roger would already be there, waiting. Things were working out exactly the way she wanted them to.

She felt totally in control. Charles had cheated on her, whether she could prove it or not, and it was about time she turned the tables.

When Roger saw Lou Anne, he stood without looking at his watch. Constantly checking his watch as though he had better things to do than to eat lunch or watch a movie with her was a bad habit that drove his ex-wife crazy. He'd learned a great deal from his ex about his bad habits. And now he planned to put what he had learned into practice.

"Sorry I'm late," Lou Anne said as she sat down.

"I've got all the time in the world, for you," Roger said, taking his seat and reaching over to touch her hand.

"You'll be so pleased," Lou Anne started to say as she opened her purse, looking for the check Charles had written for the fundraiser.

"I'm pleased to be here," Roger offered, "with you."

"Our first corporate donor!" she said, waving the check in the air before handing it to Roger to examine. "Twenty thousand. What do you think?"

"Wonderful," Roger said, taking the check in hand in order to examine it. "How very generous," he said. "Please thank Charles for me."

"He was sorry it couldn't be more."

Chapter Twenty-Five
⌘
EMILY

"First thing we need to do," Celeste said, pulling the boxes of old mailers and concert programs out from under the rickety card table, "is to sort through all this mess and save, oh, I don't know, maybe two pieces of each of whatever is in these boxes. Make a file of past events. Put them here," she said pointing to the two already overstuffed ancient grey metal filing cabinets leaning uncomfortably against the wall.

"My mother said I would be doing some kind of arts thing. She didn't say anything about cleaning and filing," Emily said, kicking at the box with the toe of her black leather motorcycle boots. She had agreed to wear a dress, and, in fact, was wearing a dress, albeit a kind of flimsy, ill-fitting, flowered thing that looked more like it belonged on the beach in Hawaii than it did in an office in downtown Raleigh. She wasn't willing to budge on the shoes.

"You're not working for your mother," Celeste said.

"And, I'm not working for you either. If you work for someone, you usually get paid," Emily shot back.

"Look, I'm barely getting paid. That's the arts 'thing' your mother was talking about."

"I'm not your janitor," Emily declared.

Celeste was in no mood to continue to engage Emily in a discussion about what she would and would not do.

"I'll clean up the file cabinets," Celeste said, taking charge, "make some room. You tackle the boxes. Two samples of each of whatever you find. Organized by the year it happened. Make a file for every year and throw out the rest. There's a dumpster in the parking lot."

"This is bullshit. I'm leaving," said Emily.

"Don't," Celeste said, "I need your help."

"You mean you need my mother's money."

Celeste looked down at her desk and the $1,000 check Binky had given her when she dropped off Emily at the office. Babysitting money. A thousand bucks was better than nothing, but in truth, it wasn't nearly enough to put up with Emily's shit and not enough to make a dent in their lack of funds. All Celeste could do with a thousand dollars for the festival was buy paper clips and postage stamps.

That said, she would deposit the $1,000 check and send a thank-you note. It was already the end of October and all she'd managed to do besides hire an orchestra was raise $21,000. There were not enough $1,000 days left between now and the orchestra's arrival in July to cover the nearly $200,000 she had now figured she needed in order to run a serious weeklong music festival.

"Any chance you're good with the computer? Social media, websites, Facebook, that kind of stuff?" Celeste asked.

"I'm guessing I'm better than you from the looks of this place," Emily said.

Celeste looked around the room, kicked off her red high heels and pulled out the bottom drawer in the first file cabinet.

"I could use some help. Okay, that's an understatement. Once this mess is cleaned up, and you've got a desk to work on, I want you to take charge of all that," Celeste told Emily.

Emily didn't say anything. Instead, she turned her head away and began shuffling through one of the boxes.

"I said I want you to take charge of the social media stuff. Are you okay with that? Do you really want this internship?" Celeste said again.

"Didn't my mother tell you about me? Aren't you afraid I'm gonna fuck it up?"

"I don't have time to worry about that. Besides, you look like you might be able to handle that and more," Celeste challenged.

"I got bounced out of St. Mary's for ditching class and fucking up."

"I grew up in Raleigh too, and I've always wondered why anyone in their right mind would want to go to a white glove girlie school like St. Mary's in the first place. No offense, but what else is there to do in a goody-two-shoes girl's school like St. Mary's but to ditch class and fuck up. Drugs?"

"Smoked some and sold a lot," Emily said, not sure why she was telling Celeste anything.

Celeste took a long deep breath and a close look at what she'd gotten herself into over a measly $1,000 check. Emily was a rather messy version of Binky. She had Binky's tendency to be a bit puffy, and the same unruly hair that needed constant help from a good hairdresser. But the girl came across as strong in the kind of way that someone who has battled all her life was strong.

Celeste did not have either the time or the energy to babysit this kid. She needed someone she could trust, but for whatever strange reason she sensed that maybe she could probably trust Emily a hell of a lot more than she could trust Binky and her socialite sorority sisters.

"I'm taking the drugs as a rite of passage, a kind of been-there-done-that sort of thing," Celeste said. "Look, if you promise not to do drugs or sell drugs while you're working for me, I promise I won't tell your mother or your father that I've discovered you're way smarter than either one of them could ever hope to be. I'm sure you've got a hundred reasons why you hate them, which is why you got bounced from St. Mary's. My father left my mother for another woman when I was a kid, and my mother's been crazy ever since. I'm not interested in hearing all about how bad your life has been because your parents fought all the time and got divorced. I need someone I can count on. This festival can either be a success or a flop, which means that you and I can be either a success or a failure."

"Why are you doing the festival?" Emily asked.

"I'm doing it because I've got something to prove to my ex-husband and maybe to myself. That, and I like the music. I suspect you've been acting out because you've got something to prove as well. I'm good with that, so take this chance with me to prove you're smarter than either Binky or your dad ever imagined. Kick a little ass if you want with those boots," Celeste said, pointing at Emily's shoes.

"If you're really serious about doing an internship with me where you get to do more than sweep the floor, stick around and I promise I'll teach you all I know and hope to learn about this business as we go along. If we're lucky, we'll learn how to do it together."

"Why would you trust me?" Emily asked. "You don't even know me."

"Because you had the good sense to get bounced out of St. Mary's, and you haven't turned around and walked out of here yet. And just maybe because I can guess that in more than one way you've had the courage and intelligence to stand up to any number of people in your life, including your bullshit parents."

Celeste rummaged around in her top desk drawer looking for the extra office key.

"The upper lock is the only one that works. The other one in the doorknob is jammed, so don't bother with it. If anybody stops you in the hallway and asks what you're doing here, tell them you're my new assistant. Unless we've got some meeting we need to go, I don't care what you wear."

"Got a Facebook page?" Emily asked.

"For the festival?"

"Yeah, for the festival."

It was past six when Celeste got home.

"You look like you've been rolling in the dirt," Millie said when Celeste walked into the house and kicked her shoes across the room.

"Been cleaning the office," Celeste said.

"Don't remember the last time I wore red stilettos to clean in. You might want to rethink that in the future," Millie offered.

"Very funny. I thought I was going to have a meeting with a potential big donor," Celeste said, plopping down on the couch in order to rub the tired soles of her feet.

"Who?" asked Millie.

"Binky Covington," responded Celeste.

"Since when did Binky become a potential big anything?"

"When she divorced Thaddeus Covington. Charles Mooreton was her lawyer."

"Wasn't he David's lawyer?" Millie asked.

"Yes, and I don't want to talk about it."

"So, you didn't have a meeting with Binky?"

"I saw Binky. Briefly. When she dropped her daughter, Emily, off at my office," explained Celeste.

"You running a daycare now?"

"She's in high school and is going to be my intern."

"So, you wore those high heels for nothing."

"Got a thousand dollars," Celeste said.

"Is that going to be enough?"

"It's a start."

Emily told her mother Celeste had asked her to come in early and that she'd do her schoolwork when she got home. Binky was not quite up to speed yet on the homeschooling front and was relieved to have the morning alone.

When Emily got to the office, the director of the Raleigh Bell Ringers Society poked her head out and asked Emily what she was doing.

"I'm the new assistant for the Chamber Society," Emily answered as she pushed her key into the lock on the office door. She was wearing a pair of tight jeans that she'd sliced the knees out of and one of her father's old sweaters that he'd forgotten to take with him when he left. She was also wearing her heavy motorcycle boots.

"You don't look like someone who likes classical music," the Bell Ringer director sneered.

"Looks can be deceiving," Emily offered, biting her tongue in order to stop herself from adding some other smartass remark. "You can call Celeste if you're worried that I'm some kind of classical music pervert or a burglar."

"Celeste hired you?" the bell ringer director asked.

"Yes," Emily said, not wanting to go through a conversation about being an unpaid intern.

"Didn't know the newly resurrected Chamber Society had two extra nickels to rub together and could afford an assistant!"

"Picked up another big donor yesterday," Emily said, smiling as she turned the doorknob and let herself into the office.

When Celeste ambled into the office at ten-thirty, Emily had already created a stack of neatly labeled folders ready to be filed. All of the boxes and extra materials were gone. She was sweeping the floor.

"I thought you said you weren't my janitor," Celeste said as she put her latte from Morning Times coffee shop on her desk.

Emily swept up the last bit of dust and junk from the floor and dumped it into the trash.

"I've made folders for ticket sales reports, concert programs, season brochures, flyers, postcards, posters, ads and articles. Twenty years of stuff. I noticed that many of the groups came back season after season...sometimes playing the same boring program," Emily explained.

"Sounds exciting," Celeste added.

Emily ignored her.

"I also made a couple charts. One shows what has been played what year. Another which group came when, and a third that shows who gave money, and how many tickets were sold. Nothing much changed in twenty years except for the audience. Seems it kept getting older and smaller which is probably why the Chamber Society shut down. The way things were going with the Society, it's not hard to understand why folks might have decided that it would have been more fun to mow the lawn and drink a beer rather than get dressed up on a Sunday afternoon to go hear a bunch of tired white men playing the same old Mozart quartet."

Celeste picked up one of Emily's charts. "Nice work."

"Whatever. You need to finish emptying the file cabinets so I can get this shit off my desk. If I'm going to be in charge of your social media, I'm going to need some room to work. By the way, I brought my own computer. Didn't think you had the money to buy me one."

Chapter Twenty-Six
⌘
LOU ANNE

"Once a cheater, always a cheater," Roger said, motioning to the waiter to refill his iced tea. "Want some?" he asked Lou Anne. They were having lunch again, this time at the private City Club Raleigh.

She touched her finger to the side of her glass, indicating she wanted a refill. She was tempted to draw a smiley face on the sweaty surface.

"And some fresh lemon," she said to the waiter.

Roger's office was on the fifteenth floor of the Wells Fargo building, a few floors down from the City Club Raleigh.

"Daddy's a member here," Lou Anne said, squeezing two of the lemon wedges the waiter had brought her into her nearly overflowing sweet tea.

"I was talking about Charles," Roger said.

"And I was talking about the Club. Such a nice view way up here above everyone and everything else."

"If Charles has cheated on you, then why can't you cheat on him? I always thought you were a feminist."

"My Daddy taught me to speak up, not to sneak out," responded Lou Anne.

"Having lunch here or anywhere else in Raleigh is hardly sneaking."

"We're hardly having an affair," Lou Anne teased.

"Your choice, not mine," corrected Roger.

"I believe Charles cheated on me. Past tense," corrected Lou Anne.

"And Jessica is just a bright, young, talented, blond office manager with killer legs. Don't you ever wonder?"

"Is there some grand rule of the universe that says a woman has to be ugly in order to be good at something other than sex?"

"So glad you brought up the topic of sex," Roger said.

"While we're talking about it, would you like to tell me how many times you cheated on your ex?"

"Never. I don't believe in cheating," answered Roger.

"Unless, of course, you're cheating with another man's wife."

"I hardly consider Charles a real husband, so I don't consider having an affair with you as cheating."

"Roger, Roger, Roger," Lou Anne laughed. "You haven't changed one bit. Your cufflinks might be polished sterling silver, but you're really the same old dirty sweatshirt-wearing wannabe jock you were at Carolina."

"I played a fine game of backgammon, thank you very much."

"And you drank like a fish, flirted like an oversexed hyena and dreamed of being the one to shoot the winning basket at the ACC tournament despite the fact that you never made the team."

"Never got tall enough," Roger answered.

"If you're hell-bent on having an affair, why not have another fun fling with Binky?" Lou Anne asked.

"Ancient history," Roger said. "Want dessert?"

"If I remember correctly, you and Binky were pretty hot and heavy."

"I was hot, and she was heavy," Roger shot back.

"Not nice," Lou Anne replied.

"Ancient history. Plus, she comes with baggage."

"Emily?" Lou Anne asked.

"I'm not interested in Binky. I'm interested in you."

"You flatter me," Lou Anne said. "But, why? Because you hate Charles? What is it about you and Daddy and your narrow-minded Carolina Blue belief that anyone who didn't go to UNC can and should go straight to hell?"

"I don't hate Charles. Frankly, I'm awestruck by the man. I mean, he didn't even get into Carolina, and yet he managed to marry you. Which means he must have something going for him, even though I can't see it. Unless the truth is that you married Charles in order to get back at your father. If that was it, you've done a superb job of it. Your father hates Charles."

"Charles happens to be one of the most successful divorce lawyers in the Triangle. Ask Binky. By the way, Mr. Carolina Blue Smarty-pants, you would have been well served if Charles had represented you when you and your ex parted company. I daresay Charles would have been able to protect your money as well as your reputation."

"My ex-wife struggled with who she was for years. I'm happy for her. She found the right person for her to love. Her leaving me for a woman had nothing to do with our relationship. Our divorce wasn't ugly. It was honest. We had a good life together and we're friends, which is a hell of a lot more than I can say for Thad and Binky. I didn't need Charles to watch my back, my bank account, or my reputation. I'm doing just fine."

"My bad," Lou Anne said quietly. She took a small measured sip of her iced tea and let her warm fingers wrap around the cold sweaty glass. She was sorry she said what she had said. She liked Roger. Their banter was playful. Exciting. She was feeling quite hungry, all of a sudden, for a good juicy affair.

"Are you saying that it's over and you're moving on? That you're not carrying a suitcase full of anger for every woman who accidentally steps into your path?" Lou Anne asked.

"You're no accident," Roger said. "I pursued you. In fact, I guess I woke up during my divorce and realized that I have always wanted to be with you."

"Ever since we first met? In third grade?"

"I was too busy learning how to tie my shoes in third grade to notice you or any other girl in my class. Call me a late bloomer. By the time I figured things out at Carolina, I thought you were out of my league, and I could never win you."

"I would prefer not to think of myself as something a man could win in a fight, a card game, or a bet," Lou Anne said.

"Bad choice of words. Let me try again," Roger said, reaching across the table to touch Lou Anne's hand.

Lou Anne left the Club and Roger in time to pick up Ryan and Rachel from Wiley Elementary. Normally she'd take the kids on some excursion after school, mainly because she hated almost every aspect of being a housewife and didn't care much for helping with homework. But today she needed to get home. Roger's questions about Jessica, along with her own growing suspicions about Charles's frequent late-night hours at his office were beginning to nag her.

"We need to get home today," Lou Anne said to her children as she pulled into the traffic and headed home.

"I want to go to the park," screamed Ryan.

Ryan was eight and Rachel ten, almost eleven.

"We can't, midget," Rachel said, punching her little brother in the arm, "Mom has things to do, and I have homework. I'm in fifth grade now. I don't have time to go to the park, so neither do you."

"Mom," Ryan wailed, "Rachel called me a midget."

Lou Anne was mulling over what Roger had said about Charles cheating on her and chose to ignore the escalating battle in the backseat.

Sensing that his mother wasn't interested in his latest squabble with Rachel, Ryan decided to take his chances.

"Dog breath," Ryan hissed.

"Ass…" Rachel started.

"Mom, Rachel said a bad word," Ryan screamed.

"No, I didn't. All I said was acidophilus, and you started screaming before I could get past ass. Acidophilus is something in milk, stupid. It's extra credit on my spelling list this week, and I was just practicing my words out loud."

"She called me stupid!" Ryan screamed again, lunging forward in his seat so he could catch his mother's attention in the rear-view mirror.

"I was practicing my spelling words," Rachel said.

"That's great, Rachel. I always say that the best way to learn new words is to practice using them. Can you use the word in a sentence so Ryan can better understand what you were trying to say?"

"Yes, ma'am," Rachel said, "happy to."

"Save it," Ryan said, slumping back into his seat.

Rachel could hardly contain her sense of triumph. As she slid back into her seat, she let her right arm fall off to the side and out of range of her mother's rear view mirror and pinched Ryan as hard as she could on the forearm.

"Ass-cidophilus," Ryan screamed.

"See Ryan, isn't it nice how willing Rachel is to help you with new words? You're going to be so smart having an older sister to help you."

Ryan rolled his right hand in the palm of his left and quickly flipped his sister the bird.

Lou Anne didn't bother looking in the rearview mirror. Instead, she kept her eyes straight ahead. She was on a mission. As soon as she got home, she was going to do a quick search around the house as well as in all of Charles's coat pockets for anything that might indicate he was sleeping with his office manager, Jessica.

She wasn't sure what she was looking for or what she would find. More to the point, she was still trying to decide what she'd do if she found anything.

Chapter Twenty-Seven
⌘
EMILY

Emily inched a tight knit dress on over her black leggings and slipped on her boots. The dress was definitely a couple sizes too small and probably the wrong season, but Emily figured the leggings and the boots would pull the look together. She was hurrying to get dressed and get out of the house before her mother took a serious turn for the worse about her schoolwork. She didn't have time to put on something that might fit and look better.

Before Emily could lace up her boots and grab her backpack, Binky was standing in the doorway of her room, blocking her exit.

"I thought we'd go over Ayn Rand's *Atlas Shrugged* before you went to your job," Binky suggested gently. Two months of the supposed homeschooling had already rolled by with not much happening in the homework department. Last night, she and Emily had had a rather unpleasant encounter regarding whether or not she was keeping up with her history and English assignments. Math would be next. Binky didn't look forward to that.

"Need to get to the office," Emily said, ignoring her.

"Not so fast, sister. We need to talk about the essay you have to write for English. Ms. Reynolds suggested, since you are homeschooling the rest of this year, that you write an essay for that Scholastic competition about *Atlas Shrugged*."

Binky stood firm, waiting for Emily's answer.

"It's a stupid book, and if that's the best suggestion Ms. Reynolds has for what I should do in order to fulfill my equally stupid English requirement, it's a pretty good indication that she doesn't know her butt from a hole in the ground. And while we are on the subject, why should I even care about entering the Scholastic Competition?"

"It would look good on your college applications," Binky said.

"That's what you said about this fancy arts internship you've cooked up for me that I'm now going to be late for," Emily replied.

"The internship is only part of what you need to do to make things look good. You've been kicked out of St. Mary's. It's on your record. You can bet that any of the colleges you decide to apply to will be happy to read all about your escapades in your high school transcript. Nothing either you or your father can do about it, short of endowing a new library for St. Mary's and naming it after you. It's time to get serious."

"I am serious," Emily said, grabbing her tattered blue jean jacket from the floor and throwing it on over her dress.

"School first," Binky said, holding tight to the doorframe.

"Later," Emily said, pushing past her mother and running down the stairs.

Emily hurried along the sidewalk past St. Mary's, down Hillsborough Street to Glenwood. She reached into her backpack and pulled out her phone, checking to see what time it was. She had told Celeste she'd be in by 10 a.m. It was only 9:30. She decided maybe she'd cut over to the coffee shop on Hargett Street, Café de los Muertos, and get lattes for both of them. She knew by the overflowing pile of empty cups in Celeste's wastebasket that lattes were either a life force or a food group for Celeste.

She paid for the two coffees, used her shoulder to push open the door in order to get out of the shop and was nearly knocked over by Charles Mooreton who was walking past.

"Hey, watch it," she said, looking at the hot liquid now splashed across the toe of her boot.

"You watch it," he shot back, scurrying up the street like a rat.

When Emily got to the office, Celeste was already there, bent over her desk looking at one of their many spreadsheets. An empty coffee cup was perched on a pile of wadded up paper in the wastebasket.

"Picked up an extra latte this morning by mistake," Emily said, placing the cup on Celeste's desk.

"What do I owe you?" Celeste said, grabbing for her purse.

"Nothing," Emily said.

"I don't pay you enough for you to buy me coffee," Celeste said, putting a $5 bill on Emily's desk.

"Correction, you don't pay me anything."

"Guilty," Celeste said, reaching into her purse and pulling out another $5 to add to the $5 she'd already given her. "Please spend it foolishly."

"Hey, do you know Charles Mooreton?"

"Yes, why?" Celeste asked.

"Seemed to be going somewhere fast this morning walking up Hargett Street. Almost knocked me down."

"He was probably going to his office on Glenwood."

"Didn't look like it. He was headed the other way, on Hargett. He ran into me when I came out of Café de los Muertos," Emily corrected.

"Walking towards the Park Devereux by any chance?"

"Could have been."

"When?" Celeste asked.

"Ten minutes ago."

"That's odd," Celeste said, taking a sip from her coffee.

"My dad thinks he's an idiot."

Chapter Twenty-Eight
⌘
MILLIE

Millie had a feeling that if she cruised around downtown, she'd catch Charles Mooreton doing something suspicious.

She didn't want Celeste to know what she was up to, so she waited until Celeste left the house before she hopped into her car.

She knew her daughter wouldn't approve.

After twelve years of an unhappy marriage to a first-class philanderer, Millie could smell a cheater a mile away. She didn't care that Charles was Celeste's boss. Charles was cheating and she was almost sure it had something to do with Celeste's good for nothing ex-husband, David.

There was something not quite right in her mind about this whole festival thing Celeste was now working on day and night with her intern Emily, scrambling to find the money she needed to do what she'd been asked to do. Millie had never seen Celeste work so hard. It was unsettling. She owed it to her only child to be sure there was nothing fishy going on with Charles before Celeste worked herself into a frazzle.

Millie had been up since six thinking about what Charles might have been doing at the Park Devereux a couple months ago, and why she had seen David go into the same building a couple months earlier. Had Lou Anne kicked Charles out? Did he have a client who lived there and needed him to make house calls? Why had she seen David going into the Park Devereux? Did he live there? Did lawyers make house calls? Lawyers like Charles?

Or, was Charles up to no good?

Since that first time she had seen Charles by the Park Devereux, Millie had taken to driving by the condos whenever she cut through town. She'd seen him two other times already, walking fast like a cheater, head down, on Hargett, as if he had someone he wanted to see and didn't want anyone to know he was going there.

Millie was pretty sure he was up to something shady, and almost positive that he had been knee deep in no good, when he promised Celeste all that money to build a festival, then didn't come through.

Twenty thousand dollars! That wasn't even enough money to pay Celeste's salary for the year. What did he think Celeste was doing, running a charity bake sale?

She was willing to bet her binoculars there was more to the story about this crazy festival idea than Celeste knew. And she was going to get to the bottom of it.

What a creep.

Chapter Twenty-Nine
⌘
BINKY AND LOU ANNE

Lou Anne was the one who called Binky and said they should go to lunch.

"So, what's up?" Binky asked, splashing vinegar, no oil, on her small house salad. Now that her divorce was over and done with, and the whole thing with homeschooling Emily was at last running more or less smoothly, she was going hardcore on the slim down. It was time to get back into action.

"How are Celeste and Emily getting along? Charles says the festival is shaping up. He expects it to be quite a success," Lou Anne said.

"For some reason, I'm pretty sure that you didn't call me to have lunch to discuss Celeste's success and Emily's new-found direction and happiness," Binky said.

"Had lunch the other day with Roger," Lou Anne said, pushing the onions from her salad over to the side of her plate.

"Roger who?" Binky asked.

"You know, Roger, Roger Matthews. I think you and he were an item at one time at UNC."

Binky kept her fork moving up from her plate to her face and managed to stuff a big piece of lettuce into her mouth so she would have to chew, then swallow before she answered. She needed a moment to figure out how she should respond to Lou Anne or what she should start worrying about.

"Sophomore year," Lou Anne said, dipping the edge of a piece of lettuce gingerly into her raspberry vinaigrette dressing. "I think you broke it off right before Spring Break. What happened? Anything I should know about him?"

"Are you thinking about going to the prom with him or something?" Binky said, hoping to skirt the issue of Spring Break and Roger.

"He asked me to help him with the big fundraiser for the museum," Lou Anne said, wondering if perhaps lunch with Binky to test the waters wasn't such a good idea after all.

"Why would my breaking up with Roger when we were sophomores at

UNC have anything to do with you working on a fundraiser with him?"

"Do you think he's cute?" Lou Anne asked.

"Cute?" Binky almost choked. "Boys are cute. Men are a lot of ugly trouble."

"I'm only asking, because you're divorced now, and I was wondering if maybe you might be thinking about…"

"Roger?" Binky blurted.

"About dating again."

"I'm thinking about dating again. However, Roger would be the last bit of thinking I'd do on the subject," Binky responded.

"You wouldn't mind?"

"Whoa, give me a minute here," Binky said, picking up her Arnold Palmer and taking a long hard drink. "Let me get this straight. You had lunch with Roger. You and Roger are working together on a big fundraiser. You think Roger is cute, so you asked me to go to lunch with you under the false pretense of wanting to know about Celeste's new success in life, all because you wanted to make sure I wasn't interested in Roger anymore?"

"Well," Lou Anne said, dunking another piece of lettuce, this time deeper into her side dish of low-fat raspberry vinaigrette dressing, "I had to ask."

"You had to ask, because?" Binky asked.

"You're my best friend," Lou Anne answered.

"And best friends?"

"You know," Lou Anne said.

"Don't tell," Binky answered.

"And, don't ask too many questions."

"Okay, so I'm not asking, and you don't have to tell, but if you happen to be thinking about or are already sleeping with Roger, please blink twice."

Lou Anne looked around the room, leaned in, smiled, and blinked twice.

Chapter Thirty
⌘
EMILY, BINKY AND THAD

"How are you and Celeste getting along these days?" Binky asked.

"Dad cheated on you, didn't he?" Emily buttered her third slice of toast.

Binky was never sure how much Emily knew or how much she should tell her.

"Is that why you screwed up at school?"

"I screwed up at school because I had nothing better to do," Emily insisted.

"I don't believe that."

"Believe it." Emily jammed her knife into the center of her toast and twisted it until the soggy bread was torn to pieces.

"You going to eat that?" Binky asked.

"Not hungry anymore," Emily said.

"And if he did cheat on me?"

"Then he cheated on me as well, which is one more reason why he's an asshole," Emily announced.

"You don't have to apply to UNC just because your dad says you do," Binky responded.

"I don't have to do anything he says. He's a cheater. Cheaters suck."

"How's your college essay coming?" Binky asked.

"How do you think?"

"Maybe Celeste could help you with your application, write a recommendation for you and all that."

Emily rolled her eyes.

"How's the festival coming?" Binky asked.

"People talk big and write small checks," Emily answered.

"I was thinking I ought to write another check."

"Feeling guilty about having Celeste babysit me every day?"

Binky considered the guilt thing for a couple minutes. She was feeling guilty, but not about the babysitting thing.

"Applications for college are due first week of November for early decision. You need to get a move on it. Friday is Halloween."

"What do you think I should be for Halloween this year?" Emily asked.

"I'm not talking about Halloween," Binky said.

"No way I'm getting into UNC," Emily answered. "No…fucking…way."

"So, don't apply to UNC."

"How about I don't apply anywhere."

Binky didn't even bother to say goodbye when Emily grabbed her backpack and slammed the door behind her.

Binky was not having a good day. To top off her fight with Emily, she was meeting Thad for lunch. Given the level of animosity between the two of them since the divorce, the judge had insisted that Binky meet with Thad on a regular basis in a neutral public place.

Thad had fought hard for this concession so he would at least have a chance to talk about Emily and keep up with what she was doing regardless of whether or not Emily wanted to spend time with him, which, apparently, she didn't. It was the one and only thing Thad won in the divorce, and he was going to hold Binky to it no matter how ugly it was between the two of them.

As Thad's lawyer had so righteously pointed out, Thad was providing a rather generous amount of financial support for both Binky and Emily, so he had some rights as the father to know how his daughter was doing.

Thad thought lunch at Big Ed's in the City Market was not only the perfect lunch, but also a place where Binky was most likely to behave herself and not cause a scene. The restaurant was always filled with legislative cronies and lawyers. In short, it wasn't Binky's audience.

It was also a cheap date. Binky usually ordered iced tea and a small house salad, blue cheese dressing on the side. To her way of thinking, there was nothing else on the menu worth the calories. Thad always ordered the fried thing of the day with greens cooked in fatback, black-eyed peas and slaw. He loved Big Ed's and was always happy to tuck into the biscuits and the complimentary dish of banana pudding that came with the plate lunch. The waitress inevitably brought two biscuits, assuming Binky would eat one of them. Thad always ate them both. Tall and football built, Thad could handle it. Binky never touched southern biscuits, or anything cooked with lard.

"You've never been able to make Emily do anything," Thad said, digging into his fatback and greens, shaking his head as though he couldn't believe he had once married someone like Binky.

"Emily thinks you're an asshole," Binky responded.

"I'm willing to bet you helped her come to that conclusion," Thad said, digging into his country fried steak.

"She figured it out all on her own," Binky corrected.

"Applications for UNC are due next week, and you better see to it that she has hers done and delivered on time. I'm holding you responsible. The UNC application is non-negotiable. I've already talked to the dean of admissions. If you remember, we both graduated from there, and I've been greasing the alumni coffers for years in anticipation of our darling daughter following in our footsteps."

Thad took the second biscuit while leaning back so he was balancing with authority on the back two legs of his chair.

"Did you tell Emily?" Binky asked.

"She didn't ask," Thad said, "and I didn't tell. I'm a big supporter of that don't ask, don't tell kind of ideology. Progressive, don't you think?"

"You should have talked with Emily before you called the dean."

"I wanted her acceptance to be a surprise," Thad said, smiling.

"Surprise, surprise," Binky said. "Emily isn't applying. Maybe you should call the dean and tell him you made a mistake. I know how hard that is going to be for you since you've never made a mistake before in your life other than marrying me.

"If that's all you have to discuss today, I need to get going. Got a hair appointment or something equally pressing. Oh, and don't forget to keep those cards and support checks coming."

With that, Binky pushed her untouched salad away, got up from the table and left.

Chapter Thirty-One
⌘
CELESTE, EMILY AND JESSICA

Celeste couldn't quit worrying about the money she needed for the festival. Nor could she quit thinking about what her mother had said several weeks ago about seeing both David and Charles going into the Park Devereux. Worrying about what David and Charles might be up to, however, did not help her with her money problems.

"Okay," Celeste said to Emily, "we need to come up with a plan."

Emily looked up from her desk, or rather, her table that was now her desk that was strewn with coffee cups, bits of paper and old concert programs. She was working on their website.

"What kind of plan?" Emily asked.

"We need money. Lots of money."

"I thought you said you got a big check from that scumbag lawyer who nearly knocked me down on Hargett Street yesterday."

"For $20,000. Plus, the Board members all pledged to give money at the meeting last night."

"How much?" Emily asked.

"Maybe all together the Board is good for $10,000 or a maybe a bit more. They signed a pledge but were noncommittal as to how much they'd give, and when they'd give it."

"So, you've got the $1,000 from my mom, $20,000 from Charles and maybe another $10,000 from the Board. That's $31,000," Emily said, adding up the list.

"But we need at least $200,000," replied Celeste.

"You said you applied for some big arts grant," Emily said, looking up from her computer.

"I'm hoping to get it, but that still leaves us short," Celeste said, tapping her pencil on her desk.

"How short?" Emily asked.

"Rather short."

"You mean I'm really not going to get paid?" Emily said, throwing up her hands in jest.

Celeste laughed. With the Facebook page almost in place, the festival website up and running, the files organized, and flow charts flowing, Emily was turning out to be a true gift from the gods.

"We've already got Charles and Lou Anne, along with your mother and the Chamber Society. We need to make a list of potential donors and go after them," Celeste said.

"What about the less-than-honorable Charles Mooreton's father-in-law? Mom says he hates Charles. Maybe he'd write an even bigger check than Charles wrote in order to pimp him."

"Good thinking," Celeste said. "Let's also make a list of Lou Anne's friends. Make it a party."

"What about some of Charles's clients? Apparently, he cleaned up for my mom and got her just about everything."

"He was my husband's lawyer."

"I heard," Emily said.

"What exactly did you hear?" Celeste asked.

"Mom seems to know some dirt about everyone in this tacky town."

"What did she say about my divorce?" Celeste asked.

"Only that you got the short end of it. Guess this job is your consolation prize, that and me. Pretty raw deal all around."

"Truth be told, you're growing on me," Celeste confessed.

"So, you're going to pay me?"

Celeste laughed.

"How do we get a list of Charles's clients?" Celeste asked.

"Easy. Call his secretary."

"My dear, dear Emily, what a brilliant idea! If it works, I just might have to promote you to assistant director and start paying you!"

Jessica hung up the phone after talking with Celeste, stepped away from her desk and softly turned the lock on the front office door so she wouldn't be disturbed. Charles was out for the afternoon. He was in court and not expected back for at least an hour. She had time.

Jessica unlocked the top drawer of her desk and began to flip through her personal copy of Charles's book, making a list of names. The more Jessica learned about the law from Charles and how to get around it, the more she despised how some people lost, and others won. Big time, as Charles would say. Jessica wasn't convinced it needed to be that way.

Of all the people Jessica had watched Charles fleece, Celeste topped the list. Celeste didn't need to know anything about Charles's side business of secret keeping. At the very least, she should have a list of potential wealthy donors to call. Charles had never come out and told her, but Jessica was pretty sure Charles had decided to resurrect the Chamber Society and make Celeste the new director in order to keep her away from some of David's secrets.

Jessica felt that providing such a list was the least she could do to make up for the measly $20,000 check Charles had written for the festival. He could have easily written a check to Celeste for $200,000 as he did for $20,000 and not felt the slightest bit pinched. Keeping secrets was a lucrative business.

In the case of David and Celeste's divorce, there had been a rather dicey bit of secret keeping and she, Jessica, had been the beneficiary of the biggest of those secrets: the condo at the Park Devereux.

It wasn't that Jessica felt guilty about the condo, only that she thought helping Celeste was the right thing to do under the circumstances. Charles had done his best to win it big time for David and leave Celeste with nothing, just because he could. It was like a showboat slam dunk in the last quarter when the winning team was six inches taller and already up by thirty points. Charles was just showing off. It was a nasty bit of a divorce if ever Jessica had seen one.

To top it off, it had always bothered her that Charles and David had set up the whole Chamber Society scam just to watch Celeste fail.

Chapter Thirty-Two
⌘
DAVID

David started laughing so hard he nearly fell out of bed.

"Does Charles know you've stuck Celeste with Emily? That's rich, really rich! This whole thing is turning out better than I ever thought it could. I can't believe it!"

"Can't believe what?" Binky asked, pulling the sheet up around her bare shoulders.

"That Emily got thrown out of St Mary's, and you've managed to pawn her off on Celeste. What'd you do, write a check for this crazy festival fantasy of hers if she promised to give Emily a job?"

"She's bringing an orchestra from Italy," Binky said.

"It's a joke," David said. "The whole thing was something I cooked up to get Celeste out of town. I had some business to take care of, needed her gone for a while, so I got this idea to have Charles resurrect that stupid Chamber Society and make Celeste the director of it in order to get her out of my hair and out of my business. I even picked up the tab for her to go to Italy. We pretended it was all Charles's idea. I needed to get some things squared away after the divorce. Dump the condo and some other assets so she could never come back and ask for anything more than what she got, which was nothing." David pulled on his pants.

"I never dreamed she'd actually find some musicians," he said. "What the hell does she know about music? Just thinking about my ex and your Emily working together to bring an orchestra from Italy to Raleigh for a music festival makes me want to laugh! What a joke!"

"Celeste has been a wonderful influence for Emily, a real role model," Binky offered.

"You mean it's been good to get Emily out of your hair. I can't believe St. Mary's told you she needed to be homeschooled or that Charles has let this whole festival thing get so far."

"Does Celeste know?" Binky asked.

"Know what?"

"That the Chamber Society job was a setup? That you bankrolled the trip to Italy?"

"I like to think of the trip as less of a setup and more of a momentary touch of kindness. As for the job, there was no way Celeste or anyone else was going to be able to fix what was wrong with that deadbeat Chamber Society.

"Given Celeste's total lack of job skills, I ought to be able to write off her trip to Italy as a charitable contribution to a hopeless situation.

"Charles was ruthless in the divorce. Top form. Celeste got nothing. That trip to Italy was a parting gift. There was no way in hell she was going to get a job on her own. What skills does she have besides hiring decorators and going to lunch?"

"What if she finds out?" Binky asked.

"If she finds out, I'll know who told her, so I suggest you keep it to yourself. That is, unless you'd like me to have a drink with Thad some night and tell him about all the good times we were having while Charles turned the screws on him. Speaking of screwing, don't you think Thad would love to know how long our little relationship has been going on? I'm sure he'd be happy to know and to share the news with Celeste."

"It's not a joke," Binky whispered.

"What?" David asked.

"The festival. It's not a joke."

Chapter Thirty-Three
⌘
BINKY

Binky waited until David left the hotel before she showered, changed into her clothes and slipped out to the parking lot and into her car. As usual, she took the back way out. If there was ever a time she didn't want to be discovered coming out of a hotel in broad daylight, it was now.

Even though Celeste had been a neighbor, someone she could call on to help her with whatever service project or charity event, Binky had never felt a twinge of guilt for sleeping with Celeste's ex-husband.

Sleeping with David had nothing to do with sex and desire. It was just the easiest way for her way to even the score with Thad. Besides, she knew for a fact that she was far from David's first dalliance and wouldn't be his last. Everybody knew David cheated. Hell, if Celeste didn't know, she should have. Binky used to think that maybe Celeste didn't want to know, or maybe she didn't care.

However, if Binky hadn't been sleeping with David, she would have never found out what David and Charles had been up to. It was no excuse for her bad behavior. But now that she knew what Celeste didn't know, it was time for a new game plan.

One thing was crystal clear: if Celeste and her festival failed, then Emily would fail as well.

Binky wasn't about to let that happen.

Chapter Thirty-Four
⌘
BINKY AND CELESTE

"Hey," Binky waved and called out as Celeste walked toward the entrance of Irregardless Café. Binky had chosen this particular restaurant because it was quiet and not at all the kind of place where David or Charles might decide to have lunch, or for that matter, Thad. There was nothing overtly fried on the menu.

"Thanks for joining me," Binky said, giving Celeste an awkward hug. "It's been way too long since we've spent some time together."

"Emily is a terrific intern. Thanks for thinking of the festival. She's wonderful," Celeste added.

"I always thought she was smart and wondered what went wrong for her at school."

"St. Mary's wasn't exactly a good fit," Celeste offered.

Binky laughed.

"You didn't tell Emily we were having lunch, did you?" Binky asked, motioning to the hostess that they needed a table for two.

"All she knows is that I'm out looking for money," Celeste said, sliding into the deep booth along the wall.

"I'd like this to be our secret," Binky said, reaching across the table in order to touch Celeste's hand as though they were forming a bond together.

"Because?" Celeste asked.

"You know what you want?" Binky tipped her head toward the waitress who was standing ready to take their order.

"I'll take the chef salad, lemon tahini dressing on the side," Celeste said, closing her menu.

"Sounds good," Binky echoed, "I'll have that also. Sweet iced tea for me, extra lemon."

"Water is fine," Celeste said.

When the waitress left, Celeste turned back to Binky.

"It's our secret, because?" Celeste asked again.

"You know how kids can be. They don't want parents interfering. Emily's kind of sensitive about that sort of thing. Plus, she likes working with you. I've never seen her so happy and motivated. She says you've given her all kinds of interesting things to do. Emily told me something about a list of potential donors. I think she said you talked to Charles?"

"It was Emily's idea to pull together a list of names from some of Charles's past clients. I thought it was a great idea."

Celeste shifted in her seat and glanced down at her purse as though her cell phone might have rung and she needed to answer it. She had this creeping feeling that maybe she'd already said too much.

Binky pushed on.

"I was asking because I thought I might be able to help, but, like I said, I will want it to be kept a secret, between the two of us. I would prefer no one, especially Emily, knows that I'm helping."

"You'd like to help?" Celeste asked.

"The festival has become really important to Emily and, I, well, I think, if you had someone like me working behind the scenes, it might be easier to get the money. As you and I know all too well, money matters. And in this case, I think Emily said you need something like $200,000. That's quite a lot of money. If you could tell me a little bit more about that list, maybe I could figure out how I can best help," Binky offered.

"Charles didn't give it to me. Jessica, Charles's office manager, did. Not sure if Charles knows she gave it to me, so I'd prefer to keep this our secret as well. It's not a long list, but it seems pretty solid, like there might be some potential there."

"If you sent me the list, I could probably add to it. I should also be able to figure out if there are other people who might know some of the people on the list. I don't know, maybe the right phone call from me can help make things happen."

When Emily went to bed that evening, Binky went to her desk in the family room and opened her email. There, as Celeste had promised, was the list. It didn't take but a minute or two to figure out what everyone on that list had in common.

They, like she, all had secrets to hide.

PART TWO
THE MUSIC

Chapter Thirty-Five
⌘
EMILY

Initially, the whole internship thing was a way to keep her out of the house as well as out of trouble, and Emily knew it and, in fact, was perfectly happy to comply. Having an internship to go to every day gave her something constructive to do. It was also a surefire reason to put off anything that had to do with school, both now and in the future.

When St. Mary's kicked her out, she was busy being angry with her parents for the mess they had made. The last thing she had on her mind when she packed her bags to come home was applying for college.

If she even pretended that she was interested in going to college, she'd be forced to apply to UNC, and she wasn't prepared to do that. The whole Carolina thing wasn't her scene.

The idea of making her father proud about anything she did was never an option for her. To that end, she had gone out of her way in high school to fail as many classes as possible in order to make sure she didn't stand a chance to get into UNC.   That is, unless her father pulled some God-almighty Carolina alumni strings to grease her way into UNC with a boatload of money. Truth: she had to admit there would have been some sweet revenge in seeing her father burn a bundle of cash trying to wedge her into his alma mater. But she wasn't quite ready to quit hating her parents, especially her father, long enough to fill out the application or write some stupid college essay.

Being a fuck-up had always been her best revenge against her parents. Getting kicked out of St. Mary's was almost more than she could have ever wished for. She was winning at hating, that was, until her mother decided she didn't want her hanging around the house and fixed up an internship for her with Celeste and the festival. The festival was bogus, but Celeste was in it like it really mattered.

The whole intern thing caught Emily by surprise.

She hadn't counted on Celeste trusting her.

She also hadn't counted on falling in love with the music.

Chapter Thirty-Six
⌘
CELESTE

Celeste had spent all her time over the last eight months doing nothing but shaking down the money. It was already April. Rather than the festival seeming months away, this morning it felt like it was only days before it would happen. They weren't even close to being ready.

"Franco," Celeste said. She was happy at last to have finally caught up with him.

"Celeste! How is it?" Franco answered.

"I need bios for all the musicians. I need copies of all their passports and papers in order to get the visas. I need a list of the orchestra's past performances and some reviews so I can write the press releases. I also need a list of what you're going to play during which concert of the festival so I can create the program. Pronto."

"Yes, yes, yes, I will get all this to you."

"I need these things now. Today. Not tomorrow. Today."

"That is not possible."

"It has to be."

"How many concerts?" Franco asked.

"Four concerts and the gala. You also agreed to play an open rehearsal the morning before the first concert in order to introduce the orchestra to our donors. Build some momentum and excitement for the festival. I don't care what you play during the rehearsals, but I have to know, right now, what you are going to play during the gala and the four concerts."

"Today?"

"I have to have something to talk about to the press and our supporters. Which means I have to know something about the musicians, as well as the music you're going to play, so I can start selling advertising in the program. Advertising is money, and money is what I want to be able to pay you. If I don't have the concert schedule, I won't have anything to say to anyone, and you won't have any money."

"I will talk now with Danielle and get all these things to you this afternoon. I promise. Ciao!"

Celeste hung up the phone.

"That was bold," Emily said.

"Necessary," replied Celeste.

"Once we know what they're playing, I can lay out the program," Emily offered.

"And then we can start selling advertising," added Celeste.

"We need the money?" Emily asked.

"We need the money."

"I took a computer design and page layout seminar at St. Mary's," Emily said.

"Great."

"You'll be happy to know that I didn't flunk that class."

"Even better," Celeste said.

"I think the posters and flyers should all have the same look," Emily offered.

"What about colors?" Celeste asked.

"I'm thinking about using colors that suggest Tuscany. Red tiled roofs, clear blue skies, bright sunshine. Make it feel like coming to the festival would be a musical mini-vacation in Italy."

"Emily, that's brilliant!"

Franco sent the concert programs late in the afternoon, but nothing about the gala.

"It's a start," Celeste said as she looked over the list.

"We could do the gala program as a separate piece if we have to," Emily offered. "I need to get started on the layout."

"How are we doing on our schedule?" Celeste asked.

Emily looked at her calendar. She had it all planned out, what should happen when in order to get everything done on time.

"It's pretty tight."

"Let's do the program now and worry about the gala later."

"I don't know any of these pieces," Emily said, looking over the list of music.

"I guess we should know something about what they're playing," Celeste offered. "Call the CD store on Hillsborough and see what they've got in stock."

"And, if they don't have one of the pieces on this list?"

"Find out who does and order it."

Chapter Thirty-Seven
⌘
EMILY

Emily recognized Vivaldi's *Four Seasons* when Celeste played it in the office. She had heard it before, but never knew what it was called. Beyond *The Four Seasons*, she was pretty sure she had never heard anything else on Franco's list.

"I'd like to take the CDs home," Emily said, shuffling through the stack Celeste had picked up on her way to work. "I'll load them into my computer and listen to them there. I'm hoping the music will inspire me to come up with a few more ideas for the program cover and posters."

Emily hummed the opening bars from Spring in *The Four Seasons* as she walked home. Working on the festival with Celeste was about a hundred times more interesting than anything she had ever done or learned at school. Today had been a bonus.

Her parents used to go to the Chamber Society concerts, but she never heard them talk about the music. They never seemed excited about the concerts and had never invited her to go along.

Until today, when she had a chance to be still and really listen to Vivaldi's *The Four Seasons*, her entire musical experience was composed of tuning out to a lot of angry rock stuff on iTunes, singing in the third grade chorus, and tapping to the driving rhythm of *Biscuits in the Oven Gonna Watch 'Em Rise*, at Arts Together when she was five.

Hearing Vivaldi's *Four Seasons* with Celeste in the office was a revelation for Emily. They first listened to it from beginning to end without stopping. Then Celeste asked Emily to play it again, pausing between the sections.

During the second time through, Celeste closed her eyes and leaned back in her chair as though the music overwhelmed her or sent her somewhere other than their crowded office, and she needed a moment between the movements to catch her breath.

It was the first time in a long time that the worry about the money was erased from Celeste's face.

When Emily closed her eyes, she could hear the seasons take form in the music. She could feel the wind, the rain, and the sun shining through. She could sense the dance of spring, the unfettered joy of summer, the melancholy richness of autumn's changing colors, and the sweet sadness of winter. In Vivaldi's artistic hand, the seasons moved purposely from one to the other as though they were woven together with a thread of hope.

When Emily got home, she went to her room and shut the door. She decided it was about time to get some serious schoolwork done. She loaded *The Four Seasons* into her computer and played it over and over again until she had made it through a dozen or so pages of the math she'd been ignoring. She let the music guide her and wash over her until she knew it well enough to be able to anticipate the next note, the next full color explosion of sound.

Feeling like she could take on both more of the schoolwork, as well as more of the music, she next loaded Tchaikovsky's *Serenade for Strings*. She had heard of Tchaikovsky, *The Nutcracker* and all that, so she thought it would be a good one to listen to while she worked. Some of the musical themes felt familiar. Others surprised her.

While she tackled the homework she'd long been neglecting, she took the *Serenade for Strings* apart, playing one musical line, then another again and again until she felt she understood it enough to allow herself to take in a whole movement. She loved the aching fullness of it, the beauty of the opening movement followed by the joyous dance and twirl of the waltz in the second movement. The haunting sadness of the Elegia, so like a prayer, nearly broke her. But it was the last movement that made her whole again as the music rose and soared and roared relentlessly like a train traveling from darkness to light.

As that last movement built to the finale, like the thrum of a herd of horses running in the rain across an open field, the music washed over her until it entered her head and became something that was not unlike her own heartbeat.

Chapter Thirty-Eight
⌘
BINKY

"So is she?" Lou Anne quickly ate through her salad, then put down her fork in order to pick up her knife and butter her second dinner roll.

"Hungry?" Binky asked.

"Ravenous," replied Lou Anne.

"Are you pregnant?"

"Are you kidding?" said Lou Anne. "Is Emily graduating?"

Binky smiled. "She's doing great."

"But is she going to graduate? I mean, it's practically May, and everyone, simply everyone has heard from colleges. UNC announced weeks ago. Not all the students who applied got in, of course. UNC is so selective these days, but I heard that both the Johnson twins got in, as did Michael Taylor, but that was expected. I don't think he's all that smart, but he's some kind of basketball star. He got a full ride."

"Emily is taking a gap year," Binky explained.

"What does that mean?" Lou Anne asked.

"It means she wants to think about what she wants to do next before she commits to college."

"Is she going to graduate or not?" Lou Anne asked.

"Of course," answered Binky. "If you're not pregnant, then are you in love? And, if you're in love, I'm guessing it's not with your husband."

Binky did not need Lou Anne to remind her that it was almost May. She knew it was almost May. She also knew she had dropped the ball with home-schooling. Truth be told, she didn't have the foggiest notion of either what or how to teach Emily anything.

For her part, Emily seemed more interested in working with Celeste than she was in graduating. But Binky was pretty sure Emily was doing some of the suggested reading St. Mary's had given her. At least Binky hoped she was.

She had pretty much decided to let Emily do her thing with Celeste and keep her distance with the festival as long as life was somewhat happy at home. That was, until David told her that he and Charles had cooked up the whole trip to Italy and directorship of the festival as a way to have one more laugh at Celeste's expense when she failed.

If Celeste failed, Emily failed.

Once Binky got hold of Jessica's list, she knew raising the money for the festival wasn't going to be hard. In fact, it was going to be a pleasant piece of cake.

It was a list full of secrets and, fortunately, people were fond of telling Binky their secrets, so the calls were easy to make, and the money started rolling in.

As for homeschooling, Emily was so involved in making the festival a success that reading Ayn Rand and applying for college and all that math and history stuff, seemed to be in a distant second place to everything else. But that was then, and this was almost May, and Binky guessed it was about time things tightened up a bit.

"Emily," Binky called up the stairs when she came into the house.

No answer.

"Emily!" Binky shouted.

When Binky climbed the stairs, she could hear music. Not Emily's usual angry rock, but something that sounded vaguely classical. She knocked on the door.

"Emily," Binky called out.

Emily opened the door. She had a long silk scarf in one hand and was moving around the room like a ballerina.

"Have you ever heard this before? It's Tchaikovsky, his *Serenade for Strings*. This is the second movement. It's a waltz. I used to think that waltzes were something that old people danced to, but this is amazing, absolutely amazing. Can you imagine what it would have been like…what I would have been like if I would have had a chance to dance to this when I was five, rather than that stupid *Biscuits in the Oven*? Can you just imagine!"

"No," said Binky. "I can't."

Chapter Thirty-Nine
⌘
CELESTE

"Are you coming home for dinner?" Millie shouted into her cell phone.

Celeste had papers spread all over her desk and was shuffling them into piles, making notes, then reshuffling them into different piles, as if by sorting them over and over again they would make more sense, or better yet, just disappear.

The grant notification arrived yesterday after Emily had gone home. They did not get the money Celeste had requested, not even close. The letter said funds were tight and requests were up, so all the applicants were getting something, but most were getting less than they had requested.

The festival was awarded $3,000.

"I can't think right now," Celeste said.

"Of course, you can't think. You're not eating, or at least not eating at home, so I guess you are either eating out-of-date junk from some damn vending machine, or God forbid, grabbing something from some fried fast food joint. It's no wonder you can't think! You're malnourished. Are you coming home for dinner or not?" Millie asked.

"I've got a lot of work to do."

"What'd you have for breakfast this morning, one of those lattes? Do you know how much sugar they have in them? And chemicals? I saw an article on the Internet just the other day that said lattes have so many horrible things in them that if you dropped a penny in your latte it would disintegrate overnight!"

"That's Coke, not lattes," replied Celeste.

"Same difference."

"Lattes are just milk and coffee, that's all, milk and coffee, and a spoonful of sugar. Milk is good for you."

"And so is home cooking. Are you coming home, or aren't you?" Millie asked again.

"What's for dinner?"

"Your favorite," Millie answered.

"What's that?"

"Takeout from Red Dragon."

Celeste had been at the office since 7 a.m. She had wanted to get in early before Emily got there. She didn't want her to know they were in trouble. Money had been coming in, but not enough. Bills were starting to pile up. It was going to cost them nearly $4,000 to process the visas, which was something she hadn't figured on. There were airline tickets to pay for, radio advertising, programs, flyers, posters, food, housing, transportation, postage, performance as well as rehearsal space, chairs and music stands to rent, and a small pile of money for whatever else she had forgotten to take into account, plus whatever surprises came along with things like running a festival. To top it off, the big fundraiser gala they had been planning was shaping up to cost so much money that she was beginning to get worried that they wouldn't even make enough from ticket sales to pay for it.

"Hey," Emily said as she walked through the door.

"Hey," Celeste answered, shoving the papers aside.

"Brought you a double shot latte to get the morning started," Emily said, placing the cup on Celeste's desk. She put her own latte on her desk and dropped her backpack onto the floor next to her chair.

Celeste drained the last of the cold latte she'd been nursing all morning and tossed the empty cup into the trash. She picked up the fresh cup Emily had given her and took a sip.

"Thanks. I put the money on your desk, plus an extra ten to cover the next couple."

"I love Tchaikovsky's *Serenade for Strings.*"

"Beautiful, isn't it?" Celeste offered.

"Amazing. I must have listened to it fifty times last night, over and over. That last movement!"

"Like a train," Celeste said.

"Like horses running," Emily suggested.

"I heard them play it in Italy. Fell in love with it, with them. Have you listened to Bartok's *Divertimento for String Orchestra* yet?"

"Not yet," said Emily.

"The adagio is a heart breaker," added Celeste.

"Your desk isn't looking so good," Emily said.

"It's nothing," Celeste responded.

"We're short, aren't we?"

"We've got a little more time," Celeste offered.

"Not much."

"Money is still coming in."

"I worked on the list yesterday. Everyone on Jessica's list has donated," Emily said.

"Everyone?" Celeste asked.

"But one," Emily said.

"My ex," Celeste offered.

"How short?" Emily nudged.

"I can't ask David," Celeste said.

"What happens if we don't have enough?" Emily asked.

"The grant letter came after you left yesterday. It isn't much but it's enough to cover the printing costs for the programs and the flyers. We've still got some money coming in from ticket sales and the gala," Celeste said.

"I have to hear them play the Tchaikovsky. I just have to."

Chapter Forty
⌘
BINKY

Classical music had blared from Emily's room the night before until way past midnight. So late, in fact, that Binky eventually fell asleep listening to Emily play Tchaikovsky's *Serenade for Strings* for what seemed like the hundredth time.

When Emily's alarm went off at daybreak, Binky heard the opening notes of the *Serenade* tumble once again down the stairs and fill their house.

Binky had never known Emily to see the sun rise. At 7 a.m., when she walked up the stairs to be sure Emily had not gone back to sleep, her daughter's bedroom door was open. The first thing Binky noticed was that Emily's bed was made and the room was clean. It had never been clean, or at least not in recent memory. Emily had always been an angry mess.

Binky quietly backed down the stairs and made a cup of coffee.

"You okay?" Binky asked when Emily finally came down for breakfast.

"We're short," Emily said.

"Short? As in not tall people?"

"Short, as in not enough money for the festival," replied Emily.

"I thought you said checks were coming in," Binky said.

"Thank you," Emily said.

"For what?" Binky asked.

"The money. I know you helped."

"Celeste promised she wouldn't tell," Binky said.

"She didn't. The people on the list. You know them, or maybe know something about them that they don't want other people to know. That's how you work."

"I didn't..."

"I don't want to know. Only want to say thank you," Emily said.

"You've worked so hard," Binky said.

"I love it. That sounds crazy, doesn't it? Me saying I love something," Emily said. "I think I'd just die, if after all this I couldn't hear them play."

Binky waited until Emily left for the office, before she called Celeste.

"You're short?" Binky asked.

"Emily told you?" Celeste responded.

"How much?"

"I've been trying to figure that out. Maybe $50,000, maybe more. There are so many things I hadn't counted on. Plus, we only got $3,000 from the City."

"What about the gala?" Binky asked.

"Probably going to cost us more than it will bring in," Celeste offered.

"You have to do a nice gala. The big donors expect that," Binky said. "I could help."

"You've already helped."

"Emily knows," Binky said.

"Was she angry?" asked Celeste.

"Surprisingly grateful," Binky responded.

"Do you know any more potential donors?" Celeste asked.

"What about David?" Binky asked.

"I can't," Celeste answered.

"Let me talk with Jessica to see if she knows anyone else," Binky offered.

Chapter Forty-One
⌘
JESSICA, BINKY AND MILLIE

When Binky called saying she needed to talk to her, Jessica told her she didn't want her to come to the office. It felt too risky. Charles would be furious if he found out she had made copies of his black book entries, then used the information to create a list of potential donors for Celeste's festival.

He would be even more furious if he discovered that Celeste had now shared the list with Binky.

"Could you come by my house? After work, maybe 7 o'clock or so?" Jessica asked.

"Of course," Binky said.

"Charles doesn't exactly know I gave the names to Celeste."

"And," Binky offered. "Charles probably wouldn't be so happy to know I've seen the list."

"Or that I'm giving you another name."

"What's your address?" Binky asked.

"Number 206 in the Park Devereux."

Celeste was a mess. She wasn't sleeping and she sure wasn't eating. She was as thin as a rail. Thinner than she had ever been, not that she had ever been fat.

Millie knew Celeste was having trouble raising the money for the festival. Something felt rotten, and Millie didn't like it. The divorce had been awful. David got everything except Celeste's fancy engagement ring. Not that he wouldn't have taken it as well if he had thought about it, but apparently, Charles had failed to include the ring in the divorce settlement.

Millie grumbled at first when Celeste moved in with her. She thought it was only right to put up a fight about her daughter moving back home in order to show her how wrong the whole divorce thing had gone.

Truth was she actually liked having Celeste around.

Millie could smell a rotten deal a mile away, and she was almost positive that Charles and David were up to no good with this festival deal.

She was hell-bent to flush them out and make them pay.

When Celeste called to say she'd be working late again and wouldn't be coming home for dinner, Millie packed a peanut butter sandwich, a thermos of coffee and her binoculars, then parked her car on Hargett Street outside the Park Devereux and waited. She was ready to catch a rat.

Charles had just closed another big divorce full of secrets and cash and was feeling good. So good, he thought he'd take Lou Anne out to celebrate.

He stepped into the Café de los Muertos to have a quick beer and call his wife to tell her to get a babysitter. When Lou Anne didn't pick up on her cell, he tried her at home.

"Hey, Ryan, is mommy there?" Charles asked his son.

"Out," Ryan said, stuffing another bite of cold pizza into his mouth.

"Out where?"

"Dunno," Ryan answered.

"Who's with you?"

"Dunno."

"Is Rachel there?" Charles asked.

"Rachel!" Ryan yelled, then dropped the phone.

"Mom, he's being an idiot," Rachel screamed, picking up the phone.

"This is dad. Where's mom?"

"Out," Rachel offered.

"Out where?" Charles asked.

"She never tells us, just says out."

"Is someone with you? Like a sitter?"

"Yeah," said Rachel.

"What's her name?"

"Hey, what's your name?" Rachel yelled up the stairs.

"You don't know her name?" Charles asked.

"I think she said her name was Stephanie or maybe Stevie."

"Do you know when mommy is coming home?"

"When she says out and orders pizza for us, it's usually late. Out and pizza means late."

"I'll kiss you when I get home."

Charles hung up and motioned for the bartender to bring him another beer.

Binky looked around Jessica's condo. She'd been there before.

"Nice place," Binky said.

"Thanks," Jessica said.

"Been here long?"

"Since last summer."

"You've got a great view of Nash Square and the city. Rent must be expensive."

Charles had told Jessica to make it clear to anyone who asked that she owned the condo. "I bought it. I'd been looking for a place downtown for a long time, and when this deal came up, I grabbed it."

"Close to work, too," Binky added.

"I've got a couple more names. Another one came up this afternoon. Charles can't know I'm doing any of this," Jessica said, changing the subject.

"I'm good at keeping secrets," Binky said, tucking the names into her purse. "If you find any other names, please let me know."

"Celeste should win," Jessica said, getting up to walk Binky to the door.

Binky was coming out of the building when Millie jumped out of her car.

"I've been watching you!" Millie shouted, her binoculars dangling around her neck as she ran toward Binky.

"Who are you?" Binky asked.

"Celeste's mother, and, I've seen you here before!"

Millie fumbled in her pocket, pulled out her notebook and started flipping through the pages.

"Tuesday, four o'clock! That's right. Tuesday, four o'clock. I made a note: saw David enter the Park Devereux with some woman. You were that woman, weren't you!"

Binky grabbed Millie by the hand and pushed her into her car.

"Yes. Now start the car," Binky shouted, sliding into the passenger seat beside Millie. "Pull out and drive slowly around to the front. Park the car on the other side of the street, there, so I can see the side entrance."

Binky slid down into her seat far enough so she couldn't be seen. But not so far that she couldn't peer over the edge of the car door and witness Charles walking toward the Park Devereux.

"Give me the binoculars."

Millie handed Binky the binoculars.

"What do you see?" Millie asked, grabbing a pencil from her purse in order to take notes.

"Exactly what I thought I'd see," Binky answered.

Chapter Forty-Two
⌘
BINKY AND MILLIE

"What does Celeste know?" Binky asked.

Binky and Millie had driven to a coffee shop a mile away in order to make sure Charles wouldn't accidentally bump into them when he left Jessica's.

"I told her I saw David going into the Devereux on more than one occasion, and that lately I've been seeing that scumbag lawyer Charles coming and going from there as well. Seems like quite a hot bed of activity," Millie said.

"Did you tell her about me?" Binky asked.

"No. I just remembered seeing you going in there when I saw you come out tonight. And I pretty much remember it was one of those times when I'd seen David. I had it in my notebook and all. I was spying on him. Celeste was pretty sure David was up to no good. He and Charles really did a job on Celeste."

"You're right. I've been at the Park Devereux before, with David. I regret that," said Binky.

"Well, I'm her mother and I'm out for revenge."

Binky laughed.

"I like you. Now, tell me what you know about Charles and the Park Devereux."

Millie had enough information in her notebooks for Binky to be pretty sure she knew how and when Jessica got her condo. She also knew, for certain now, that Charles was cheating on Lou Anne.

"You were sleeping with David, weren't you," Millie said.

"I'm not proud of what I did," replied Binky.

"Celeste doesn't know, does she?"

"Not yet, but I'll tell her when the time is right. I promise. I owe Celeste a lot for what she's done for Emily, the least of which is the truth," Binky assured her.

"If it weren't for that lousy divorce, there wouldn't be any festival," Millie said.

"That's true, isn't it?"

"I tease Celeste about her babysitting job, but truth is, she likes Emily. She says she's funny and smart." Millie paused. "Do you think you can get Celeste the rest of the money they need for the festival?"

"After tonight and what you've just told me, I'd say I'm about 100 percent sure of it."

Binky made Millie swear she wouldn't tell Celeste she had seen her with David at the Park Devereux, or that she'd been there tonight.

"If we work together," Binky told Millie, "we should be able to guarantee Celeste will get all the money she needs and then some."

ChapterForty-Three
⌘
ST. MARY'S

Dear Mrs. Covington:

*I have been unsuccessful in my attempts to schedule
an appointment with Emily regarding her plans for next year.
I assume, since neither she nor you have requested transcripts
from St. Mary's, that Emily has decided to postpone
applying for college. Many of our students opt for a gap year
in order to better prepare for that next step into adult life.
When Emily is ready, we will be here to help.
On that note, I met with the Dean of Students today
to talk about Emily's graduation. I'm hoping this year
of homeschooling has gone smoothly and Emily is ready
to take her exams and graduate.
If Emily wishes to walk with her classmates at St. Mary's
we would be happy to help make that happen. There are two
options. Emily can either take our final exams or she
can complete and pass North Carolina's exams.
Either way, once we have the results, we can move
forward with her graduation plans.
Senior pictures will be taken next week. You
should have received the information in the mail.
Please have Emily call to make an appointment.*

Sincerely,
Allison Whitehall
Director of Counseling
St. Mary's High School

"Emily!" Binky screamed.

Emily turned down the music and opened her door.

"Yes?"

"Do you know anything about pictures at St. Mary's?"

"Threw it in the trash," answered Emily.

"Graduation?" Binky asked.

"What about it?" Emily asked.

Binky stood at the bottom of the stairs.

"You need to come down," Binky said.

Emily turned off the Dvorak *Serenade* and came down.

"I'm guessing you're going to say that we need to talk about graduation," Emily said.

"I've let things slide with the homeschooling thing," Binky confessed. "Any chance you've read Ayn Rand? Have you kept up with the math? History? Any of it?"

"I told you Ayn Rand sucked," replied Emily.

"You read it?"

"How else would I know it sucked?"

"You've got to take your exams."

"And you're afraid I'm going to fail," Emily offered.

"What about…"

"My last exams? The ones I did fail. You don't need to worry. I'll call tomorrow and get it all set up. I'll pass my exams and I'll walk at graduation, that's the least I can do for all you've done for the festival. However, I won't sit for any stupid senior pictures."

Chapter Forty-Four
⌘
LOU ANNE AND ROGER

"I've never done this before," Roger said, reaching around Lou Anne's shoulders to unzip her dress.

"Unzipped a woman's dress?" asked Lou Anne.

"Had an affair," answered Roger.

"I don't believe you."

"Believe me, I was loyal, am loyal, it's part of who I am. I'm a lifer."

"What about college?" asked Lou Anne.

"Fortunately, not everything you do in college gets noted on your transcript. And most of what you do outside of the classroom magically disappears once you leave those hallowed halls."

"What about your college fling with Binky?" Lou Anne asked.

"Like most things I learned at Carolina, Binky is forgotten."

"What does that mean?" asked Lou Anne.

"That means, I'm yours. All yours. We're an item."

"We're a secret."

"You mean Charles doesn't know?" Roger slipped his hand down Lou Anne's bare back and pulled her close. "What does he think you're doing when he comes home at night after a hard day's work and finds a babysitter?"

"Out with a friend," answered Lou Anne.

"A half-truth," Roger whispered in her ear.

"Better than the whole truth."

"When are you going to tell him?" Roger asked.

"Tell him what?"

"That we are seeing each other."

"Why should I tell him?" asked Lou Anne.

"Because he should know," Roger suggested.

"He already knows we're working together and that we're friends."

"I want us to be something better than friends."

"How about best friends with benefits?" Lou Anne offered.

"How about I want to marry you," Roger said.

Chapter Forty-Five
⌘
BINKY AND LOU ANNE

"He what?" shouted Binky

"Not so loud. Someone might hear us," Lou Anne shushed.

Binky and Lou Anne were sitting in the corner booth of the Hayes Barton Café having lunch. It was two o'clock in the afternoon. The crowd at the restaurant was thinning and the chatter around them was dying down enough where people might, in fact, be able to hear them talking. Binky leaned in.

"So, it's official, you're s-l-e-e-p-i-n-g with Roger?" Binky whispered.

"Shhhh, call him Mike, just to be safe," Lou Anne said.

"How about we call him Charles, since that's who you should be sleeping with."

"Since when did you get to be so uptight and righteous?" Lou Anne asked.

"Okay, so you're sleeping with Mike and he wants to marry you. Did you remind him that you're already married? In fact, married to Charles and you have two lovely children?"

"When did you get so all-fired concerned about Charles?" asked Lou Anne.

"You need to slow down and think this through. Charles could probably ruin you if he knew you were sleeping with rah-rah UNC Roger. Look what he did to Celeste," offered Binky.

"Was Roger sleeping with Celeste?" Lou Anne quipped.

"I was using Celeste as an example of what might happen to you if Charles dragged you into court. You want to move back home and live with your parents? That would be cozy! Have you thought about the kids?"

"Like you were you thinking of Emily when you divorced Thad?" challenged Lou Anne.

"I'm not happy about what either Thad or I did to Emily. But that's done and over with and I'm trying to make amends. Right now, I'm talking about you and your children."

"What about my children?" Lou Anne asked.

"If Charles knew you were sleeping with, what's his name, Mike, he could paint you as an unfit mother and get custody of the kids."

"Like he's never had an affair," Lou Anne scoffed.

"Which makes it okay for you to have an affair?" Binky asked.

"You need to help me think this through."

"What do you want?" asked Binky.

"I don't know."

"Well, you better get your thinking straight before things get out of hand."

"I'm afraid they already have," said Lou Anne.

Lou Anne paused, took a deep breath and went on. "What would you do if Roger..."

"You mean, Mike?" Binky corrected.

"Yes, if Mike asked you to marry him?" Lou Anne asked.

"Fortunately, I'm not married to Charles and my relationship with Mr. Mike was a million years ago. I wouldn't be tempted on either account, so I'm not the one to ask. However, I'll do whatever you think you want me to do and help in any way, once you know for sure what you want."

"You'll keep my secret?"

"As long as I need to," answered Binky.

Binky did not tell Lou Anne what she now knew about Charles and Jessica. That would have to wait until Lou Anne knew for sure what she wanted.

Right now, however, Binky needed to talk to Roger.

Chapter Forty-Six
⌘
CELESTE

Emily walked into the office.

"I'm going to do the graduation thing at St. Mary's, and I need a letter from you about my community service with the festival," Emily informed Celeste.

"Happy to call the work you've been doing either an internship or community service, whatever you need. Your work has been excellent. Impressive."

"It needs to say I've done a hundred hours of community service," said Emily.

"It's been more like a thousand. If you count getting coffee, then I'd say at least a thousand, maybe two," offered Celeste.

"There's something else," Emily went on.

Celeste stopped what she was doing.

"I want you to be there," Emily said.

"I wouldn't miss it for the world," said Celeste.

"I couldn't have done it without you."

"That's not true," Celeste protested.

"You're right. I wouldn't have done it without you," Emily corrected.

"Good luck on your exams tomorrow."

"Thanks."

Emily left a few minutes after five o'clock in order to meet her mother for dinner at Vic's Italian Restaurant. Celeste sat at her desk for a long time watching the light fade from the day. Emily had asked her to join them for dinner, but she had declined. She needed to read through her remarks and make copies of the report Emily had prepared for the Board of Directors' meeting.

Celeste had a lot to tell Charles and the Board. There were only a few weeks left before the festival and with any luck, they would nail it. Binky said at least two more checks were promised, and they still had the gala and the ticket sales to come in, so she was pretty sure they would close the books of the festival in the black. Binky had told her they had at least another $10,000 coming in from the names Jessica had just given her, maybe more.

She and Emily had done it, with a little help from Binky and Jessica, and she couldn't wait to give her report.

Celeste was pleased Emily had invited her to the graduation. If she hadn't been invited, she'd figured she would go anyway and stand in the back of the room in order to watch Emily cross the stage and get her diploma. She was so proud of her.

David hadn't wanted children. Celeste wasn't sure anymore if she had wanted children or not or had just known instinctively that it wouldn't have worked with David.

That train had long ago left the station of her life's possibilities.

Chapter Forty-Seven
⌘
CHARLES

"Celeste has done it, well, almost. She's still forty thousand shy of what she needs but says she's got more money promised plus the gala and the ticket sales, which should be able to take her over the top," Charles said, while pulling on his pants and tucking in his shirt. "I didn't think she could do it."

"Want some coffee?" Jessica asked, rolling to her side of the bed and grabbing her robe.

"Celeste is only forty thousand dollars shy of almost two hundred thousand. That's big. Quite a list of big donors too. Impressive," Charles announced.

"What happens if she doesn't get the forty thousand?" asked Jessica.

"I don't know, I never gave it much thought until now."

The Board meeting had been a relatively short one, which gave Charles plenty of time to drop by Jessica's before going home.

He had originally planned to go straight home after seeing Jessica. However, something about Celeste's report nagged at Charles.

"Hey, Ryan," Charles said when his son picked up the phone. He was walking toward his office rather than home. "Is Mom home?"

"Out," Ryan said.

"Where?" Charles asked.

"Just out."

"Did she say when she'd be home?"

"She ordered pizza again," Ryan answered.

"I've got some work to do in the office. I'll kiss you when I get home."

This was the third time in the last two weeks that Lou Anne was out for the evening. Not that he was counting, and not that he came home all that often himself. But it was the third time in the last two weeks she had ordered pizza.

Charles switched on the lights and went into his office. Then he locked his door, unlocked his top drawer and took out his book of secrets. He reached into his pocket for Celeste's report and spread it out on his desk. Celeste had done a great job. The report listed all the donors in alphabetical order along with the amount each of them had given.

The list was impressive. There were the usual small checks for $25 or $50, and a half dozen $100, $250 and $500 donations here and there. Charles drew a line through each of these. Chump change.

He also crossed off all the donations made by the Board members, along with the one he and Lou Anne had made, and the $3,000 grant from the City of Raleigh Arts Commission. When he finished, what was left was a list of names that felt oddly familiar to him.

He opened his black book and started going through the remaining list of donors. Binky Covington had made two donations: one for $1,000, another for $5,000. Given that Celeste had mentioned in her report that Emily Covington was working with her as an intern, the two checks made sense. The first was probably the check Binky wrote in order to get Emily the internship. The second would have been a kind of guilt money, or perhaps an incentive for Celeste to keep Emily busy and out of Binky's hair.

The other donations were a bit harder to explain away or understand as some kind of coincidence. He was familiar, in fact, all too familiar, with each of the remaining names on the donor list. Except for David, Celeste's ex, everyone in his black book of secrets had donated at least $1,000 to the festival. In fact, a couple of them, who had rather large secrets to hide, had written checks for $5,000 or more.

Charles had no idea so many of his clients were music lovers.

Chapter Forty-Eight

⌘

BINKY, JESSICA AND CELESTE

Emily had been the one who prepared the report.

"We're still a couple dollars short," Emily told her mother when their pizza came.

Emily pulled a piece of hot pizza off the pan and onto her plate. She picked off the three greasy circles of pepperoni and ate them before cutting into the slice.

"You want my pepperoni?" Binky asked, holding out a couple on her fork. "How short?"

"Depends on how you look at it, I mean, if the festival is going to cost us $200,000, then I guess you'd say we are $40,000 short. That is, if the festival is only going to cost us $200,000."

"You think it could cost more?" Binky asked.

"Celeste and I keep going over the expenses, you know, plane tickets, hotels, printing, meals, rental, all that, and every time we do, we think of something else. Like she says, there's always those thousand-dollar 'what ifs' that can get you."

"Like?" Binky asked.

"What if we need to rent a van to cart around the instruments? What if all the money that we've been promised doesn't arrive? What if we don't sell enough tickets? What if we don't sell any tickets?"

"Maybe you're really $50,000 short," Binky offered.

"That's what I'm thinking."

Emily went straight to her room when they got home. She said she needed to review for her exams before going to bed.

"I'm going out," Binky called up from the bottom of the stairs.

"My first exam is at nine. Can you wake me at seven?" Emily asked.

"Will do," Binky called back.

Binky heard Dvorak come rolling down the hallway the minute Emily shut her bedroom door.

Binky's first stop was Jessica's.

"You can't ask for any more names," Jessica said, standing in her apartment doorway.

"But, we're still short," Binky said.

"Forty thousand, I know," Jessica offered.

"Celeste told you?"

"Charles. He knows about the list, or at least, I think he's beginning to get suspicious," said Jessica. "There was a meeting tonight. Celeste gave some kind of report."

"And the report has the list in it," Binky said.

"But someone would only be on the list if they've already given, right?"

"They've all given, except for the last name you gave me, and David," said Binky.

"You can't come back here again," Jessica said, stepping back and closing the door.

After she left Jessica's, Binky sat in her car thinking about what she could or should do next.

On an impulse, or maybe a flicker of guilt, she pulled out her phone and called Celeste.

"It's Binky. Can you meet me at the Raleigh Times Restaurant? We need to talk."

"What's up?" Celeste asked, as she sat down at Binky's table. Even on a weekday night, the place was hopping. The waitress came over.

"I'll have a gin and tonic," Celeste said, "and the nachos."

"Merlot," Binky added.

The waitress took their orders and left.

"Didn't have time for dinner," Celeste offered as an excuse for the nachos. "By the way, Emily did a great job with the report."

"We need to talk about the list we got from Jessica," Binky said.

"What a great list. Everyone on Jessica's list wrote a big check."

"Except for David, and he didn't write one because you told me not to ask him. I can't ask Thad either, but you see, David was on the list. I'm not quite sure how to say this. They were all Charles's clients."

"I knew that. That's how Jessica had their names. So what?"

"It's more complicated than that. The list was a rather select list of Charles's clients. David was on the list because he had secrets that he wanted Charles to keep. Secrets he was willing to pay Charles to keep secret.

"I was on the list for the same reason. I hired Charles to be my lawyer because he has a reputation for keeping secrets. The kind of secrets that could ruin a divorce settlement," Binky said.

"Like?" Celeste asked.

"Lots of things. Like infidelities. Past indiscretions. Hidden bank accounts. Property. Things that might hurt you in your divorce if they were disclosed."

"Let me guess. You knew something about everyone's secrets. That's why you wanted to make the calls. You told them you'd continue to keep their secrets in exchange for a donation to the festival. The bigger the check, the bigger the secret?"

"There's more."

"I don't want to know any more," said Celeste.

"This isn't easy for me."

Celeste finished off her gin and tonic and motioned for the waitress to bring her another. "I'm getting a feeling that you know a lot more than I know about my own divorce. Why did Charles arrange for me to get this job? Why did he send me to Italy?" Celeste asked.

"Do you remember when your mother told you she saw David and Charles going into the Park Devereux?"

"What does that have to do with the festival?" Celeste asked.

"Everything."

Binky told her what she had pieced together once she discovered that Jessica now owned the condo that had once been David's.

"Jessica paid a dollar for it. Charles acted as the attorney. He drew up the papers." Binky drained her glass of Merlot and motioned for another.

"Once I discovered Jessica owned the condo, the rest was easy. It's all in the public records. My guess is you were in Italy during the second week of July when the deed was transferred. I'm pretty sure the condo wasn't on any of David's financial disclosures."

Celeste laughed. "You must be kidding. Charles and David acted in court like he was close to financial ruin because of my bad decorating habit. In case he didn't tell you, I was the bitch of the universe because I was too involved in spending his money and doing charity work to get a real job in order to help pay all the bills I was racking up making our house look like a showplace.

"The truth is that David demanded that I make the renovations, keep up with whatever was the latest trend: granite countertops, then expensive hand polished soap stone countertops, five burner gas range, double wall ovens, bamboo flooring, white walls, grey walls, wallpaper, no wallpaper, you name it. He wanted to be able to bring his clients around and show them what they could do with their new houses. He was always pushing me to redecorate, buy top of the line this or that. Money was no object. He wanted our house to be a real-life *Better Homes and Gardens* showcase. He often used our place, adorned with my decorating ideas, to help him close the deal.

"When I tried to explain in court how David used our home to build his business, and that he insisted that I didn't work so I could keep up the constant remodeling, as well as be involved in all kinds of community projects so he could be the big man in town, he laughed and called me a liar."

"And you didn't shoot him?" Binky asked.

"Too many witnesses," Celeste said, draining her second gin and tonic.

"Always the problem."

"You knew about the condo because you'd been there before," Celeste guessed.

"With David," Binky offered.

"That was the secret you paid Charles to keep from Thad?"

"Charles didn't know I was sleeping with David," Binky said.

"Neither did I."

"David was good at keeping his own secrets," Binky offered.

"So, Charles paid for me to go to Italy in order to get me out of town so he could get rid of David's hidden love nest. That's why he got this wild idea to resurrect the Chamber Society and give me this job. This job he thought was so impossible to do and therefore would keep me too busy to start snooping into any other things David might have failed to mention in his financial disclosure."

"Charles didn't pay for you to go to Italy. David did," Binky said.

"You know this because?" asked Celeste.

"David told me."

"When?"

"A couple of days before Emily got the idea to get the list from Jessica," explained Binky.

"Please don't tell me," Celeste begged.

"I'm not sleeping with him now. In fact, not ever again," Binky promised.

"Because you think we're friends now, and to keep sleeping with my ex-husband would be some sort of betrayal?"

"I hope we're friends. I really do. Something happened."

"What could have possibly happened to make you change your mind to quit sleeping with my ex?" Celeste asked.

"He laughed at you. At you and Emily. He said it was all a joke, the trip to Italy, the job, and especially the festival. That none of it was supposed to succeed. That he and Charles had set you up to fail. Like it was all some sort of middle school prank. Just something else to get away with and laugh about."

"Nice. And, you're telling me now because you feel guilty about the part you've played in all of this? And by telling me you'll somehow feel good about having extorted money from Charles's clients in order to make Emily feel smart and successful?"

"I can just imagine how this all sounds right now. But don't you want to prove David wrong? Don't you want the festival to succeed?"

"I did," Celeste said, almost too tired to care one way or the other.

"Well, I do, more than ever," countered Binky.

"We're short forty thousand dollars," said Celeste.

"Not for long."

They talked and plotted and ordered more drinks while they polished off the pile of cold nachos Celeste had ordered.

"We're closing," waitress said as she brought them their check rather than another round of drinks.

"I'll get this," Binky said, handing the waitress her credit card.

"I've got a job; I can pay for my part."

"And I took Thad to the cleaners, so I could pay for the whole restaurant tonight if I wanted to."

Celeste let Binky take the check.

After they closed the place, Binky and Celeste stood outside talking.

"I like the idea of Millie being the one to catch Charles with Jessica," Celeste said, laughing. "She's been spying on him ever since my divorce. She'll be thrilled to know she was right."

"Charles will be the last one on our hit list. There are some other issues that have to play out before we let Millie catch Charles coming out of Jessica's place," said Binky.

"What about Jessica?" Celeste asked.

"The fact that she gave us the list makes me think she knows even more than we know. Kind of interesting that she'd risk her relationship with her sugar daddy Charles in order to help you and the festival succeed."

"You said there was one more name you could tap," Celeste said.

"That's my secret," Binky answered.

Chapter Forty-Nine
⌘
EMILY

The grades were posted a week after the exams.

Emily's were good. Better than good. She'd taken top marks in all her subject areas except math, but she had only missed that by a couple of points.

"We're impressed," Ms. Whitehall said, when she handed Emily her grades. "The decision to try homeschooling for the last bit of your senior year seems like it was a good one. Looks like it gave you a chance to really apply yourself."

"You could say that," Emily said.

"I'm afraid, however, even these outstanding final grades won't quite make up for your other three years with us. I'm afraid it will be hard for you to get into the kind of school you deserve."

"I want to take classes at the community college in order to bring up my grades. I also plan to continue to work a second year with the festival, hoping that might give me a chance," Emily explained.

"A chance," Ms. Whitehall agreed. "The classes might not transfer, depending on where you want to go and what you want to major in, but it would be a good way of showing you're a serious student. I think it could help. Do you know what you want to do?"

"Yes."

Chapter Fifty
⌘
LOU ANNE

"You're home!" Ryan turned off the PlayStation and quickly hid the controls between the couch cushions.

"You're supposed to be in bed. I told you no PlayStation on school nights," said Lou Anne.

"But you weren't here, and you ordered pizza, so I thought…"

"Where's the sitter?"

"Up in Rachel's room, they're surfing hot boy sites on her computer."

"Rachel!" Lou Anne called up the staircase.

"You're home early," Rachel called back, surprised.

"Turn off the computer, send the sitter down, and get ready for bed. It's nine-thirty."

Charles had called Lou Anne earlier on her cell and left a message telling her he would be working late. She didn't expect him until ten-thirty at the earliest. Probably more like eleven.

Lou Anne paid the sitter and sent Ryan and Rachel to bed. Then she threw away the left-over pizza, picked up and put the house back in order. When she found the controls for the PlayStation she hid them in the back of the silverware drawer. Then she poured herself a generous serving of wine, opened her purse and took out the small square box Roger had given her.

When Roger had first tried to give it to her, she'd pushed it away. He had cooked a special meal for the two of them, lit candles and poured her favorite wine: the whole works.

"I'm serious," he said when he put the box back into her hands a second time.

The box was a Bailey's jewelry box wrapped in black and white striped paper and tied with a red satin ribbon. Bailey's had this stupid car that drove around town with a big gaudy copy of the box, just like the one Roger had given her, stuck to the roof of the car, which made the car look ever so much like a wedding cake on wheels.

"I can't," was all she said.

"Take it, think about it. That's all I ask. Whether you say yes or no, the ring is yours to keep. I want you to have it. You deserve it and more."

She took the unwrapped box, stuffed it into her purse and left with the candles burning and her dinner getting cold. It was all too much.

The house was quiet. The kids were asleep. She drained her wine glass and poured another. Her head was spinning.

She pulled the satin ribbon off the box and slipped her finger under the tape. The paper fell to the floor. She held her breath and then opened the box.

The lid of the box was stamped with the Tacori logo. Inside was a stunning platinum engagement ring with a two-carat, princess cut solitaire diamond surrounded by a glimmer of round pave diamonds and three rows of pave set diamonds prominently adorning the band on either side of the big diamond.

The ring was dazzling.

Lou Anne slipped off her gold wedding band and put the diamond ring on her finger. Her affair with Roger had started as just a fling, something to even the score with Charles. A lark. A kind of secret dare-to-do something bold for once in her life.

She had never thought things with Roger would go so far so fast. She had not anticipated that her heart would race, that she would doubt her marriage. That she would or could ever want something more.

She picked up the phone and called Binky.

"Where is it?" Binky asked Lou Anne the next day. They were having lunch at a corner table in the Hayes Barton Café. Binky was jabbing French fries one after another deep into the pond of ketchup she'd squirted onto the side of her plate. The place was packed and noisy as usual. No one could hear what she and Lou Anne were talking about.

Binky ate the fries nervously while she waited for Lou Anne's reply.

"Can I have one of those?" Lou Anne asked, pointing to the fries.

"Tense times call for French fries. Big thighs and diets be damned. What in the world were you thinking of when you ordered a salad?" Binky motioned for the waitress to bring more fries.

"Thanks," Lou Anne said, grabbing another fry.

"So, where is the ring?" Binky asked.

"I hid it in my underwear drawer."

"What if Charles goes looking for something there?"

"Why in the world would Charles go rummaging through my underwear?" Lou Anne asked.

"You never know about men," Binky cautioned.

"It's beautiful," Lou Anne said.

"No doubt expensive, too," Binky offered.

"That's not the point," said Lou Anne.

"What's the point?"

"The point is I like it."

"What's not to like about a two-carat diamond ring set in platinum?" Binky asked.

"What am I going to do?" asked Lou Anne.

"Have a French fry," Binky offered.

"Charles doesn't even know I'm seeing Roger, that we're, as Roger said, an item." Lou Anne picked up another fry.

"Charles is pretty smart for a divorce lawyer," offered Binky.

"Divorce!" Lou Anne cried out.

"Do you want a divorce?"

"There's this crazy part of me that thinks I should be able to stay married to Charles and keep Roger and the ring on the side."

"Now you're thinking like a man," said Binky.

The waitress delivered a fresh basket of fries to their table and refilled their tea.

"Sex with Roger is fun."

"Now you really are thinking like a man!"

"And why not?" asked Lou Anne.

"Because we can't all act like men. If we did, the world would be a total mess and we'd all have sexually transmitted diseases. Plus, you've got two children to think about."

"Ryan and Rachel don't know what's going on," Lou Anne said.

"I'm sure they love having pizza for dinner with the babysitter who lets them do whatever they want and stay up as late as they want. Why would they ask questions, or care about why you're not there? However, Charles is eventually going to ask some questions, and the kids are going to get tired of eating pizza, and you're going to be forced to figure out what you want."

"Why did you break it off with Roger?" Lou Anne asked.

"We made some mistakes together," said Binky.

"Am I making a mistake?"

"Do you like being with Roger?"

"It's easy."

"Of course, it's easy, all you're doing is going out for dinner and having sex. If all marriages were like having affairs, no one would ever get a divorce."

"He never cheated on his wife."

"Well, that's a plus," said Binky sarcastically.

"And he likes me. I'm not sure Charles likes me. I'm not even sure I like Charles. Daddy's right, Charles is a pretty sleazy divorce lawyer."

"Good point," Binky said laughing.

"I think he's sleeping with Jessica. I've been snooping around, but I haven't found anything yet," Lou Anne said.

"What would you do if you knew for sure he was sleeping with Jessica?" Binky asked.

"I'd divorce him for cheating on me!"

"But, you're sleeping with Roger."

"It's complicated," Lou Anne said.

"Always."

They picked through the basket of fries and polished off a couple more glasses of sweet iced tea.

"What do you want?" Binky asked for the tenth time.

"I want some time to sort all this out."

"Keep the ring in your underwear drawer. Cool it with Roger for a bit and quit ordering pizza for dinner. Spend some time with Ryan and Rachel. Go back to normal for a couple of weeks."

"What about Charles?" Lou Anne asked.

"Divorce can be pretty ugly, so you should be damn sure that's what you want before you act on it. Sleazy or not, Charles is the best at what he does, and he could ruin you."

"You know something, don't you?"

"Maybe."

Chapter Fifty-One
⌘
CELESTE

Celeste was sitting at Millie's kitchen table opening the various containers of takeout Thai food. It was a noodle kind of night. She decided to tell Millie what she knew.

"You were right about Charles and David," Celeste said, filling her bowl with Pad Thai.

"Well, hallelujah and pass the Sriracha!" cried Millie.

"That unit you've been watching at the Park Devereux used to belong to David. It was his secret love nest. When we got divorced, he sold it to Jessica, Charles's secretary. He didn't exactly sell it. He gave it to her in a deed transfer for $1, probably as part of some deal with Charles to keep other things secret from me. That is why they, I mean, David, paid for me to go to Italy so I would be out of the way while he cleaned things up a bit."

"That sneaky bastard. You ought to nail him!" Millie declared.

"I want you to do it, at least nail Charles. But not right now. Later, once we know how things are going to play out with the festival."

"We?" Millie asked.

"Binky Covington is helping me with a few things," Celeste explained.

"You trust her?" Millie asked.

"She told me the truth, which wasn't easy."

"I think she was cheating on you and sleeping with David."

"Technically, David was the one cheating on me," Celeste corrected.

"You were not only cheated on. You were cheated!"

"As far as I'm concerned, I'm the winner in all this. The whole thing couldn't have been more perfect."

"You like living with me that much?" Millie asked.

"If David hadn't cheated on me and didn't have so much to hide, he wouldn't have sent me to Italy. I wouldn't have a job, wouldn't have met Franco and the orchestra, Binky wouldn't have paid me to take Emily on as an intern, and there wouldn't be a festival."

"What about living with me?" Millie asked again.

Celeste took another helping of noodles then leaned over and gave Millie a kiss.

"And I wouldn't be living with you. You're a great mom and a great cook, and I love you."

They were forty thousand dollars short of what they needed for the festival, and Celeste had never been happier in her life. She called Binky.

"I told Millie she could do all the spying she wants. She needs to figure out when and where Charles comes and goes. See if there's some pattern. I told her she could watch him, but she couldn't catch him, at least not yet. She's already trying to figure out what she should wear for the showdown. I told her we would handle David."

"Perfect," Binky said. "Are we okay?"

"We're okay, but we're still forty thousand dollars short."

"Not for long."

Chapter Fifty-Two
⌘
EMILY

"Do you think you could get a hair appointment for me with Steven?" Emily asked.

Binky was buttering toast and pouring tea for breakfast.

"Today?"

"I want a new look," Emily said.

"Get it cut, maybe some highlights?" Binky offered.

"Nothing old lady or slutty looking, but something, I don't know, that wouldn't make me look like a high school dropout."

"Let me call him."

Steven was running his hands through Emily's hair, pushing it this way and that, trying to get a feel for how it moved and how best to maximize Emily's features.

"I'm thinking short or at least shorter and sassy, maybe some sun-kissed highlights around your face. You've got a lot of pretty about you that you've been hiding for far too long."

"Short?" Emily asked Binky, who was sitting nearby.

"It's hair. If you don't like it, it will grow," replied Binky.

"Okay," Emily instructed Steven. "But nothing too wild. I've got a job."

"While I'm doing the highlights, I want to do some conditioning as well. You've not been good to what you've got. Let's make it better."

While Steven worked, Emily flipped through fashion magazines.

"Is Celeste expecting you in the office today?" Binky asked.

"Told her I'd be in later, that I had some things to do. Thought we could do some shopping when we finish here."

"If you're asking if I'd go with you," Binky said. "That's a yes, I'd love to take you shopping."

"I'm going to need some new clothes for the festival, but I don't know what exactly."

"Something more than new jeans?" Binky asked.

"Nothing Junior League," Emily insisted.

"If that's the case, then we're both going to need something!"

After getting a good selection of basic business clothes at Ann Taylor, they finished up at Banana Republic for some clothes that were a bit more office casual.

"I like that jacket on you," Binky said. "The hair, the jacket, stunning."

"How about these pants with this jacket, and maybe something classic like this white shirt. I'll need some things for rehearsals and last-minute meetings," Emily said.

"Smart, but simple. Nice."

"I think I'll wear these now," Emily said, holding up the white shirt and the dark blue dress pants.

"I've got a few things I need to take care of."

Emily had her mother drop her off downtown, but she didn't go to the office; instead, she walked to Big Ed's Restaurant to meet her father.

"Hello," she said, sitting down across from her father. "I passed. Better than passed, I did really well. I wanted you to know." Emily handed Thad her grades.

Thad looked at them, then pushed them back across the table.

"I had it all arranged for you to go to UNC," replied Thad.

"It wasn't what I wanted," Emily insisted.

"You're just like your mother."

"That wouldn't be a bad thing, but I suspect I'm more like you," replied Emily.

"If you're not going to go to Carolina, then what are you going to do?" Thad asked.

"That's what I wanted to talk with you about."

Emily ordered a veggie plate. Thad ordered his usual fried meat and two sides. Today's choice was fried chicken or country fried steak. He went for the steak. They both opted for biscuits rather than cornbread.

As soon as she ordered, Emily started talking about the festival and the plans she had for her future. Thad listened.

"You're a vegetarian?" Thad asked when her food came.

"You must be kidding!" Emily laughed. "I'm counting on some fatback in these green beans."

"You had me scared there, girl. After all this talk about the festival and wanting to be some kind of arts administrator, I was starting to get worried you were becoming a Democrat."

Emily finally got to the office after two. Before she sat down at her desk, she handed Celeste a check.

"What's this?"

"A check," Emily said.

"Your mother has given us enough money, not to mention all the help with…" Celeste was saying.

"It's from my father."

"I thought your mother wasn't going to ask him," Celeste said.

"My mother didn't ask him. I did."

"It's for $10,000!" Celeste exclaimed.

"Apparently, Mom didn't get all of Dad's money. He considers the check an investment in my future. I told him about you, about the music, the festival, about how I've found what I want to do. And that I'll need your help."

"With what?"

"Next year. I want a job, with you, doing another festival. I told my dad that if he helped me make this year's festival happen, I promised him I would go to school year after next."

"At Carolina?"

"At Lawrence University. It's a really good liberal arts school in Wisconsin with an emphasis on music. I've talked with them already. They know my situation. The guidance counselor at St. Mary's helped me with the call. If I take some classes at Wake Tech and do well, I can apply to Lawrence next year. All the students at Lawrence have to study music in some form or another. I can sing. That's my ticket. I want to learn everything I can about music and arts management. I want to do this, what we've been doing. To make things happen."

"You sing?" Celeste asked.

"I'm pretty good," Emily answered.

"I don't doubt it."

"I told my dad that the festival had to happen, that I had to have another chance."

Chapter Fifty-Three
⌘
FRANCO AND DANIELLE

"Replace her!"

Danielle and Franco were sitting at an outdoor café.

Franco waved to the waitress to bring him another beer. Danielle had barely touched hers.

The orchestra rehearsal had not gone well. Although Franco was pleased with how the music was coming together, Danielle, as concertmaster, kept asking for sections to be played and replayed over and over again. Each section she wanted repeated were places Danielle claimed Gabriella, the cellist, was either coming in late or early, playing a wrong bowing or missing a note.

It had been a battle between the two women, and Franco was caught right in the middle of it.

"You were out of line," Franco said.

"She can't count!" Danielle protested.

"We leave in two weeks for the festival. I can't replace her."

"She made me miss my entry in the third movement of *The Four Seasons*. I can't concentrate with her around. I can't play with her in the orchestra."

"Why?"

"She can't count."

"You don't need anyone to cue you in for your entry in the third movement or any movement of any piece."

"I don't like her."

"She's a good cellist. We play well together," said Franco.

"I bet you do!"

"Don't you trust me?" Franco asked.

"I saw how you touched her arm."

"To get her attention, to make sure she saw the bowing and fingerings I had marked into the score this morning."

"The bowing! The fingerings!"

Danielle pushed her beer away.

"Why aren't you drinking?" Franco asked.

"I thought going to America would be a good time for us to start a baby," Danielle answered.

"We have concerts to play."

"We will always have concerts to play."

"No," Franco declared emphatically.

"No, we won't always have concerts to play, or no, we can't have a baby?"

"We've talked about this already," Franco said, draining his beer.

"You promised me a baby."

"Not now, Danielle."

"When?"

Franco motioned for the bill. His phone buzzed in his pocket.

"I have to meet with Manuel to copy the scores," he said.

"You promised," Danielle challenged.

Franco shouldered his cello and left the restaurant. As soon as he was down the street and safely around the corner, he called Manuel. Manuel didn't pick up, so Franco left a message.

"See you in two hours to copy the scores," he said.

When he hung up, he called Gabriella to let her know he was on his way.

Chapter Fifty-Four
⌘
BINKY AND ROGER

"Nice to see you," Binky said, sitting down across the table from Roger.

"I figured you must have told Lou Anne something, which is why you wanted to see me all of a sudden," Roger said quietly.

"Told her what?" Binky responded innocently.

"How about a secret or two?"

"That's none of her business."

"I don't believe you," Roger scoffed.

"You should. As promised, I've kept it secret. It's nothing I'm proud of, so why tell?"

"I don't believe no one knows." Roger said.

Binky took a minute to let Roger cool down.

"There were circumstances, like when I got pregnant with Emily, and I let my OB-GYN that I had once had an abortion. But I'm telling the truth when I say that I have never told anyone that you were the father."

"I wanted children, but we weren't able to conceive. I let my ex believe I was the reason. I never told her what happened between us, about the abortion," Roger confessed.

"Trust me, I never told Thad about you and never will and hope you'll be kind enough to do the same and not mention our complicated love business to Lou Anne."

"I've always wondered. What did you do with the money?"

"Let it sit in a Swiss bank account collecting interest."

"I'm willing to bet Thad never knew about that either."

"He had enough, there was no need to share."

"Why won't Lou Anne see me?" Roger asked.

"The ring," Binky answered. "She was stunned by it. Thunderstruck. Gob smacked. She didn't see it coming, and it knocked her out."

"And you told her to do what?" Roger asked.

"To hide it in a drawer and think about what she really wants," Binky said.

"I want to marry her."

"There's this tiny problem of Charles. Her husband. The meanest divorce lawyer in town?"

"Thad was happy to tell me what Charles had done to him," Roger responded.

"Charles would be happy to do the same to Lou Anne."

"The whole town knows Charles is cheating on her," Roger said.

"Excuse me, I thought Lou Anne was cheating on him. Or, was that just a friendship ring?"

"Why did you ask me to lunch?" Roger asked. "You said you had some deal I might be interested in."

"If Lou Anne is serious about you and wearing that ring, she needs to make it harder for Charles to find out about you, at least for the moment. She needs time to figure out what she wants to do."

"And you're offering to help me convince Lou Anne that she should leave Charles if I help you with something."

"Something like that, but not quite as calculating as you make it sound. This may be hard for you to believe, but I actually like you. Always have. Thought you were noble in all of our troubles. You didn't brag. Didn't even get drunk and let your frat brats know that I was easy, and you knocked me up."

"Easy is a word I would never use to describe you."

"Lou Anne needs to make it impossible for Charles to find out about your affair or your fling, or whatever you want to call it, until she has some hard evidence against Charles and a plan. She also needs to think about the impact all of this is going to have on her kids."

"He's not much of a father."

"Divorcing Charles is going to be ugly no matter how you paint it."

"It might be hard for you to believe, but I have always been in love with Lou Anne. I didn't think I was good enough for her when we were in college."

"Now you think Charles isn't good enough to keep her?"

Roger laughed.

Binky told Roger about the festival, but not everything. Only that Charles had set Celeste up to fail and that it was important for Roger that she didn't.

"The festival is still a tiny bit short of funds," Binky said.

"How much?" Roger asked.

"About the price of that ring you bought Lou Anne."

Roger pulled out his checkbook.

"This is no guarantee," Binky said, taking the check.

"Neither was the ring, but I believe in investing in my future."

Chapter Fifty-Five
⌘
THE MONEY

"One more happy donor," Binky said, putting Roger's check on Celeste's desk.

"For?" Emily asked. She was working on their tally sheet.

"Five thousand. How are ticket sales?" Binky asked.

"Getting there," Celeste said. "We have a pretty good house for the opening gala, not full, but better than I expected. I'm hoping they'll drink some champagne, relax and enjoy the music, then buy tickets in order to come back for more."

"Or at least tell their friends," Emily offered.

"Ready to go?" Binky asked Emily.

"Need anything else?" Emily asked Celeste.

"I'm good."

"You sure you don't want to join us for dinner?" Binky asked.

"I can't tonight, but thanks for all your help," Celeste said.

"My pleasure," said Binky.

The posters were up, the ads were running on the radio, the programs were back from the printers, and with this last check, Thad's check and a few others that had at last arrived, Celeste now had enough money to pay for everything. As long as nothing went sideways.

She called Charles. It rang a couple of times, then went to his voicemail. She left a message.

"I wanted to let you know we made it."

Charles checked his messages while Jessica was in the shower.

"Celeste called," Charles said.

Jessica stepped out of the shower.

"Who?"

"Celeste. She left a message."

"Oh," Jessica said, wrapping the towel around her. "Want some coffee?"

"She said she made it," Charles said.

"Made what?" Jessica asked.

"She has all the money she needs for the festival."

"Hey, I put on a fresh pot of coffee right before you came over, thought you might like a cup before you go," Jessica offered.

Jessica walked into the kitchen and started fussing with the coffee machine.

Charles stood in the doorway, blocking her way out of the room.

"Two hundred thousand dollars. That's a lot of money. Any ideas where all that money came from?" Charles asked.

"Not sure. Why?"

"Maybe Celeste has had some help," Charles offered.

"I heard Binky's daughter, Emily, was helping her."

"How about Binky?" Charles asked.

"Celeste couldn't have done it on her own, no one could," Jessica said.

"You've got a really nice place here," Charles said, looking around the condo.

"What are you saying?"

"And a pretty easy job," Charles added.

Charles pulled off Jessica's towel and dropped it on the floor.

"I had no idea so many of my clients liked classical music," Charles said. Then he slapped her hard on the ass and left.

By the time Jessica grabbed her phone to call Binky, the welt of Charles' handprint was clearly visible.

Millie was sitting in her car watching out of her binoculars. She made a note in her book: Charles arrived at Park Devereux at 5:25, left promptly at 6:15. Short visit. She also wrote down the date beside the entry just like Celeste had instructed.

She slumped down in her seat and watched through her binoculars as Charles walked toward either his office on Glenwood or his home in Cameron Park. She wasn't sure which. She was tempted to follow him, but Celeste had told her to be careful and not to do anything crazy, so she waited until she thought Charles was far enough away that he wouldn't notice her behind him and drove slowly up the street.

"I told you not to follow him," Celeste said. "He could have seen you, could have called the police."

"I wasn't breaking the speed limit. Even used my signal when I turned onto Glenwood from Hargett. You'd be surprised how many people don't use their turn signals these days."

"You could have gotten caught," Celeste added.

"He looked like he had other things on his mind. He was walking fast. Like he had someplace to run from or run to, not sure which, but fast, much faster than usual."

"How do you know how fast he usually walks?"

"I've followed him before. He usually goes straight home when he leaves Park Devereux, but this time he went to his office. I saw the lights in his office go on, so I knew he was there," Millie said.

"How long did he stay?"

"Fifteen minutes or so. Twenty tops. Then he left and headed home."

Charles rummaged through Jessica's desk looking for some evidence of a list. That's when he found her folder. After he shredded the pages of his secrets she had copied, he put the empty folder on top of her desk and went into his office, unlocked his top drawer and removed his black book. Then he locked his desk, put the key in his pocket, and put the book into his safe.

Jessica sent a photo of the angry red handprint Charles had left on her backside to Binky, and then she called her.

"He thinks you had something to do with the festival getting all the money," Jessica said.

"What did he say?" Binky asked.

"That I have a nice condo, a pretty easy job."

"Are you okay?"

"I've sent you a photo. We weren't playing around. He's slapped me before, but never like this."

Binky called Lou Anne.

"I think it's time for lunch," she said.

Lou Anne heard Charles come in the front door and walk straight into his office at the back of the house.

"Tomorrow, noon?" Lou Anne asked.

"Irregardless Café?"

"Grammatically right or wrong, Irregardless."

Chapter Fifty-Six
⌘
JESSICA AND CHARLES

When Jessica got to the office the next morning, she was not surprised to see her empty folder on top of her desk and Charles sitting in her chair.

"I have two weeks' vacation coming," Jessica said.

"What makes you think I'll pay you?" Charles asked.

"What makes you think I'll keep quiet about the notes you've made in your black book?"

"The condo," Charles sneered.

"Not much of a threat. My name is on the deed, fair and square. I think I paid a dollar for it."

"I'm sure there are people who would like to know how you got it."

"Probably the same people who might be interested in this."

Jessica pulled out her cell phone.

"What's that?"

"A picture of your handprint on my ass."

Chapter Fifty-Seven
⌘
BINKY AND LOU ANNE

"Nice ring," Binky said, spearing a large lump of blue cheese off the top of her salad. Irregardless didn't serve French fries, which left Binky with little recourse in times of stress. She ordered the chef salad with a double dose of blue cheese dressing and lathered an extra smear of butter on two rolls.

"What do you think?" Lou Anne asked, admiring her hand that was adorned with Roger's ring.

"I think you're going to have to keep your nails manicured. Something deep scarlet might be a nice touch. Red looks so good with big diamonds and platinum," Binky replied.

"Can you prove Charles has been sleeping with Jessica?"

"Here," Binky said, finishing off the first of her buttered rolls and handing Lou Anne her cell phone.

"What's this?" Lou Anne asked.

"Charles's handprint on Jessica's rear end. Jessica sent it to me."

"When?" Lou Anne asked.

"Last night," said Binky.

"Charles was home by seven."

"I know," Binky offered, grabbing her second roll.

"You followed him?" Lou Anne asked.

"Millie did," answered Binky.

"Who's Millie?"

"Celeste's mother. Charles has become a special project of hers ever since Celeste's divorce from David. By the way, Millie takes great notes. She will be an invaluable resource in your divorce from Charles."

"I'm listening," Lou Anne said.

"Last night Millie followed Charles. He arrived at Jessica's at 5:25 pm, which is just about the time he arrives most days, but last night he only stayed until 6:15. After leaving Jessica's, he walked to his office rather than going home, like he usually does," explained Binky.

"Why did he go to his office?" Lou Anne asked.

"My guess is to shred some secrets," offered Binky.

"I know about Charles's book of secrets, and also know it's too valuable for him to ever think of shredding it."

"More than likely, he shredded the copies Jessica had made of the various secrets Charles was being paid to keep. They were copies he didn't know she had. FYI, Jessica gave Celeste a list of names of potential donors for the festival from Charles's book of secrets."

"Was Jessica sleeping with David?" Lou Anne asked.

"No, I was. Which is not something I'm particularly proud of these days. It's over, and I hope you can keep that bit of information to yourself. In any case, David needed to dump the condo before Celeste found out about it. Charles took it as partial payment to keep some of David's other secrets," Binky explained.

"Charles owns the Park Devereux place and Jessica sleeps there?" Lou Anne asked.

"Jessica owns it," Binky explained.

"Charles gave it to Jessica?" Lou Anne asked.

"Technically, it was David's condo and he sold it to her for a dollar. It's all there in the public records. Charles was the attorney on the deal."

"Why did Jessica give Celeste the list of names?" Lou Anne asked.

"She figured it was payback time. She didn't like what Charles and David had done to Celeste. When David started bragging to me about how he and Charles had sent Celeste to Italy in order to get her out of the way, and that he and Charles thought the whole festival thing was a big joke, I didn't like it much either. That's when I quit seeing David and started helping Celeste."

"I know for a fact that Charles didn't pay to send Celeste to Italy. I've been keeping track of his money," Lou Anne said.

"As for keeping track of Charles's money, all of the secrets are paid for in cash. Let's just say, Charles has money you don't know about. He may not have graduated from UNC, but he has gotten a pretty good education from his clients about hiding money as well as lovers.

"As for Celeste's trip to Italy, David paid for it. Which is why you couldn't find anything. When David told me, he had paid for the trip and told Charles to give Celeste the job of revitalizing the Chamber Society, he laughed. Said they did it knowing Celeste would fail. They thought it was all a big joke.

"That's when I got angry and cut it off with David and started helping Celeste."

"Because if Celeste failed, that meant Emily would fail as well," Lou Anne concluded.

"Yes. When Emily told me that Celeste had gotten a list of potential donors from Jessica, I suspected the list had come from the black book."

"And you offered to help because you knew the people on Jessica's list had a few things they'd be happy to pay to keep secret," Lou Anne offered.

"Getting the money was easy. Kind of ironic that Charles's clients could write a fat check to the festival in order to continue having their secrets kept hidden, get their names in the program as good citizens, and snag a nice tax deduction in the deal. Kind of a weird win-win."

"Are you in his black book?"

"Yes."

"What if Charles finds out you're involved in all of this and threatens to tell your secret?"

"He already knows I'm involved. Thanks to Jessica and Millie's fine detective work, I don't think I'll have to worry about that. Telling my secret would unleash a whole can of whoop ass on Charles."

"What do you think I should I do?"

"First, you need to put that ring back in the drawer for the moment. Jessica quit this morning. Or Charles fired her, depending on who is telling the story. I talked with her right after she left the office. She's ready to tell you everything and then some. She's not a bad person. I believe Jessica got caught up in something ugly, really ugly, and would like to make at least part of it right. She's going to need our help."

Chapter Fifty-Eight
⌘
JESSICA AND LOU ANNE

Jessica told Celeste and Binky that she wanted to meet with Lou Anne alone. She was tired of all the secrets and ready to come clean.

"Ask me anything," Jessica told Lou Anne.

They were sitting together in Jessica's condo having a cup of tea. Jessica had pulled out all the stops and had even baked a batch of cookies. She'd felt a kind of giddiness when she left Charles's office that morning, knowing he might be able to fire her, but she still owned the condo. She'd be okay, which was reason enough to bake cookies.

"How long?" Lou Anne asked.

"Charles hired me three years ago."

"How long has he been sleeping with you?"

"Three years," Jessica answered.

"Oh," Lou Anne said, beginning to grasp the situation. She picked up a cookie and took a bite. "What about the secrets?"

"When clients would come in, and Charles would close his door and tell me to hold his calls and not bother him, I pretty much knew what was going on. After they left, he always kept his door closed for a while. I guess that was when he'd take notes in his black book.

"Whenever he went to court and won a big settlement, he would come back to the office bragging about how he had really stuck it to someone. The first week I started working for him, he had one of those secret keeping divorce cases. He stopped at a bar before he came back to the office. It was a big win, and he had had one too many drinks. Anyway, he started talking, telling me stuff about the case: bragging a bit, trying to impress me."

"What did he tell you?" Lou Anne asked.

"That the poor sucker who just lost in court didn't know half the story about what his wife was up to and he never would. That her secrets were safely hidden. Like it was a ruthless game of winner take all. Charles liked to talk about divorce being all about who wins and who loses."

"Charles liked winning. The bigger the better."

"That was the first and only time he talked about his black book. He was pretty loose and happy that night. Full of booze and brag."

"And you made copies of his black book," Lou Anne guessed.

"He didn't know about the copies."

"I bet he didn't," Lou Anne laughed.

"After a big divorce was finalized, and Charles was out of the office, I'd take a look in the black book. If there was anything there, I'd make a copy. I figured as long as I knew about the secrets Charles was keeping, I could pretty much get what I wanted."

"Which was?" Lou Anne asked.

"To keep my job. Save enough money to go back to school."

"Why did you help Celeste?"

"Charles always played to win. And he knew how to hide something in order to get what he wanted in court. After a while I began to realize that he did it more to score than to help anyone. Like it was some big game, and he always had to be the winner. What he and David did to Celeste was the worst. I knew I'd lose my job if I helped her, but I didn't care. She got nothing for no reason," Jessica explained.

"Binky showed me the picture. He hit you?"

"Last night, when he figured out that I must have given Celeste a list from his black book. Binky said you might divorce Charles and that you needed my help."

"I don't want to lose like Celeste did," Lou Anne confessed.

"You won't have to," Jessica reassured her.

Jessica told Lou Anne everything, or at least everything she thought Lou Anne needed to know in order to help Charles make the right decisions.

"It's all here," she said, handing Lou Anne a folder. "All the gifts, the dates we traveled together, all of it."

Jessica handed Lou Anne a second folder.

"What's this?" Lou Anne.

"The secrets. In case Charles has second thoughts about being generous."

"I thought he shredded your copies."

"Why would Charles think I'd be stupid enough to only make one copy?" Jessica laughed.

"He clearly underestimated you."

"There's something else you need to know. He has a safe deposit full of cash from the secrets he's kept. You'll see when you look through the copies that there's a number in the upper right-hand corner on the first page of each secret. No dollar sign, just a number. I suspect it represents the amount of money each person had to pay him in order to keep their secrets hidden. Charles always paid for our trips and dinners together in cash. Made him feel big, I guess. He even paid for my plane tickets in cash. There was no paper trail with any of it, so you couldn't catch him. Since I kept the books in the office, I happen to know for certain that none of the secret-keeping money was ever reported as income. I bet the IRS would love to know how much is in that safe."

"Nice work," Lou Anne said, thumbing through the papers.

"I'm sure Charles would be happy to give you just about anything to keep this information a secret and his ass out of jail. Would you like another cookie?" Jessica offered.

"I think I have all I need. What are you going to do now?" Lou Anne asked.

"Finish my undergraduate degree, then go to law school," Jessica answered.

"I'd hire you in a heartbeat."

Chapter Fifty-Nine
⌘
CELESTE AND MILLIE

"Put on your shoes," Celeste told Millie when she unlocked the door.

"What do I need shoes for?" Millie asked.

"So, I can take you out to dinner."

"Why?"

"Because I want to. Because I can. Because I need to say thank you," Celeste explained.

"For?"

"Taking me in," Celeste said, searching for Millie's other shoe so they could leave. "We've got reservations. At seven. Bloomsbury Bistro."

"Seven! I can't go to Bloomsbury looking like this. I need to change!"

"No, you don't. You're perfect."

Celeste ordered a good bottle of wine and suggested they have appetizers before their main course. She told Millie to be sure to save room for dessert.

"Who's paying for all this, Charles?" Millie asked.

"I am."

"Didn't know being a festival director paid so well."

"It doesn't. Which is something I want to talk with you about," Celeste said.

"Are you still short? You need a loan? If you do, I'm good for it," Millie offered.

"I don't need a loan, but I'll need a place to live."

"Where?"

"With you. I promised Emily she would have a job next year, working with me to create another festival. I've really liked working with Emily, and even Binky. I don't know what I would have done without Binky. I'm new at this job, but together, Emily and I have learned a lot. Next year we won't have the list, not like this year's list, but I'll find another list."

"You're happy?" asked Millie.

"Surprisingly happy," Celeste responded.

"Living with me?"

"Living with you."

"I was hoping you'd stay."

They shared the fried green tomato appetizer and Millie ordered the chicken special. Celeste had the crab cakes. They let the meal stretch out through the bottle of wine.

"I caught Charles red handed, didn't I?" Millie said.

"Yes, you did. Lou Anne is probably going to divorce Charles. She's got enough evidence now with what you saw and what Jessica knows," Celeste explained.

"I don't know anything about Lou Anne, but I know for sure that any woman deserves better than Charles. What about David?"

"I don't need to hurt him. What's done is done and I'm moving on! I've got a festival to run."

Chapter Sixty
⌘
THE TUSCAN CHAMBER ORCHESTRA

The flight to North Carolina was a rough one. Miguel, the youngest orchestra member, had forgotten to set his alarm and showed up ten minutes before the plane was about to board, unshaven and smelling of alcohol. When Franco stepped out of the boarding line to grab him in order to drag him forward to join the rest of the musicians, Miguel started swinging.

Words were exchanged, and the two men were about to come to serious blows when Manuel, the calmer and taller of the two violas, stepped between them and stopped the fight.

"I'll sit with Miguel," Manuel said, putting his arm around Miguel's shoulders in order to steady him and get him into the back of the line and out of Franco's reach.

"He's drunk," Franco said.

"And you're angry," Manuel answered. "What makes you think they're going to let any of us board this plane if the two of you are going at it?"

Danielle pulled on Franco's sleeve, urging him to get back in line. Franco jerked his arm away from Danielle.

"Forget it, Franco," Danielle said, drawing upon all the authority she could muster as concertmaster. "If we don't board this plane, we don't go to the United States, and if we don't show up for this festival, we won't be asked to play another festival ever again."

The other musicians fell quietly in line behind Franco and Danielle, making the distance between the warring factions greater.

The ticket agent walked over to their group.

"Is there a problem?" the agent asked.

"No problem," Danielle answered, linking her arm with Franco's.

"I need to see your tickets. I'm going to have to make some changes in your seat assignments in order to accommodate the instruments. I'll take the two passengers with the cellos first. You'll have to sit together in the middle section with the cellos in the seats between you in order to keep them away from the aisles. The bass goes in back, last seat on the right, please."

Danielle frowned and grabbed Franco's hand.

Franco spoke up, "My wife is afraid of flying. It's important that I sit with her."

"If you're one of the cellos, then you'll have to sit with your cello in the center with the other cello and its owner. Someone else will have to sit with your wife. The airline cannot take responsibility for your instrument, and we won't let you fly unless you are seated next to it. The violins and violas will fit in the overhead compartments."

"What about my wife?" Franco challenged.

"She'll be fine," Gabriella, the other cellist said, stepping forward with her cello. "Surely she can live without you for a couple of hours."

Danielle let go of Franco and glared at Gabriella. Franco stood frozen between the two women.

The ticket agent turned to Franco.

"If you want to fly with us today, you'll fly sitting next to your cello in the middle row of seats with the other cellist and cello. Those are the rules."

Sophie, the principal second violin, stepped out of line and linked her arm with Danielle's. "I can sit with Danielle," she said.

"Are you fine with that?" the agent asked.

Danielle shook her head yes. Gabriella showed the agent her boarding pass and got on behind Franco.

Shortly after dinner was served on the flight, Gabriella started feeling queasy and began throwing up.

Chapter Sixty-One
⌘
CHARLES AND LOU ANNE

Charles arranged to have a small private dinner party at their home for a few of his clients and the Board members before the opening gala for the festival. Lou Anne hired caterers to handle the food and flowers.

"Make it nice," Charles had said.

Lou Anne decided to pull out all the stops. Instead of serving buffet style, the food would be plated and presented at the table. First class, elegant was the ambience she was going for. It turned out to be an excellent decision.

David had been invited, but Binky, of course, had not. In fact, none of Lou Anne's close girlfriends had been invited, which turned out to be fine. She had made some plans of her own for the evening.

The quiet sit-down elegance of the event was exactly what she needed to ensure her plan would work. With a room full of Charles's old clients, and Board members he wanted to impress, Lou Anne was pretty certain he would be on his best behavior. There wouldn't be a scene.

The kids were out seeing a movie with the sitter. Except for the caterers in the kitchen, plating the salad, the house was empty. Lou Anne went into their bedroom and closed the door.

"Jessica and I had tea and cookies this afternoon. In her condo. Nice place." Lou Anne sat down on the edge of their bed.

"I told you I fired Jessica."

"Have you seen this?" Lou Anne asked, taking her phone out of her pocket.

"What?" Charles asked, grabbing Lou Anne's phone.

"Your handprint on Jessica's bare ass. I believe you hit her. Last night."

"She's lying," Charles said.

"Thought you'd say that, which is why she gave me a folder filled with interesting information, plus a copy of the notes you made in that book of yours," Lou Anne said, recapturing her phone. "I am sure all your guests this evening would love to see what you've written about them. I'll be happy to share."

Charles turned his back on Lou Anne and walked to his closet. He started searching for a tie.

"Jessica is such a clever girl. She made two copies of everything, kept one copy in her desk and another at the condo. She was a good bookkeeper too. She had all the dates you slept with her, places you went with her, presents you bought her. You shouldn't have hit her. For the right price, I'm sure she won't press charges. She wants to go to law school. I think she'd make a damn good lawyer. I suggest you help her."

"This is ridiculous."

"Hardly. I'm filing for divorce, and you're not going to make a fuss, not this evening in front of all our guests, not ever. And you're not going to cheat me like you cheated Celeste."

"What makes you think for a minute that you'll get anything, including the kids?" Charles asked.

"The numbers," Lou Anne said.

"What numbers?"

"The ones in your black book. That and the tidy bit of corresponding cash you've kept secret from the IRS. Karma's a bitch. You should know that," Lou Anne said.

"You can't prove anything."

"Your clients can, and I'm pretty sure they would be happy to help verify the numbers once they understand the situation with the IRS and all. I'm betting they have no idea you've kept tabs on them. By the way, I've made a copy of David's entry for Celeste. I plan to give it to her this evening at the gala. A petit cadeau, as the French would say. I think it's about time she understood what happened to her. She's really a rather remarkable woman."

"What does Jessica want in order to keep this photo and these records a secret?" Charles asked.

"She hasn't said exactly, but I'm thinking a nice round figure, say, a hundred thousand. Isn't that where hush money usually starts?"

"It can be that high," Charles answered.

"A hundred thousand should sound like a bargain, given Jessica's bookkeeping skills and her attention to details. She keeps great records. I'm impressed, really impressed. Dates, times, activities, even kept track of all the gifts. She must have been a wonderful office manager. What a shame she won't be helping you anymore."

"A real shame," Charles interjected.

"Of course, the condo is still hers free and clear."

"Free and clear. Her name is on the deed," Charles said.

"That was rather nice of you."

"Glad you think so," Charles answered.

"Then there's the issue of the festival for next year. I'm thinking it would be a nice gesture to give Celeste a start on raising money for next year. I was thinking $50,000 might get the ball rolling."

"Fifty thousand?" Charles choked.

"Cash would be fine. Jessica wasn't sure exactly how much you have in your safe at the moment, but I'm betting it's a lot, probably plenty to start making amends. If you think you might not have quite that much, I'd be happy to count it for you. Maybe get an exact figure for the IRS?"

"I think $50,000 would get the ball rolling," Charles offered.

"Exactly, let people know the festival is here to stay and that you're backing it. Might make it easier for you to pick up the pieces and shine up your sterling silver reputation after our divorce. I'm afraid that scandalous bit of news about the dissolution of our marriage might grab a headline or two: Prominent Lawyer Sued for Divorce Over Secret Love Nest. Could get ugly. You know how people like to gawk and gossip."

"How much money were you thinking it would take to keep things quiet? Make our separation amicable?"

"Such a good question, Charles, one that I will get to in a minute. I have some other items on my list that we need to talk about first."

"Such as?" Charles asked

"How much money were you paying Celeste to build this festival of yours?"

"It isn't my festival," Charles corrected.

"It is now, and forever will be," Lou Anne informed Charles. "As the festival grows, it will need more money, and you know it's going to grow. I love Celeste's idea about building a yearly summer festival rather than a season of boring Sunday afternoon concerts. It is really something, what Celeste has done, don't you think?"

"Quite something," Charles stammered.

"Binky's daughter, Emily, can't quit talking about the music. Says it's magical, absolutely breathtaking. That it has changed her life, that and working with Celeste. Celeste has been a real inspiration for her.

"Celeste was right to spend all the money to bring that orchestra here. It was really genius on her part. I can't wait to hear the concert tonight. Just imagine what Celeste could do if she had more money!"

"I can't imagine," Charles echoed.

"I believe Celeste needs a raise," Lou Anne said.

"A raise?"

"As in, a higher salary. We wouldn't want to lose her, now would we?" Lou Anne asked.

"The Board is paying her $40,000, which is in line with what other area arts organizations pay their directors."

"That's hardly a living wage in this town, don't you agree? Besides, if we want good things, quality programs, shall we say, then I believe we should be willing to pay for them."

"How much am I willing to pay?" Charles asked.

"I think $75,000 is more like it for starters. Raleigh is an expensive town. That, plus the fact that you and David really did a number on her with the divorce, and from what I understand, left her with no real viable means of support. Seventy-five thousand will make her life more comfortable. But, as the festival grows, and Celeste's responsibilities grow, I believe her salary should grow as well. I'll put that in writing for you, so you won't have to remember it on your own."

"Thank you," Charles said, pulling a red and grey striped tie from his closet.

"Celeste is going to need help building the next festival, and luckily, Emily has agreed to stay on for another year. I believe Emily should be paid next year. After her gap year working on the second festival with Celeste, she's made arrangements to go to college at Lawrence University in Wisconsin. Turns out that UNC doesn't have what she wants. She plans to go into arts administration. It's really wonderful what working with Celeste and this festival has done for her."

"Wonderful," said Charles. "How much?"

"Well, I've only started looking into that this afternoon. What do you think?"

"How about $30,000?" Charles offered.

"Let's say $35,000," Lou Anne countered.

"Thirty-five it is, then," Charles said.

"And, another $5,000 as a thank you to Emily for the work she's done this year as an unpaid intern."

"Cash?" Charles asked.

"Cash is always nice," Lou Anne agreed.

"Are we done?"

"No, no, no. Not yet. I really liked the trip to Italy thing you gave Celeste last year. What a nice idea. It sure did shake things up a bit with the Chamber Society, really put them back on the map, big time."

"David paid for Italy. It was his idea," Charles said.

"Would you like to get David involved?" Lou Anne asked.

"I don't think that will be necessary. Let's say it cost $5,000."

"Nice. Five thousand dollars it is for traveling expenses," Lou Anne wrote that down on her list.

"Every year?"

"Every year. How else can Celeste get inspired and find new talent? I mean, as a lawyer, you go to conferences and workshops in order to stay informed and on top of your game. As director of the festival, why shouldn't Celeste visit other festivals to do the same?"

"Why not?" Charles agreed.

"Then there's Binky," Lou Anne said, looking up from her list.

"Binky?"

"She doesn't want, nor does she need any money. Thanks to the great job you did with her divorce. But there's this sticky matter with some secret you've sworn to keep for her. I know you're angry at her for all she did to help Celeste, but I want you to keep in mind that she already paid you to keep that secret."

"And?"

"If you don't, I can promise you, it won't be pretty. It's a deal breaker."

"And the deal is?"

"You keep Binky's secret, and Jessica and I keep yours."

"And all the money you're asking for?"

"Keeps us happy and out of your business."

"Are we done?" Charles asked.

"Let's see, we've taken care of Binky, Jessica, Celeste, Emily and the festival. I guess that just leaves me."

"What do you want?"

"What all your clients usually get."

"What's that?"

"Everything."

Chapter Sixty-Two
⌘
THE GALA

After Celeste figured out what it would actually cost if they went all out on the gala, she decided to make the evening simple but elegant with champagne and passed hors d'oeuvres in the lobby before the gala concert, followed by dessert, coffee and brandy with the musicians afterwards. There would be no open bar and carving station.

When the orchestra had arrived the day before, they balked at having to play for the gala. When Celeste had a moment to talk privately with Franco, he let it slip that there had been some problems in rehearsal, and they had only been able to prepare music for four concerts. They hadn't prepared anything special for the gala.

Celeste calmly explained that the whole point of the gala was to give the big donors a chance to hear the orchestra. There was going to be a gala, and the orchestra was going to play for it. She stood firm and didn't budge.

After a rather heated discussion, it was decided that the gala performance could be a teaser for the festival. The orchestra would play something they had prepared for one of the other concerts as a kind of special preview of coming attractions. Franco reluctantly agreed and chose two pieces: the Tchaikovsky *Serenade for Strings in C* and Mendelssohn's *Capriccio in E*.

Both pieces were scheduled for the final concert. The *Serenade for Strings* would be the last piece they would play in the festival. Franco was pleased with the idea of an opening and closing of the festival marked by this piece.

Celeste had wanted more than two pieces for the gala but accepted Franco's proposal. The orchestra agreed to play two pieces and mingle with the crowd after, although Danielle thought they should be paid extra for the event. Given the late change of plans, not to mention the cost of printing yet another program, Celeste told Franco he would announce the pieces from the stage. He wasn't pleased but agreed.

The programs were back from the printer and looked beautiful. Emily suggested using them, arguing that having the full program in hand, rather than a separate program for the gala, would give the attendees a first look of what was to come during the week of the festival.

"Chips and dips would have been cheaper," Emily said, watching the waiters weave their way through the crowd, passing food and filling champagne glasses.

"I should have thought about that," Celeste said.

"How can you tell if they're having fun?" Emily asked.

"Never easy with this crowd," Celeste answered. "Let's hope they buy more tickets."

Emily had sold twenty concert tickets when people first came in, but things had slowed down once the champagne corks popped.

"The champagne was a mistake," Emily informed Celeste, rattling her nearly empty cash box.

"Champagne is never a mistake," Celeste said.

"Once they started drinking, they quit buying tickets."

"You need to give folks time to socialize and enjoy themselves. Ticket sales will pick up once they hear the music and loosen up with a brandy or two."

"That's your plan?" Emily asked.

"It's all I've got."

Millie came racing around the corner, the hem of her long dress clutched in her hand so she could run rather than walk.

"Backstage," she stammered. She was out of breath from running.

"What happened?"

"You've got a sick musician."

Celeste linked her arm in Millie's and drew her close to her so she could whisper in her mother's ear.

"Straighten your dress. Have a glass of champagne, smile and mingle with the crowd. Not another word about someone being sick. I'll be right back."

Celeste found Binky.

"I've got to take care of something backstage," Celeste told her.

"Nice crowd," Binky said.

"Keep them drinking and eating. I might need to hold the curtain ten more minutes."

Celeste grabbed a waiter. "I need a can of ginger ale or coke and some crackers," she told him.

The waiter came back with a coke and a napkin full of crackers.

When she got backstage, the orchestra was milling around tuning. Franco was standing outside the bathroom door and Danielle was pacing angrily back and forth.

"I think Gabriella has food poisoning," Franco said. "She got sick on the plane right after she ate dinner."

Danielle glared at Franco. "I told you to replace her!"

Celeste knocked on the bathroom door.

"Please let me in. I have something for you to drink, and some crackers to help settle your stomach."

"That drink had better do more than settle her stomach. Maybe you can teach her how to count while you're in there," Danielle hissed.

Gabriella opened the door. Celeste brushed by Danielle and Franco and closed the door behind her. She took one look at Gabriella and instinctively knew.

"It's not food poisoning, is it?"

"I feel sick," Gabriella answered.

"How many weeks?"

"Six, maybe eight."

"Who knows?"

"No one. It's Franco's."

"Franco's? Is that why Danielle wanted him to replace you?"

"She doesn't know. Franco doesn't either," Gabriella bent over the toilet and retched again.

Celeste handed her the coke.

"The coke and the crackers will help settle your stomach. Have a couple more sips and take the crackers with you. I need to get everyone on stage."

"I can't play," Gabriella said.

"You have to play. There are no options here. Take your time, wash your face and rinse out your mouth. I'll handle Franco and Danielle, at least for the moment."

Celeste left Gabriella in the bathroom so she could get herself together.

"She's feeling much better. I told her she could have five minutes to wash up and give her stomach a moment to settle. I can hold the curtain for another ten minutes or so. Are we good?"

"We are good," Franco said, relieved.

"We would be better with a different cellist," Danielle replied.

"We are good," Franco snapped and walked away.

"Quite a party," David said, coming up behind Celeste and sliding his hand down her back in order to give her butt a squeeze. Celeste angrily pushed his hand away.

"What are you doing here?" Celeste whispered.

"Charles invited me," David offered.

"How thoughtful. Where's Charles?"

Celeste had seen Lou Anne's mother and father come in, but not Charles and Lou Anne.

"Probably still at the house taking care of some sticky domestic details. Charles and Lou Anne hosted a fancy dinner party for a few folks to kick off the festival."

"How nice," said Celeste, stepping away.

"Aren't you going to say thank you?" David asked.

"For what?" Celeste asked.

"Sending you to Italy, getting you this great job. I thought it was the least I could do."

"I'll bet you did," Celeste said sarcastically.

"How did you persuade so many rich people to give you money? I hear that's not easy."

"You didn't think I could do it, did you?" Celeste challenged.

"Oh look, Binky Covington is here! I was so surprised she wasn't invited to the dinner party. Any idea what that was about? If you'll excuse me, I need to talk with her."

Millie came up alongside of Celeste and handed her some champagne.

"Just say the word." Millie said.

"I'm fine," Celeste said, downing the drink.

"Son of a bitch thought you couldn't do it. Binky told me Charles fired Jessica," Millie said.

"Something like that," Celeste said.

"I guess he won't be going to the Park Devereux anymore," Millie chuckled.

"I think you've had enough champagne." Celeste grabbed Millie's glass and polished it off. "Could you grab me another?" Celeste asked. "This is going to be a long night."

"Binky, Binky, Binky," David crowed. "What a surprise!"

"The surprise is all mine," Binky said, smiling.

"Look at all these people with all their crazy secrets. Why didn't you call me?" David asked.

Binky took a sip of her champagne.

"I had no idea you liked classical music," Binky offered.

The house lights flickered.

Charles and Lou Anne slid into the lobby right when Emily stood up to announce that people should get ready to move into the auditorium and take their seats. Roger came in, striding ten steps behind Charles and Lou Anne.

"You and I need to talk," Roger said, taking hold of Binky's arm.

Binky broke away from David and went off with Roger.

David turned and walked away.

Millie found a waiter and swiped the last two glasses of champagne from his tray. She handed one to Celeste.

"Show time," Millie said, clinking her glass against Celeste's in a toast.

"Give me a minute to get backstage," Celeste told Emily and Millie. "When everyone is in, close the house doors and take a seat in the back row. I want to be able to look out over the crowd and see the two of you."

Celeste saw Charles and Lou Anne come in. Lou Anne flashed Celeste a smile and waved. Charles turned his back on Lou Anne, which meant he had also turned his back on Celeste. Celeste tried to get his attention, but Charles didn't acknowledge her.

Celeste headed down the hallway.

It was time to close the house doors.

"Is there room for one more?" Thad called out to Emily.

"I can't wait for you to hear the Tchaikovsky!" Emily said.

"Wouldn't miss it for the world," Thad answered.

Millie came into the lobby.

"All accounted for?" Emily asked Millie.

Jessica came running in at the last minute.

"Am I too late?" Jessica asked.

"For champagne, but not the music," Emily said.

"I don't have a ticket," Jessica confessed.

"From all I've heard from Celeste about what you've done," Millie said, coming up behind Jessica and ushering her into the auditorium. "Your ticket is covered. I'd be honored if you'd sit with me."

Celeste was surprised by what you could see when you stepped to the front of the stage and looked out beyond the stage lights. She let her gaze roll over the crowd until she could focus on Millie and Emily. That's when she caught sight of Thad sitting next to Emily. Jessica was there as well, next to Millie.

She had not expected to see Thad with Emily or Jessica sitting next to Millie. Nor had she anticipated that David would show up. The world had shifted on her a little and was demanding her to speak out. There were old scores to settle.

Celeste had thought that if she could keep looking at Emily and Millie while she talked, she could get through this introduction with some sense of grace and style. It had been a rough time getting where she was on that stage, and she didn't want to ever lose ground again. She had found her place, and she liked it.

Celeste scanned the crowd until she could adjust her eyes to the strange dark and glare from the stage in order to locate Charles and Lou Anne. Roger and Binky were sitting together a couple of rows behind them. David was five rows behind Binky, sitting on the aisle by himself.

All the people who had brought both trouble and joy into her life were now seated before her in the audience. It was time to acknowledge them and move forward.

The applause died down.

"Welcome to the gala opening of the first festival of the newly revived Chamber Society. This is a fresh start, and I hope, it will be the first of many festivals to come. Before I introduce you to the delightful and talented Tuscan Chamber Orchestra, I need to thank the City of Raleigh for their generous support not only of this festival, but all of the arts in Raleigh.

And I also want to thank my incredible assistant, Emily Covington. Emily, will you please stand? And her mother, Binky Covington."

Applause filled the auditorium.

"This festival would not have happened without the help of these two amazing women. By the way, Emily will be out in the lobby selling tickets right after the concert. Please go by and say hello and thank her for all she's done."

Laughter.

Emily stood, graciously threw Celeste a kiss and sat down. Thad squeezed Emily's hand and kissed her cheek. Binky, who was sitting with Roger several rows in front of Emily and the crew, waved to the crowd like the queen she was and would always be.

"I'd also like to give a special thanks to the two men who sent me to Italy last summer in search of a way to ignite this great new beginning for both myself and the Chamber Society."

Celeste looked straight at Charles and motioned for him to stand. Charles sat frozen in his seat. Lou Anne sat quietly beside Charles, a Cheshire Cat grin spreading across her face as if she knew what was going to happen next.

"Charles, will you please stand?" Celeste called out.

Lou Anne gave Charles a nudge and he stood.

While the applause rose, Celeste turned her gaze to another man.

"And David. Please join him!"

David stood, straightened his coat, and nodded to the crowd.

Celeste raised her hands in applause.

"I'm sure the two of you had no idea what all of this would cost you when you cooked up this crazy idea to hire me! But thank you."

The audience laughed and applauded.

"And, of course, many thanks to all of you here this evening. We couldn't have done any of this without your generous support. I hope once you hear these wonderful musicians play, you'll tell all your friends and help make this, our first summer festival, a sustainable success. As a special thank you, we would like to invite all of you to join us in the lobby after the performance to have brandy and dessert with the orchestra. And of course, to buy more tickets!

"And now, it is my great pleasure to introduce to you the Tuscan Chamber Orchestra!"

Celeste turned to welcome the orchestra onto the stage. Franco came out first. As the other musicians filed onto the stage and found their places, Franco took Celeste's hand, kissed it and raised it, then brought it down in a gracious bow, allowing Celeste to catch the applause.

"Thank you," Franco said, letting go of Celeste's hand so she could leave.

When the musicians were in place, Franco moved to the front of the stage.

"This is our first time playing in the United States. It is a pleasure to be here. This evening we will be giving you just a taste of what is to come this week. We hope, of course, that you will come back another evening for the full dinner!"

The audience applauded.

"The first piece we will play is Mendelssohn's *Capriccio in E*. Mendelssohn wrote the Capriccio for a quartet, but I have arranged it for our orchestra. I believe you will be pleased. It is a short, but powerful piece. One that lends itself to a big sound. The second is a favorite of ours, the beautiful *Serenade for Strings* written by Tchaikovsky. I hope you will enjoy."

The Mendelssohn played out, as planned by Franco, like a bewitching spider web that spun itself around and through the audience leaving them breathless.

"Wow," Thad said, when the applause died down.

"Wait until you hear the Tchaikovsky," Emily whispered to her father. "It's like, I don't know, like magic, like nothing I've ever heard before. It's what I told you, why I have to do this."

Thad put his arm around Emily and leaned in as the music began.

The orchestra struck the first grand chord, it hit like a bolt of lightning: sure, and deep. Then came the lyric promise of the waltz, a gentle sashay that wooed Thad to sit back in his chair and let go. The slow movement touched a nerve. He leaned over and kissed Emily on the cheek in order to keep from weeping.

"I'm so proud of you," he said.

"Close your eyes," Emily whispered in her father's ear before the start of the last movement. "Keep them shut, and imagine horses, wild horses, running, a train barreling through a mountain pass, a storm building. It's magnificent." As the last movement began, Jessica quietly rose from her seat and made her way to the back of the auditorium. Celeste was standing alone by the door.

"I best get out of here as soon as you open the doors," Jessica said, giving Celeste a hug. "I suspect all hell is going to break loose once the music stops and Charles gets to drinking."

"Thanks. I hope it was worth it for you," Celeste said.

"You bet. And then some. This was really something, something wonderful that you've done. Thank you!"

As soon as the applause began, Celeste opened the doors so Jessica could make her escape.

The audience stood and clapped and called for more until Franco came back on stage and motioned for the orchestra to return for an encore of the last movement of the Tchaikovsky.

Celeste noticed that Gabriella was missing for the encore.

Chapter Sixty-Three
⌘
CHARLES, LOU ANNE, DAVID AND THAD

Charles picked up a second snifter of brandy and downed it.

"Clever," he said, leaning in close to Lou Anne so he could whisper, except he'd already had too much to drink, so the whisper came out more like a bark. "You think you're so clever, wearing that gaudy ring, telling me you're going to leave me, when there are all these people around. You can't."

"You're drunk, and I can. You need to sober up, write a few checks, and bow out gracefully, or you might risk being publicly exposed as both a philanderer and someone who physically abuses women. Once the fog of the alcohol subsides, I believe you will be able to clearly see that you could possibly be disbarred for some pretty sleazy misrepresentation on the part of your clients, and most probably go to jail for tax evasion. Not to mention how angry your clients will be if they ever discover those secrets you've promised to keep for them have leaked out. I wonder what the losers in your divorce cases might think of all that information. All those hidden secrets. Could be interesting, don't you think?

"By the way, while you are deciding how quickly you want to move out and move on with our divorce, Jessica has graciously agreed not to press charges. At least for the time being. That photo is pretty damning."

"What were you saying, Charles?" Binky said, sidling up to Charles and linking her arm through his. "I missed it."

"Don't touch me," Charles growled and pulled away from Binky. "I kept your secrets! I kept all of them, every one of them!" he shouted, twirling around to encompass the room. "I kept them all!"

The crowd quieted. People stepped back to make room for Charles as he stumbled out the door. No one offered to comfort or help him.

"Coffee, anyone?" Celeste asked in the silence.

The crowd began talking again.

"You okay?" Lou Anne asked Binky.

"Shouldn't I be the one asking you?" Binky responded.

"Knowing the truth is so much better than not knowing or wondering. I've always wondered if Charles was cheating on me and now that I know, I'm relieved. At last I can quit wondering and thinking about it all the time. I feel great."

"This isn't going to be easy," Binky warned.

"No, but it will be worth it," Lou Anne said.

"I think I have some long overdue truth telling to do before Charles beats me to it," Binky said.

Roger came up behind Lou Anne and slipped his arm around her shoulders.

"Are we okay?" asked Roger.

"We're fine," Lou Anne said.

"If you'll excuse me, I need to give something to Celeste," Lou Anne said, leaving Roger and Binky alone.

"Lou Anne told me what you did in order to help her make the decision to leave Charles," Roger said.

"It needed to be done," Binky replied.

"Secrets," Roger said, taking a sip of brandy.

"I'm going to have to tell Thad about the abortion before Charles does. He's pretty angry about what I've done to help Celeste. I wouldn't put it past him to tell what he knows in order to get back at me. Fortunately, he doesn't know about you. Thad needs to know about the abortion, but he doesn't need to know about you and neither does Lou Anne. What happened between us was nobody's business but ours. I plan to keep it that way."

"For what it's worth, I loved you then, and I like you now," Roger said. "The music was magnificent. What you did to help make this happen is really something. Admirable in a twisted Binky kind of way. Thanks for asking me to be part of it."

"That might be one of the nicer things anyone has ever said to me," Binky said. "Thanks."

Lou Anne found Celeste standing off to the side watching the crowd.

"The Tchaikovsky was amazing," Lou Anne said.

"It was really something, wasn't it," replied Celeste.

"Pretty brave and smart of you to call out both Charles and David. You've got class. I like that. I have to apologize for dropping you after your divorce," Lou Anne said, reaching out to take Celeste's hand.

"Apology accepted," said Celeste.

"Pretty shallow and bitchy on my part. I plan to make it up to you, help you with the festival next year. The festival and the music have been inspiring, as well as what you've done for Emily. You've been quite the role model."

"It was my pleasure, but thanks," Celeste answered.

"I've read David's entry in Charles's black book. It's pretty disgusting. I made a copy for you. Thought you should have it. You deserve to know what happened. Don't know what you can do now that the divorce is over and all, but I thought you should know all the things David and Charles hid from you."

Celeste took the envelope from Lou Anne.

"Do I want to know?" Celeste asked.

"Up to you. But you have it now. You might need it. Knowledge is power and all that," Lou Anne added.

"Good luck with Charles," said Celeste.

"Thanks for your help with that. Thank Millie for me also. I hope I'll have the guts to stand up for my children the way she's stood by you. You're lucky to have her on your side."

Celeste laughed. "I'm stuck with Millie and pretty happy about it these days."

"I need to see Emily and buy some festival tickets while there are still some left. I have a number of people I want to bring to the concerts, people without secrets who might be willing to help us make this happen again next year. Lunch soon?" Lou Anne asked.

"Lunch soon," responded Celeste.

After Lou Anne slipped away, Millie walked over to Celeste carrying two snifters of brandy.

"Want one?" Millie asked Celeste. "What did Lou Anne want?"

"To give me this." Celeste showed the envelope to Millie.

"More money?" Millie asked.

"Better than money. A guarantee."

"More secrets?" Millie asked.

"The kind that can set you free," Celeste answered.

"To you," Millie said, clinking her glass with Celeste's in a toast.

"And to you," Celeste answered, taking a sip of her brandy.

"What happens next?" Millie asked.

"I think I'll ask David."

Things seemed to be falling into place. The orchestra members were weaving through the audience. Franco was in his element being adored by the crowd. Danielle was drinking brandy with Manuel and Carmen. The three of them were caught up in an animated conversation with Lou Anne and Roger. Roger was entertaining all of them with his charming, but patchy, knowledge of classical music and French.

Miguel had pulled up a chair and was sitting next to Emily. Miguel was drinking brandy and talking with patrons while Emily sold them tickets. It seemed innocent enough from a distance. Emily had, as promised, stayed away from trouble while she was an intern, and Celeste was pretty sure, with both Binky and Thad around, all would remain copasetic.

Celeste took another sip of her brandy and made a quick inventory of the crowd, trying to get a sense of what was developing. People looked like they were having a good time. Thad and Binky were talking with each other over in the corner, and it appeared to be friendly.

While Franco held court, the other musicians inserted themselves among the big donors, smiling and nodding as they drank and ate dessert, doing their best to keep up with the English conversations around them. They were pros at working the after- performance crowd. Gabriella was nowhere to be seen.

Celeste didn't know whom she should worry about more: Emily or Gabriella. She was pretty certain Emily could handle herself and fairly certain Miguel had enough sense to behave, or at least she hoped he did.

She was less sure, however, that Gabriella could manage both the situation of having to play a series of concerts battling morning sickness and Danielle's wrath if she found out the baby was Franco's. Celeste didn't have a clue how Franco would respond to the announcement of Gabriella's pregnancy, and she sincerely hoped that he'd find out later rather than sooner. Like maybe once their plane took off for Italy.

She had a festival to run.

Celeste walked over to Emily.

"How's it going?" Celeste asked.

"Your plan worked," Emily said, taking another order for more tickets.

"The music was wonderful," Celeste said, turning to Miguel.

"You liked?" he asked.

"Very much."

"Tomorrow the Dvorak," said Miguel.

"I can't wait," Emily replied.

"Can you give me a set of tickets for the rest of the concerts?" Celeste asked Emily.

"It's going to cost you," Emily teased.

"It already has."

David had picked up a fresh snifter of brandy and was standing off to the side alone.

"Nice move," he said, lifting his glass to Celeste. "Were you thinking, if you put me on the spot I'd go away."

"Or write me a check," Celeste said.

"Why in the world would I do that?" David asked.

"This," Celeste offered, showing David the envelope Lou Anne had given her.

"What's that?"

"A page out of Charles' book of secrets. Your page. Lou Anne gave it to me tonight."

"You've read it?" David asked.

"Don't need to. I already know about the condo. Jessica told me about that. Lou Anne said there were other things as well."

"The divorce is final. Don't think you can cash in anymore," David announced.

"I don't think I ever cashed in," responded Celeste.

"You had a good life," David said.

"I had a nice house and a lousy marriage. Good wasn't part of the equation."

"Were we ever happy?" David asked.

"Probably not," replied Celeste.

"Should I apologize?"

"Too late," Celeste answered.

"I cheated you out of everything."

"Sending me to Italy, cooking up this weird idea of resurrecting the Chamber Society in order to get me out of town and out of your business might have been the best gift you or anyone else has ever given me. Better than the house and the diamond necklace. All of it."

"What do you want?" David asked.

"To give you this. I don't need to read it."

"Everybody wants something," David said.

"I want this festival to go on. It's good. Maybe the best thing I've ever done in my life," explained Celeste.

"I don't understand," David said.

Celeste stuffed Lou Anne's envelope into David's jacket pocket.

"Am I supposed to thank you?" David asked.

"After you hear the rest of the concerts," Celeste said, handing him the tickets she'd just gotten from Emily.

"I can't take your tickets," David protested.

"They're a gift. You have to take them. As they say in Italy, it's bad luck to turn down a gift."

The crowd was beginning to thin. Celeste was saying goodbye to the last of the guests and starting to close up shop. Emily was packing up the tickets.

"A good night?" Celeste asked.

"Amazing," Emily responded. "The brandy was brilliant, as was the music."

"The perfect combo," Millie chimed in. She'd had one too many, but not so many that she couldn't pitch in and help Emily with the clean-up. She was smiling.

Celeste sent the orchestra to their hotel. She had been busy working the crowd in the front and hadn't had time to check in with Gabriella to see if she was feeling better. Since both Danielle and Franco were in good spirits when they boarded the bus, Celeste figured that at least for the moment they had dodged the sure-fire explosion of the baby bomb. She hoped Gabriella would hold up through the rest of the concerts.

Binky and Thad had slipped out earlier, telling Emily they were going to catch a late dinner together. Emily didn't ask any questions. She was just happy to see they weren't snarling at each other for a change.

"Emily is something else," Thad said to Binky.

He and Binky were sitting at a corner table at Five Star having a plate of Heat Seeker Shrimp, one of Binky's favorites, and a generous concession on Thad's part. He claimed he only ate seafood in restaurants where he could see water. Lots of water, like the ocean. At least, Binky had argued when she ordered, the shrimp was fried.

"Yes, she really is something wonderful," Binky offered. "Did you know she listens to classical music all the time?"

"Emily told me. Also told me she isn't going to go to UNC."

"But she's going to go to school. Did she tell you that? Binky said, spearing another shrimp.

"You've done a good job," Thad said.

"If you're going to thank anyone, thank Celeste. She's the one who turned things around. Emily has worked her butt off for her. We should both be thanking Celeste."

"I told Emily I'd help with the festival next year. Write some checks, spread the word, anything she wants."

"I want to tell you something," Binky said, putting down her fork.

"We were never good at talking, were we?"

"I want to be the one to tell you, not Charles," Binky offered, almost in a whisper.

"What could Charles possibly have to say to me that I would care about now?"

"He knows something. Something I asked him to keep out of the divorce."

"That you paid him to keep secret?"

"I was afraid if you knew something about my past, I'd lose Emily. I couldn't. I didn't want to take the chance. So yes, I paid Charles to keep my secret. I paid him a lot."

Thad didn't say anything. Instead, he leaned back in his chair until the two front legs lifted off the floor.

"Does Emily know this secret?" Thad asked balancing lightly in his seat.

"No," replied Binky.

"We put her through a lot. I can see that now," Thad said.

"We did, but no more secrets," Binky said, reaching across the table, hoping for whatever reason to be able for that moment to hold Thad's hand again.

"Tell me," he said. He shoved his hands deep into his pockets in order to avoid touching Binky's hand. He let his chair fall gently back to the floor, so it was once again firmly on four legs.

"I was young, stupid, got pregnant, and I had an abortion."

Binky took a deep breath and held it.

Thad slipped his hands from his pockets and leaned forward. He cradled Binky's outstretched hand in his two hands.

"Did your parents know?" he asked.

"No. No one knew, except the boy and his parents. I had to sign an agreement that I would end the pregnancy and keep it a secret."

"Did the father of your baby go with you?"

"No," Binky whispered.

"You were alone?" Thad asked quietly.

Alone. That day in that dark room with people she didn't know who didn't know her came back like a rush of cold wind and blew through her. She couldn't speak.

Thad got up and moved his chair next to hers. He put his big arms around her.

"I can't imagine," he said, stroking her hair.

Binky started crying.

"You shouldn't have been alone. He should have gone with you. Someone needed to be there with you."

Her tears were warm and bitter, deeply sad and terrifying. She couldn't stop them.

"I don't know how you did it by yourself and kept it inside all these years," he said, pulling her closer. "I can't imagine. I would want someone to be there with Emily if this ever happened to her. Can you tell her? Would you tell her, please? Tell her I would be there for her. I wouldn't let her be alone."

Chapter Sixty-Four
⌘
EMILY

Emily heard her mother come in shortly after 1 am.

"Hey," Emily called out from her room.

"Hey," Binky called back.

"You okay?" Emily asked, getting out of bed.

Binky started up the stairs.

"Better," Binky said. She was standing in the doorway to Emily's bedroom thinking about all the times she had stood there before and had been angry at Emily because her room was a mess or school was a mess or life in general was a mess.

"The music was amazing, the whole evening was amazing," Emily said, plopping herself back onto her bed.

"Amazing," Binky echoed. She wanted to hug Emily. To tell her how much she loved her. To thank her for managing to live through all the terrible things she and Thad had done to her and still come out kicking and willing to take on the world. Binky wanted to tell Emily that she was beautiful and full of grace and that she loved her more tonight than she had ever loved her before. She had wanted to say all those things but couldn't for the moment speak.

"I'm glad Dad came," Emily offered.

Binky stepped into the room and sat on the edge of Emily's bed.

"He's not a bad person," Binky managed at last.

"He said he'd help me, help us with the festival. That he'd make sure it happened again."

"And he will," Binky said. "You can count on it. We both will."

"I saw you talking."

"And now," Binky said, "we should talk."

Binky told her about the abortion. About how hard it had been holding that secret from Thad and how that secret had simmered and rotted their marriage in a way she had only now come to understand.

She also told her how hard it was to be alone in the world and how being alone with her own secrets had made her tougher than she needed to be and maybe too quick to judge others. She also told Emily that she never wanted her to have to feel like she was alone ever again. She said she knew both she and Thad, in the confusion of their own troubled relationship, had pushed Emily away when she probably needed them most, and she was sorry about that. Very sorry.

"I wanted you to hear about the abortion from me, not from Charles or from anyone else. I owe you that and much more. Charles is pretty angry about the list," Binky said.

"The festival wasn't supposed to happen, was it?" Emily asked.

"It appears that Charles and David had intended otherwise," Binky replied.

"Celeste wouldn't quit. Even when we didn't get the money we needed from that grant; she wouldn't quit. Whenever things were falling apart, or the money wasn't coming in, Celeste would start talking about that night she heard the orchestra play in the piazza in Italy. How it was like magic, like nothing she had ever heard or experienced before. She made me love the music and the idea of creating a festival where other people could feel that same thing she had when she first heard them play. After a while, I felt like the world would fall apart if I couldn't hear the music that she had heard. Making the festival happen for Celeste became the most important thing in my life."

Binky reached out and took her daughter's hand.

"I could see that loving something and wanting something that much mattered more than anything else in the world to Celeste," Emily continued. "Celeste didn't care whether Charles or anyone else understood it or not. She made me feel it too, and it made me feel alive."

"The two of you made something quite special happen," Binky said, stroking her daughter's hair.

"Thanking Charles and David this evening before the concert was Celeste's way of declaring her independence from them, wasn't it? It was her way of telling them they could fuck off. She didn't need them or anyone else to define her anymore."

Binky laughed.

Chapter Sixty-Five
⌘
GABRIELLA AND THE OPEN REHEARSAL

The front rows of the auditorium were filling up.

Binky came up beside Celeste and put her arm around her. "The open rehearsal was a brilliant idea."

"I'll be happy when we get through it. Franco and Danielle were a bit touchy this morning. Danielle doesn't like the idea of people hearing their mistakes."

"Mistakes make it real. This crowd is ready to hear more. Last night was stunning," Binky offered.

"I'm sure Charles and David loved it," Celeste said.

"David's a big boy and deserved what he got. Charles needs some time to adjust. He took quite a hit from the combined forces of Lou Anne and Jessica, not to mention Millie's damning detective work."

"Well deserved," Celeste added. "I need to get backstage and get this thing started."

Emily was in the lobby selling tickets.

"Going well?" Celeste asked as she breezed by Emily's table.

"Could be better," Emily replied.

Millie was standing by the door greeting folks as they entered. "You've got more coming in," she called out to Celeste.

"If anyone walks up after we get started, tell them to be quiet when they come in and to sit in the back," Celeste instructed.

"Will do," Millie said, opening the door for another rush of people. "Looks like a full house coming down the street!"

Things were tense backstage.

"We've got a nice crowd," Celeste said as she approached Franco.

Franco and Danielle were off to the side arguing. The rest of the orchestra was churning around tuning, trying hard not to get sucked into the argument.

"I told you to get rid of her," Danielle shouted at Franco.

"We're about to get started," Celeste said, trying to force a smile.

"No," Danielle snapped.

Franco put his hand on Danielle's shoulder.

"It's almost one," Celeste said. "I'm going to give a couple more minutes for people to get seated then I'll go on stage, make the introductions, and you can come on stage and get started."

"We need to wait," Franco said.

"For?" Celeste asked.

"Gabriella," Danielle answered for Franco. "Her head is in the toilet where it belongs."

Celeste made a beeline for the women's bathroom. Gabriella was there, exactly as Danielle had described, with her head in the toilet retching.

"The rehearsal is about to start," Celeste whispered.

"I can't," Gabriella gasped.

"You have to," Celeste pleaded.

"Find someone else," Gabriella wailed.

"Like I told you last night, quitting is not an option. Do you want Danielle to win? Or the orchestra to think she was right to want to fire you? That you're not as good as she is, or they are?"

"I can't," Gabriella protested.

"What's done is done. Own up to it and move on. Don't let Danielle beat you, and for heaven's sake, don't let Franco walk away from this. No matter how this plays out, if you don't go on that stage, you're the loser. Do you want that?"

"No," Gabriella said, pushing away from the toilet. "Give me a minute."

"You've got two minutes to wash your face and get on stage."

When Celeste returned backstage, Danielle was standing in the middle of a knot of sympathetic musicians. She was ranting about Gabriella faking being sick, being irresponsible, being a second-rate musician. The others were listening.

Celeste grabbed Franco.

"Get a handle on this situation, now," Celeste said. "It's your job to make sure the orchestra, including Gabriella, is on stage, smiling and ready to play. I've got an audience full of people eager to hear you rehearse."

"How can Gabriella play? She's sick. We have to cancel this rehearsal," Franco said.

"She's not sick," Celeste said.

"The food on the plane. She has food poisoning. There will be no rehearsal until you take her to see a doctor," Franco demanded.

Celeste pulled Franco to the side of the stage to make certain the others wouldn't hear what she was going to say.

"She doesn't have food poisoning," Celeste informed Franco.

"You're not a doctor," he responded.

"True, but I do know what's wrong with her, and it's not going to stop this rehearsal."

"Why has she been sick ever since we got on the plane to come here?" Franco asked.

"She's pregnant. And you are going to manage this because I have risked my future and my reputation to bring you and your orchestra here, and I'm not going to fail now. If you do not get on that stage and do this rehearsal in two minutes, then I will tell your wife that Gabriella is carrying your child. Do you understand?"

"My child?" Franco asked.

"Yes."

"But how?"

"I believe you know how and can probably guess when."

Celeste left Franco standing by himself and walked out on stage.

"Good afternoon," she called out to the nearly full auditorium.

"Good afternoon!" the crowd shouted back.

"Welcome to the first open rehearsal of the first music festival of the newly revitalized Chamber Society. My name is Celeste Anderson and I'm proud to be the new director of the Chamber Society. Thank you for coming this afternoon," Celeste announced.

"An open rehearsal is not a concert. Rather than playing a piece from beginning to end, the orchestra will work through certain lines and parts in a variety of pieces they will be performing during the festival. The orchestra may work on pieces for this evening's concert, or some other piece for another night. They'll stop from time-to-time to discuss how to play something a different way. The group works without a conductor, so they talk about things and make decisions together. Who knows, they might even have an argument or two. Nothing is scripted or polished. This is not a performance, per se, but a special backstage look into how an orchestra works."

Celeste took a deep breath and went on. "If you have to leave before the rehearsal is over, please do so quietly. The orchestra has asked that you hold your applause until the end of the rehearsal. The concerts this evening and tomorrow are nearly sold out, so if you're interested, my assistant Emily will be in the front lobby selling tickets. We still have tickets left for the final two concerts. Please tell your friends. Better yet bring your friends!"

Laughter.

"And now, it is my special pleasure to introduce the truly amazing Tuscan Chamber Orchestra."

Celeste turned and stepped to the side to make room for the musicians to come on stage in order to take their seats. Franco nodded to Danielle. She stood and played a clear fine A. The violins tuned to Danielle's A, then the violas, the cellos, and last, the bass. Satisfied, Danielle took her seat. Franco sat down and tapped his stand.

"Dvorak, from the beginning," Franco called out.

The quiet sound of pages being turned fluttered through the waiting audience as the orchestra members searched their respective folders for the Dvorak's *Serenade for Strings in E Major.* Eventually, the musicians slid back into their seats, ready to play. Franco nodded and the music rolled out from the stage: a warm wave, an ocean full of sunshine, fat with color and the promise of brilliant fireworks of chords and emotion.

"Amazing," Binky said as Celeste slipped into the back of the auditorium and stood next to her.

"I love this piece," Celeste said.

"You, you were amazing. You're there, all there, in control. You've done it. You don't need anyone to tell you what to do. You're in charge. It's electric!"

"I'm in trouble," Celeste said, grabbing Binky's hand and dragging her out into the hall.

"Charles?" Binky asked.

"Gabriella," Celeste whispered.

"Who's Gabriella?"

"The cellist, the one sitting next to Franco. No, sleeping with Franco," Celeste corrected.

"But," Binky started.

"Franco is married to Danielle. Franco is also sleeping with Gabriella."

"Who am I to judge? I slept with David," Binky said.

"Gabriella's pregnant. Danielle doesn't know, or at least isn't positive about the affair but certainly doesn't know about the baby. In the meantime, she's suspicious. Keeps demanding that Franco get rid of Gabriella. She was backstage trying to get the other musicians to stand with her. There's more," Celeste said.

"More?" Binky asked, leaning closer.

"Franco wanted me to cancel the rehearsal. Take Gabriella to the doctor. He said she was in the bathroom throwing up because she had food poisoning from the food on the plane."

"You told him that it wasn't food poisoning," Binky said, filling in the blanks.

"And, that the baby was his and if he didn't handle the situation, get Danielle to back off, get the orchestra on stage and the rehearsal started, that I'd tell."

"Bold, but effective," Binky offered.

"I've never threatened anyone in my life," Celeste confessed.

"Not even David?" Binky asked.

"Not even David."

"Talk about firsts," Binky said, giving her a high five.

"How long does morning sickness last?" Celeste asked.

"Depends on how far along she is," Binky explained.

"She thinks she's maybe six weeks. Could be as many as eight. Gabriella said traveling all the time and being onstage was stressful, and she often missed a period," Celeste said.

"She could be sick for a couple more days or a couple more weeks," Binky said.

"How about a couple more concerts?" Celeste asked.

"Keep her hydrated. Give her crackers to nibble on," Binky offered.

"What do I do if Danielle finds out?" Celeste asked.

"It won't be the first time some stupid husband has slept with another woman and gotten her pregnant."

"But it might be the first time it played out on stage in front of a packed auditorium during the second movement of the Dvorak."

"True," Binky said.

"What am I going to do?" Celeste asked.

"Take a break. Emily and I can handle the rehearsal. Things will settle down."

Chapter Sixty-Six
⌘
CELESTE

Celeste walked across the street to get a cup of coffee. She couldn't remember the last time she had been outside during daylight hours. The sun felt good on her face. She slipped off her sweater and pushed back her shirt-sleeves. Her arms were pasty white. She hadn't been to the beach since her divorce.

Her divorce. It had seemed like such a tragedy a year ago. The humiliation. Moving in with her mother. Having to get a job.

But now, in the light of all that had happened in the last twelve months, getting a divorce from David had more perks than being married to David ever had, in spades.

Working invigorated her. She loved the rhythm of the day, of waking up, driving downtown, getting coffee, opening the door to her office. She even loved her dingy hole in the wall office. She looked forward to hearing Emily coming to work, walking down the sacred arts hallway in her motorcycle boots.

Emily and she were, Celeste had to admit, quite the pair: the ex-socialite divorcee who had never worked before posing as the director of a festival and her homeschooled high school dropout intern in rumpled clothes and attitude.

She had cried when she saw Emily walk across the stage at her graduation. When Emily shook hands with the principal of the high school and took her diploma in hand, she had looked out across the audience, then waved defiantly as if to say, I did what all of you thought was impossible: I'm not who you think I am.

If Celeste ever got drunk enough to get a tattoo, she'd have that inked across her ass: I'm not who you think I am.

That's what she'd learned from Emily, and she was falling down grateful for it. Grateful, too, that Emily wanted an extra year to get her ducks in a row in order to go off to college. She needed that year as much as Emily did.

Celeste was not anxious to let go of her assistant, at least not yet. They were just hitting their stride together.

She hadn't had a chance to give Emily her graduation present. It was a check. She had already written it, rolled it up like a proper diploma, tied it with a ribbon. Emily might have thought her graduation came when she walked across St. Mary's stage, but in reality, her real graduation day was going to be the last day of the festival. Celeste intended for the two of them to be on stage together, taking their bows.

Chapter Sixty-Seven
⌘
THE END OF THE OPEN REHEARSAL

Emily ran out of the front door of the auditorium just when Celeste came walking up the sidewalk.

"Come quickly," Emily yelled.

Celeste started to run.

"Is Millie okay?" Celeste called out in panic. She had been worried about losing Millie since the day her father ran away with that other woman. She had been dreading this moment her whole life.

"Millie is fine. But you've got to stop the rehearsal. They're fighting!" Emily wailed.

"Who's fighting?"

"Danielle, Franco, Gabriella," Emily shouted. "The whole orchestra."

By the time Celeste made it backstage and peaked through the curtain, Danielle was hovering over Gabriella's music stand, shouting at her. The audience was watching.

"It says, crescendo," Danielle screamed. "From the top. Play it again, but this time, play it right or get out!"

Fortunately, she was screaming in a mad tangle of Italian and French, so few people in the audience knew what was going on.

Celeste glared at Franco. Gabriella sat frozen; stone-faced.

"Backstage," was all he said as he stood up and motioned that Danielle should follow him.

Danielle left in a rage.

Celeste stepped out onto the center of the stage.

"The orchestra will be taking a break," she calmly announced. "Which will give all of you a chance to buy tickets in the lobby. Emily will be out there to help you."

The orchestra stood and filed off the stage. The audience began to stream out of the auditorium. Gabriella didn't move.

"Come," Celeste said, helping Gabriella from her chair. "It's time to put a stop to all of this."

"She hates me," Gabriella whispered.

"Do you think she knows about you and Franco?" Celeste asked.

"Perhaps," Gabriella replied. "But that is Franco's and my business."

"Your business has unfortunately become my business."

"It is unfortunate," Gabriella said.

"Quite."

Celeste went backstage with Gabriella in tow and pulled Danielle and Franco aside.

"Can they rehearse without the three of you?" Celeste asked.

Franco hesitated.

"Can they?" Celeste asked again.

"They could do a sectional, the violins and violas, with the bass," Franco said.

"On the Tchaikovsky," Danielle offered.

"Manuel could run it. He's done that before," Franco said.

"Tell him. Get them back on stage in ten minutes. I'll announce that the orchestra will be doing a sectional without the three of you. It's a sectional, right?"

"Yes," Franco answered.

"Good enough. In the meantime, I want the three of you to get your instruments and put them away. Do not say a word to each other until I get back, and do not talk with anyone else. Not a word."

Celeste ushered the remainder of the orchestra on stage.

"As I explained before," Celeste told the audience, "this is a rehearsal. And, part of rehearsing is conducting sectionals. The violins and violas, along with the bass, will be working on the Tchaikovsky. Manuel, the first viola, will be in charge. This will be a wonderful opportunity for you to hear a small part of this incredible piece, the whole of which will be played during the last concert. Again, tickets are going fast, so please be sure to buy yours today before you leave."

Once the orchestra got started, Celeste led Franco, Gabriella and Danielle to the privacy of the loading dock outside.

"We need to talk," Celeste said. "No, actually, I need to talk, and the three of you need to listen and listen well."

Danielle folded her arms and glared at Gabriella. Franco began to fidget.

"You need to get rid of Gabriella," Danielle blurted.

"It's too late for that," Celeste said calmly. "What the three of you decide to do once I put you on the plane when this festival is over is your business. But what you do today, tonight and for the rest of this week is my business."

Danielle crossed her arms and glared at Celeste.

"As concertmaster, I am in charge," Danielle informed Celeste.

"As the director of the festival and the one who will be signing your checks, I think that I am the one in charge at the moment," Celeste announced.

Franco closed his eyes, let out a whoosh of breath, and took a step back.

"I'm pregnant," Gabriella said.

"Merde!" Danielle shouted.

"Are you sure?" Franco whispered, stepping back into the circle.

"Sure?" Danielle gasped. "Sure? As in, is it yours? Is it, Franco? Is it?"

"Yes," Gabriella said.

Franco's shoulders slumped and he stepped away from the three women.

Celeste held up her hands as if to stop a fight. "There are four concerts ahead," she said. "That's my business. It's also your business, and you will handle it professionally. There will be no more outbursts on stage if you ever want to play in the U.S. again. Understood?"

"Understood," Franco offered.

"Danielle? Gabriella? Do I have your word?" Celeste asked.

The two women looked at each other.

"Do I have your word?" Celeste demanded.

"Is it really Franco's?" Danielle asked again turning first to Franco then to Gabriella.

"Yes," Gabriella said. Franco shrugged his shoulders and nodded his head.

"I would appreciate it if this conversation and the information regarding your pregnancy, Gabriella, as well as whatever affair that has been going on between you and Franco, be kept confidential. Completely confidential, understood?" Celeste asked.

"Understood," Gabriella said.

"I don't want to hear anyone in the orchestra talking about it. In addition, I don't want anyone on my Board or in the audience talking about it. Do you understand, Danielle?" Celeste asked.

"I understand," Danielle said.

Celeste left the three of them standing on the loading dock talking. If there was shouting and screaming, she didn't hear it. If there was bloodshed, she didn't want to see it. She wanted this day to be over and to live long enough to see the curtain fall on the first concert and know that all was going to work out. It had to work out.

She took the long way around the outside of the building and came in the front door. She needed the walk. She was desperate for five more minutes of sunshine on her face as well as some time alone in order to regroup. There would be questions to answer and people to talk to as soon as the rehearsal finished. She had no idea what she was going to say to the audience or how she was going to spin the whole shouting match on the stage. She had worried so much about the money she had completely forgotten to worry about the orchestra and the music. She hadn't anticipated there might be even bigger problems to solve once the money was in place. She didn't have a clue about how to handle what was going to happen next.

When Celeste finally stepped into the lobby, Emily was putting things away and packing up.

"Going somewhere?" she asked.

"You won't believe it," Emily said.

"Have people started asking for their money back? Do we even have a refund policy?"

"We're sold out," Emily announced. Every concert. Standing room only. As soon as you broke up the altercation between Danielle and Gabriella, people started pouring out of the auditorium buying tickets like this was going to be the fight of the century, and they absolutely had to have front row seats."

Chapter Sixty-Eight
⌘
WHAT IF...

Emily was recording ticket sales for the day and entering names in the database. Celeste had been on the phone for almost an hour and had just hung up. Emily couldn't help but overhear what Celeste had been trying to negotiate.

"Sounds like we have one of those 'what if' situations on our hands," Emily said.

"Yeah, like what if Franco gets thrown out of his hotel room," Celeste said.

"We didn't budget for that, did we?" asked Emily.

"Couldn't have even imagined it," Celeste added.

"Probably not a typical line item on a grant application or budget report," Emily offered.

"I don't blame Danielle for throwing Franco out of her room and can't quite fault Gabriella for sleeping with him. He is charming."

"How much is this going to cost?" Emily asked, stopping her work for the moment.

"More than any of the other rooms. The hotel is apparently booked. The only thing they had left was the bridal suite."

"Pretty funny," Emily said.

"Hope we can laugh about this tomorrow," said Celeste.

"Maybe next week," Emily offered.

"That's what I'm thinking."

"Bridal suite as in?" Emily asked.

"King size bed, satin sheets, heart shaped tub, a complimentary bottle of champagne," Celeste answered.

"Bottom line?"

"Two hundred and fifty dollars a night. We've got the orchestra here for four more nights. This little dalliance of Franco's is going to cost us something over $1,000. With tax and tip, I believe the bottom line is about $1,200.

I sent Millie over to finalize the deal, move Franco out of the hallway and into the bridal suite, and capture the champagne. As far as I'm concerned, it's ours and we are going to chill it, lock this door, pop the cork and drink all of it the minute the festival is done and the orchestra is safely up in the air and out of our hair."

"Am I invited?" Emily asked.

"No question. It's going to be a graduation party of sorts with you, your mom, Millie and me," Celeste said.

"What about Jessica?"

"She deserves a bit of celebration for all she's done for us and all the crap she's taken from Charles."

"Chips and dip?" Emily asked.

"Bring it on," laughed Celeste.

Millie knocked on the office door. She had a big carryout bag in one hand and two bottles of champagne tucked under her other arm.

"Got two bottles," Millie said glowing. "The manager threw in a second bottle because we're renting the suite for so long. I brought Chinese for lunch."

"Nice," Emily said, clearing a space on her desk for the food.

"Figured the two of you probably were on some kind of festival hunger strike."

"How's Franco?" Celeste asked.

"He can't decide if he should be angry or contrite. I suggested he keep a lid on it and his pants zipped until he gets back to wherever," Millie said.

"How about Danielle?" Celeste asked.

"Happy to have Franco out of her room. She's one angry lady right now. Seems like she's been after Franco for quite a while to have a child. She appears to be angrier about Gabriella getting to have Franco's baby than she is about their affair. Cheating is one thing, babies another."

"How's Gabriella?" Celeste asked.

"Resting."

"I need you to be Franco's private chauffeur for the rest of the festival," Celeste said.

"Figured as much. Told him I'd be by a half hour early. Thought I'd get him up and out of there before the others gather in the lobby for the van."

"Do you think Miguel is cute?" Emily asked.

"I'm starved," Celeste said.

"Let's eat and worry about whether or not Miguel is cute later," Millie offered.

Chapter Sixty-Nine
⌘
GABRIELLA

On the way back to the hotel, Gabriella sat in the front of the van by herself. Her stomach was rocking and rolling, and her head was reeling. As soon as she got to the hotel she went to her room, shut the door, turned off the light and got into bed.

She couldn't sleep.

She couldn't stop thinking about what would happen next.

For sure, as soon as the orchestra got on the plane to go back to Italy she was going to be fired. Danielle wasn't about to let Franco and her affair become public as the pregnancy became more obvious. She didn't show now, but she would soon.

The Tuscan Chamber Orchestra wasn't her only gig. She played with a couple of other groups, but Tuscany was a small region. Word would get around.

Truth was, she didn't have to stay in Tuscany. She could go anywhere she wanted. There were other orchestras to play in. There were a hundred new lives out there for her to discover.

She curled up into a tight ball and rolled from side to side. Rocking the baby.

She was thirty-two, single, and going to have a baby. Franco's baby. Did she care that it was Franco's? Did she want the baby? Could she raise the baby by herself, traveling around the world playing concerts? What did people do with babies? What would she do with her baby?

It was her baby. Not Franco's. Hers. She slipped her hands under her shirt and pressed her fingers against the soft mound of her belly. She wondered how big the baby was already. How big it would have to be before she could feel it moving inside. She closed her eyes and pressed the fingers of her left hand against her bare skin as though she were working the fingerboard of her cello playing a scale up and down the neck of her instrument. Could the baby feel that? She let the fingers of her bow arm trail from side to side gently stroking her stomach.

Could the baby hear the cello when she played? Did it startle when she struck the first hard chords in the Tchaikovsky? Did it sway back and forth to the rhythm of the waltz in the second movement? Weep in the adagio? Run with the horses as the resolution of the melody rose in a wild crescendo to the ending?

She closed her eyes and let her body rest. Let the baby settle safely inside of her.

Chapter Seventy
⌘
THE CONCERT

Celeste was waiting backstage when the van pulled up. The members of the orchestra got out, pulled their instruments from the back of the van and filed into the auditorium. As soon as their cases were opened, they began to move away from each other, finding corners where they could be alone to tune, to get focused.

Franco had gotten to the auditorium before the rest. Millie had dropped him off early. He was on stage working through scales, warming up. If the other members of the orchestra wondered why Franco hadn't traveled with them, no one asked. Danielle acted as though there was nothing unusual at hand.

Gabriella was off in a corner, shoulders slumped across her cello, her arms cradling the instrument as she plucked and tuned, occasionally bouncing her bow across the strings.

Celeste loved the quiet commotion of the musicians preparing to play. Bees buzzing. Honey gathering. Eyes closed. Bodies focused. She could feel the tension of the tightened bows and the gently plucked strings being brought into tune. She felt her throat tighten and her heart skip a short beat in the wonder of what was about to happen once the curtain rose and the music started. Being backstage in the excitement of what was to come when the curtain was lifted was a gift she had not anticipated when she had agreed to be the director.

Celeste leaned her back against the wall. She closed her eyes and wondered what it would be like to stay on the stage tonight, to be there as the music rose and fell and filled the room. What if, she thought...what if she took a chair and sat down in the middle of the musicians after she introduced them so she could hear the music being made? The rough hair of the twelve bows pulling against the smooth metal strings, the breathing in and out as the musicians and the instruments wove their sounds together, and there were no longer twelve voices on stage, but one righteous sound. One giant wave of emotion disguised as music that would touch every person sitting in the audience.

She might have made this week happen, but more than anything, she wished she could be there, for just one night, in the middle of the music.

"Celeste," Gabriella said touching her arm.

Celeste opened her eyes.

"Thank you," Gabriella said.

"For?"

"Not letting me off the hook."

"I didn't have any other choice," Celeste said.

"Neither did I."

The tuning and fiddling died down, and Franco nodded to Celeste that they were ready. She stepped out on stage.

"Thank you for being here this evening and for helping to spread the word about the festival. The first of many, I hope. By the way, we are sold out tonight and for the other concerts as well. We have no more tickets to sell. Who would have ever been so crazy as to dream this could happen? That classical music lovers could fill an auditorium for four nights running in the middle of July in downtown Raleigh. Don't you people have beach houses to go to?"

Laughter and applause.

"And now, it is my great pleasure to present the Tuscan Chamber Orchestra!"

The orchestra filed onto the stage, and, as they did, the audience stood and applauded. Franco took a bow and held his hand out for Danielle to take her position as concertmaster. She tucked her violin under her chin and struck an A. The perfect A traveled through the strings from the left to the right. One-by-one each instrument responded, then rested on a knee waiting for Franco's nod to begin.

The audience sat back in their seats. Some closed their eyes. Others leaned forward as if that would help them to be the first to hear the notes as they tumbled from the stage.

Celeste stood at the back of the auditorium remembering that night in Pietrasanta when she first heard them play. The magic was still there.

When it was time to play the last piece in the program, Vivaldi's *Four Seasons*, Danielle, as soloist, dug into her violin and played like she was possessed, like nothing mattered in that moment but the music. Like there was nothing else holding her to the earth. With each note she dug more deeply, finding the strength to let go of her anger and her sadness, and Franco.

She set herself free.

Gabriella took a deep breath and hugged her instrument close to her body, folding her arms in an embrace around her cello and opening her heart. Her knees pressed lightly against the sides of her cello, holding the polished wood in place as she rocked and played. While her fingers danced up and down the neck of her cello and her arm drew the bow across the strings, the vibrations of the strings, in turn, passed through the bridge and sound port to the back of the instrument. Each clear note washed over her body with new life. Every movement of her fingers and stroke of her bow was another soft caress for her baby, another kiss.

When Danielle came to the moment in the music when the solo violin and the cello play their duet, it was as though a door had opened and whatever she had ever held back from her playing burst forward in an avalanche of warm sound. Gabriella followed suit. All that had ever been unsaid between the two women poured out across the stage.

As imagined by Vivaldi, this was to be a duet with the soloist and the first cello. Franco, however, in reimagining the work for his orchestra had written it with both he and Gabriella playing together with Danielle. He had wanted this particular moment in the music to resonate with power.

From the first note of the duet, when Gabriella leaned into her cello and drew her bow across the strings, Franco leaned back allowing Gabriella to take the lead. The two women looked up from their stands and acknowledged each other, heads nodding, bows moving up and down, hearts beating together with the music.

The orchestra fell in with Danielle and Gabriella as if the two musicians had somehow woven a spell and taken control of the stage. Franco sheepishly followed.

When the last note hung in the air, and the audience had jumped to their feet to applaud, Franco stood and motioned first for Danielle to take her bow, then for the orchestra to take theirs. The audience clapped and shouted. Danielle took a second bow, and then she walked across the stage and put her arms around Gabriella.

"You were magnificent," Danielle whispered in her ear. "Brava!" she said and kissed her cheek.

The orchestra members tapped their bows on their stands and joined in on the applause. Franco stood to the side so the two women could take another bow together.

"You liked?" Miguel asked Emily.

The orchestra had come from backstage to join the audience in the lobby. People stood in clusters and talked. Even though the concert was over, the music hung in the air like a sweet dream. No one seemed to want to be the first to leave, for fear of breaking the spell.

"I liked," she said.

"The music makes the world more beautiful. You are beautiful," Miguel said, leaning close and lightly kissing her cheek.

Danielle and Gabriella came into the lobby together. People stepped back to make room for them and applaud. Celeste joined in the applause.

Franco moved away from the crowd. Millie followed.

"I've got someone I'd like you to meet," Millie said, grabbing Franco's hand.

"A donor?" Franco asked.

"The big enchilada," Millie said, dragging Franco towards Charles Mooreton.

Chapter Seventy-One
⌘
CHARLES AND LOU ANNE

Millie and Franco ambushed Charles just as he was trying his best to smile, make nice and find his way first to Lou Anne and then to the door.

"Thank you, Charles, for all you did to make this happen and for hiring Celeste," Millie said, grabbing Charles's hand.

"The orchestra is so happy to be here," Franco said. "We can't thank you enough. We have always dreamed of coming to the States to play. This is a dream come true. Did you like the concert? Danielle is amazing, isn't she?"

"A wonderful violinist and a beautiful woman," Charles said.

"She is my wife," Franco replied.

"You're a lucky man," Charles said, smiling.

"And your wife?" Franco asked.

"Is threatening to leave me."

Charles excused himself and looked for Lou Anne. She was busy talking with Celeste. Charles stepped back and waited until Lou Anne finished talking with Celeste before he tried to get her attention. He had no desire to be caught in a shit storm right now with these two women. The only thing worse would be a free for all with Jessica and Binky thrown into the mix.

"Let's go," Charles mimed, giving a quick flip of his head towards the door, when Lou Anne at last turned around.

She shook her head no and turned lightly on her heels in order to go over to talk with a particularly overly jeweled knot of women.

Charles was getting antsy and anxious. He needed to get out of this crowd. If one more well-meaning musician or seemingly well-meaning music lover came up to him and asked him if he liked the concert, his charming public face was going to unravel to something more sinister. He needed a drink and he wanted to talk with Lou Anne.

Laughter and spontaneous outbursts of applause rumpled through the air as the musicians worked the crowd. It seemed to Charles that this merry music love fest was only getting started, and no one was going to leave any-time soon. He began to hope that security would come along and boot out the lot of them, or at least dim the lights so people would get the idea that the evening was over and would leave gracefully.

It was over.

Binky Covington came up behind him and slid her hand around his arm, linking them in combat.

"What do you have to say?" Binky asked.

"Nothing to you," Charles barked.

"Don't be such a sore loser. You're the hero tonight. The festival is a sold-out success. You should be glowing."

"Why did you do it?" Charles asked.

"Because I could. Because you and David shouldn't have screwed Celeste, and you know it."

"She was a fool," Charles said. "She knew who David was from the get-go and if she didn't like the fact that he was cheating on her, she shouldn't have married him in the first place."

"Is that what you're going to tell Lou Anne?"

Charles wiggled away from Binky and walked over to confront Lou Anne.

"It's getting late," he told her in no uncertain terms. Then he grabbed her hand, pulled her away and out the door.

"That was rude," Lou Anne told Charles as he escorted her to their car.

"We need to talk," Charles said.

"We're done talking," Lou Anne reminded him.

"I've agreed to everything you've asked. I've written checks, signed your silly contracts swearing to support the festival and keep Binky's secrets, along with giving you the cash for Emily's intern bonus. Everything you told me you wanted me to do for you."

"Silly contracts?" Lou Anne said. "I have brokered a sweet deal for you. Those silly contracts and checks are there for you to keep Jessica from drag-ging you to court for assault. The checks and promises to Celeste are in place to keep her and your other losers out of your secret keeping business. Not to mention, keeping the IRS out of that tidy stash of cash of yours, hidden in your safe. You should be falling down grateful that those checks and con-tracts now guarantee that I will do my best not to tell Daddy as well as the Bar Association about what you've been up to these last few years. Those silly contracts will also keep your name out of the papers for a wide variety of offences, including your three-year affair with Jessica. I daresay the story of David's ex-love nest, along with a picture of your handprint on Jessica's backside would not look good in print for a high priced, highly regarded divorce lawyer such as yourself. David wouldn't care too much for it either. Those contracts and checks are anything but silly. In fact, I am doing my best to salvage your tacky legal career," Lou Anne explained.

"What about our marriage?" Charles asked.

"Over and done with," Lou Anne announced.

"What about our children?"

"Perhaps you could arrange the same visiting rights you worked out for Thad in Binky's divorce. I believe you were quite pleased by what you managed to do there for Emily."

"How long have you been sleeping with Roger?" Charles asked, smiling.

"Not nearly as long as you've been sleeping with Jessica. By the way, speaking of sleeping, until you have had the chance to make other arrangements, you will be sleeping in the guest room."

Lou Anne gave Charles the money to pay the babysitter and dropped him off at home.

"Where are you going?" he asked.

"Funny question," she said. "I'll be back in a couple of hours."

She was going to see Roger. She had the ring in her pocket.

They needed to talk.

"Why have I been dreading this?" Roger asked when he opened his front door.

"Aren't you going to ask me to come in?"

"Please," he said, opening the door wider so she could pass without the two of them touching.

"It's not what you think. I'm also pretty sure it's not what you were hoping for, but it is as good as I can do right now, and it's not only what I want, but what I think both of us need."

She reached into her purse and pulled out the Bailey's box and placed it on the coffee table.

"You don't like it," he said.

"I love it," she answered.

"Then you don't like me," he countered.

"I like you. Which is why I want to do this the right way. I want you to keep the ring for now. Let me get through my divorce with Charles. Allow the dust to settle. Then I want us to date."

"Date?"

"Have a proper romance. Not something where we have to sneak around.

I don't like what we've done, but I'm beginning to understand why Charles had all those affairs. An affair is pretty exciting. It's both naughty and nice. Much more exciting than a by-the-book, boring marriage with parent-teacher conferences and bills that need to be paid. The everyday is what life is about, and I'm looking for the everyday to be better than just another married day. I want my children to see what it looks like to be truly in love with someone. I don't want them to grow up believing that marriage is a trap that needs to be escaped through deception and deceit. They've had enough babysitters and eaten enough bad pizza in the last few months to be sick of it. I can't live through another empty marriage full of deception and affairs, and they can't either," Lou Anne paused.

"I want to be wooed by you," she announced.

Chapter Seventy-Two
⌘
CELESTE AND DAVID

"One down," Emily said, putting a fresh latte on Celeste's desk.

"Three to go," Celeste responded. "And not a ticket left to sell."

"What now?" Emily asked.

"We start thinking about next year."

"The Tuscan Chamber Orchestra again?" Emily asked.

"What do you think, dear Emily, other than that Miguel is cute?"

"Cute, but not my type," Emily said.

"And your type is?" Celeste asked.

"Not sure yet."

"Good for you," Celeste said, taking a careful sip of her hot coffee.

"Do we want to bring them back a second year?" Emily asked.

"Now that Danielle has thrown Franco out and Gabriella is pregnant, who knows if there will even be a Tuscan Chamber Orchestra come next July?" said Celeste. "I'm thinking we should start looking."

"No old men," Emily cautioned Celeste. "I need to start looking for a boyfriend."

"Who's looking for a boyfriend?" David was standing in the doorway.

"How did you find us?" Celeste said, closing her computer screen and turning in her chair so she could face him. "I would ask you to come in, but we only have two chairs."

"Thought maybe you'd go to lunch with me," David said.

Celeste looked at her watch.

"It's 10:45," she said.

"How about coffee?" David asked.

Celeste lifted her half empty cup.

"If we walk towards Moore Square from here and take the long way around, it will be 11 o'clock by the time we get to Sitti. It's a civilized restaurant that has the good sense to open early for those of us who work strange hours. No offense, but I'm willing to bet you haven't been out of this rat's nest in months. When was the last time you even had a hot meal?" David asked.

"Millie brought Chinese takeout for us just yesterday," Celeste offered.

"I'll have you back in an hour. You're all out of tickets, so what else do you have to do this afternoon?"

"Okay with you?" Celeste asked Emily.

"Fine with me. I've got a noontime date with Mom and Dad at Big Ed's."

"You buying?" Celeste asked David, grabbing her purse and slipping on the high heels she'd earlier kicked off that were now underneath her desk.

"My pleasure."

The day was hot and muggy in that crazy way July can be in Raleigh, when the humidity is higher than the temperature, and it doesn't have to rain in order for it to be wet outside.

"I remember now why I haven't left my office in weeks," Celeste said, wiping the sweat off her upper lip.

"It can be humid here. July and August make it mighty hard to sell a house to someone from San Francisco," David offered.

When they crossed the street, Celeste could see a couple of tables and chairs sitting on the sidewalk in front of Sitti.

"I hope we're eating inside," she said.

"I called and asked for a quiet table, the one there, in the window, off to the side."

"I hope you don't think this is a date," Celeste said.

"Depends on what you want," David said.

"Lunch is good enough," Celeste responded.

David smiled at the hostess who was busy at the bar and waved his hand to indicate both that he knew her and that he was at home in this restaurant. Celeste was not surprised. She figured David was probably sleeping with the hostess. She was pretty enough and just his type. David grabbed two menus and ushered Celeste to the table.

"Service with a smile," he said, pulling out a chair for her.

"What's the occasion?"

"No occasion," he said.

"Except for the gala the other night, I haven't heard from you nor seen you since our divorce. Not that I was expecting you to keep in touch or deliver roses to my office every Wednesday or anything like that. Heaven knows, I haven't called you."

David threw his head back and laughed.

Celeste had forgotten how she had loved being wrapped in that laugh.

How, when it happened, David's warm gust of laughter made it feel like a door had just swung wide, allowing sunshine to flood the room. When he laughed, nothing else in the world mattered but that moment with him. She missed that.

"Do you know what you want?" he asked.

The waitress was standing by the table waiting for their order.

"Not sure," Celeste said, studying the menu.

"She'll have the Sitti Salad, no onions with a well-done salmon filet. House dressing on the side. I'll have the chicken kabob. We'd like an order of hummus to start. We're in no hurry. Thanks."

"Drinks?" the waitress asked.

"Unsweetened iced tea, extra lemon," Celeste said.

"Sweet for me," David said.

The waitress took the menus and returned with a basket of hand-sized, hot out of the oven pitas.

"Was I that predictable?" Celeste asked.

"When it came to ordering lunch, you were. Thought that you'd be pleased I remembered what you liked."

"I probably need to get back to the office pretty shortly," Celeste said.

"What for? All the tickets are sold. The programs printed. Advertising done. It's all done. You've done it. Beautifully, I might add. You're pretty impressive up there. Totally in control. It's quite sexy."

"Thanks for the sexy comment. Not sure about in control. There have been some bumps lately."

"By the way, you've really done a great job with Emily. Even Thad has been singing your praises. Never thought I'd hear him crow about Emily taking a year off, then choosing to go someplace other than his beloved alma mater."

"UNC wasn't right for her," Celeste offered.

"What about St. Mary's?"

"Not a good match, especially during the throes of Binky and Thad's divorce. That was a pretty bad time for her. I didn't do much but pay attention to her and challenge her. She's really smart. She saved my bacon more than once this last year. She's a wiz at spreadsheets, email messaging, you name it."

"Thad told me Emily's going to work with you again next year while she gets her grades up at Wake Tech."

"Truth is, I'm not ready to fly on my own yet. I'm hoping Emily can teach me a thing or two before she leaves for school. We were scrambling this year to raise money, get our feet on the ground, plus figure out how to sell tickets. We didn't have much time to kill with how-to seminars or chit-chats about what to do better. It was quite a year. I even wrote my first grant and got a little money. Emphasis on little."

"Sounds like you've been busy."

"I've never been happier. How's business?" Celeste asked.

"Great. Raleigh's got a buzz. Real estate is booming. Big houses are an easy sell. People with money are moving here. We've got a great ballet company and orchestra, a couple of fine museums, exciting theatre, and now a first-rate summer music festival. People coming here from bigger cities are impressed."

"Who would have ever thought our divorce would help you sell houses," Celeste laughed.

The waitress brought the hummus and some more bread along with their drinks.

"Speaking of houses," David said. "I sold ours last week."

"The big house of bad taste!"

"Here," David said, handing her a check.

"What's this?"

"It's the net proceeds from the sale of our house."

"I didn't think I was getting half," Celeste said.

"It's not half, it's all of it."

"I wasn't expecting anything," Celeste said, folding the check and tucking it into her purse.

"Aren't you going to look at it?"

"Maybe later," she said, squeezing a wedge of lemon into her iced tea.

"After the divorce I didn't change anything. Basically, lived in a couple rooms and put more beer in the refrigerator when I ran out. The people who bought the house loved what you'd done to it. They don't plan to change much except maybe the fronts of the kitchen cabinets. They prefer painted white cabinets to cherry. They didn't haggle on the price. There's enough there for you to buy any house in town you want."

"Living with Millie on the southside has been good. It's not a bad location. Turns out she needs me, and I need her. She's a terrible cook but has good taste in takeout. It's a nice arrangement. We have a surprisingly quiet life together with the cats."

"Buy yourself a beach house then," David said. "You've got the money now."

"I'm sorry, I didn't say thank you. Thank you. I'm overwhelmed."

The waitress brought their food. They ate in silence for a moment.

"Were you ever happy being married?" David asked.

"Ever?" Celeste asked.

"You don't have to answer," David said, picking at his chicken.

"I never really had a father, and I guess I never managed to figure out the best way to do the marriage thing or what to expect. But there were good times, like when we were out walking in the neighborhood or having dinner together, just the two of us. I loved that. Those were the moments when I felt like we were really a couple. It was especially nice when you weren't always looking at your watch as if you had someone else to see, somewhere else to go."

"I guess I'm not good at staying focused," David said, cutting his chunks of chicken, then pushing them around in his rice. He took a sip of his tea.

"That's funny," Celeste said.

"What's funny?"

"That you cheated because you couldn't stay focused."

"Ouch," David said.

"That was ugly, and I'm sort of sorry I said it, but by god, it felt good. Like it was a stone in my shoe I've been walking on for years and at last kicked out."

"Ugly, but well deserved. I can't possibly apologize for all the times I failed you, not to mention that crummy divorce thing Charles and I maneuvered. Talk about having a stone in your shoe. I've been walking on that one all year. Seeing you on stage last night made me rethink some things," David said.

"If the job was your idea, it was a good one, and I thank you for it. Feel free to kick that nasty bit of history to the side of the road. I don't care why you did it. Sending me to Italy was a gift. For the first time in my life I have a life that is mine. You don't need to feel sorry for me or for the divorce."

"Now that you've kicked that stone out of your shoe, would you have dinner with me?" David asked. "I'd like to celebrate your success. Dinner and drinks after the last concert? I was thinking Bloomsbury. You always liked having dinner there."

"Just friends," Celeste emphasized.

"Friends would be an honest start," David agreed.

Chapter Seventy-Three
⌘
CHARLES AND THE BOARD

The second concert went off without a hitch and was even better than the first. The musicians played like their hair was on fire. The audience loved them and kept clapping and hooting until Franco brought the orchestra back onstage for an encore.

Like the first night, the audience hung in the lobby afterwards hoping to talk with them. Celeste could see how much the musicians were giving and got worried they were going to burn out before the last concert, so she did her best with Emily's help to usher them out of the lobby as soon as possible and into the van to go back to the hotel in order to get some rest.

Charles managed to catch Celeste as she came back into the lobby after she sent the musicians to the hotel.

"The Board would like to meet with you," he said, trying to keep his interaction with her as neutral as possible. He was still raw from his recent encounter with Lou Anne. "Tomorrow, before the concert. We're meeting in my office. Lou Anne has arranged for drinks and sandwiches. The meeting starts at five o'clock. You'll be first on the agenda."

Celeste had not been adequately prepared for the demands a gala and four concerts would have on her wardrobe. Somehow, in the chaos of creating the festival and finding the money to pay for everything, she had overlooked the now pressing reality that for five nights running she was going to have to be dressed to kill. Unfortunately, kill was hardly an overstatement given the recent disclosure of Jessica's involvement in their fundraising efforts and Lou Anne's decision to dump Charles.

Being first on Charles's agenda at this particular moment was not exactly her idea of a good time. She thought it best to be dressed for the occasion and the possibility of a scene.

To top it off, David's odd reappearance in her life had significantly upped the ante. She didn't want to get back with him, but it had been a long time since anyone had taken her out to dinner. Dinner, with no expectations or commitments would be perfectly fine for one evening.

"It's almost 4:30," Millie called out from the kitchen. "Didn't you say you had to go to some important meeting at 5?"

"I do, but I don't know what on earth I'm going to wear!"

"The dress last night looked good," offered Millie.

"That was last night," Celeste answered.

"You look smashing in the emerald green."

"I'm wearing that tomorrow. David's taking me out to dinner after the last concert, to celebrate," Celeste let that little piece of information slip, then instantly wished she could call it back.

"David? The one you used to be married to. The one who screwed you in court and nearly ruined your life?"

"No, the one who sent me to Italy in order to get me out of his life, then arranged for me to get this great job. That David," replied Celeste as she pawed through her closet. "What about pants. A pair of tight black pants, and...?"

"How about your white silk blouse? Black and white is classic. Wear that silver necklace I gave you for Christmas last year and those big silver earrings. Black and white and good jewelry says power. What does the Board want?"

"Don't know, but they're serving sandwiches."

Chapter Seventy-Four
⌘
THE BOARD

When Celeste stepped into Charles's office, she was surprised to see about a dozen of her biggest festival donors: all ex-clients of Charles's who had made Jessica's magic money list.

"Look what you've done!" Lou Anne said, grabbing Celeste's hand and dragging her through the crowd and over to the refreshment table.

"Let's get rolling," Charles said, calling the meeting to order.

Celeste took a chicken salad croissant and grabbed a bottle of water in lieu of a glass of wine. She found a seat at the end of conference table near the door. Lou Anne walked past the sandwiches and helped herself to some wine, then strode to the head of the table and sat down next to Charles.

"I believe the first order of business this evening," Charles said, "is to thank Celeste for bringing the Chamber Society back to life. The second is introducing our new Board members."

Celeste took a bite of her sandwich and a sip of her water. She regretted not taking the offer of wine.

The introductions went around the table, starting at Charles's right. Lou Anne was the last to speak.

"I can't tell you how thrilled I am to be a member of this Board and to take a leading role as the chair of the fundraising efforts next year," Lou Anne said.

Charles forced a smile. Lou Anne stood up and assumed control of the meeting.

"I'm happy to announce that Charles and I have already made a significant donation in order to get the ball rolling for next year. With the Board's approval, of course," Lou Anne went on, "Charles and I would like to propose that we earmark part of our initial donation to pay for an assistant for Celeste and to bring Celeste's salary in line with the responsibilities of the festival. Can we have a round of applause for Celeste?"

The people sitting around the table all turned to Celeste and applauded warmly.

"I'm overwhelmed, thank you," Celeste said. "I'm sorry that my office assistant, Emily, isn't here to share the applause. I couldn't have done it without her."

Lou Anne continued, "Do I have the Board's approval to use the money Charles and I have recently donated for next year's festival to be used to pay for an office assistant for Celeste and to raise Celeste's salary to be in line with the growing responsibilities of the festival?" Lou Anne asked. "Can we have a show of hands?"

All hands around the table went up, all except for Charles's. Lou Anne placed her hand on his shoulder and gave it a squeeze.

"Do you have something you want to say?" Lou Anne asked.

Charles stood.

"I, ah, didn't know what to expect or what would happen when Celeste first called me and proposed we create a festival. But she did, and we went along, and ah, with the help of everyone sitting here, we made this happen."

Charles paused.

"What about Binky?" Evelyn Meyers, the woman sitting to Lou Anne's left, asked. "Shouldn't we be saying something about her, shall we say, contribution to the festival?"

"She was a wonderful..." Celeste started to say.

"Chief fundraiser?" Evelyn suggested.

"Persuasive advocate?" Arthur Collins offered.

"Secret keeper," another shouted out.

"Here, here," several others echoed.

Charles shifted in his chair, clutched his plastic wine tumbler, and looked as though he might be having a stroke.

"A highly successful fundraiser for the festival," Celeste interjected. "We wouldn't be here tonight without your generosity and support, and I want to say, thank you."

To Celeste's great surprise, the whole Board, except Charles, stood and started to applaud.

"So," Lou Anne said, calling the meeting back to order, "can we hear about your plans for next year?"

Celeste managed to eat half of her chicken salad sandwich, drink her bottle of water and talk for ten minutes about a second festival she hadn't yet planned. Her heart was racing. She was late.

When she finished and excused herself from the meeting, Lou Anne walked out with her, handed her an envelope with the money and gave her a hug.

"I hope we can start again. Be friends. Real friends this time. Work together on the festival. I think I have a lot to learn from you. Next year is going to be a challenge for me."

"Binky mentioned that you're leaving Charles," Celeste said, stuffing the money into her purse.

"Charles and I left each other long ago. I was just the first one to be honest enough to call it like it is. I haven't told the kids yet. I don't think they'll be surprised. I'm keeping the house. Not much will change for them. As for me, I'll be starting over."

"Starting over is full of surprises, for sure," Celeste laughed. "By the way, I know you and Binky felt sorry for me because I had to get a job after my divorce and had to move in with my mom, but you can forget about that. I love working. It's been the best year of my life, all of it, even the bit about living with Millie. It's weird."

"I'm worried about the kids," Lou Anne said. "I've been so busy hating Charles, being suspicious of him and Jessica or whoever else he was sleeping with, I really haven't paid that much attention to them lately."

"Emily survived. Thad and Binky's divorce might be the best thing that ever happened to her. That and getting kicked out of St. Mary's."

"I wish my kids could have someone like you in their lives," Lou Anne said.

"They've got you. You'll be fine. They'll be fine. It won't all be pretty, but some of it will be great. I've got to say, it's refreshing to see someone take Charles to the cleaners for a change. Talk about amazing."

"Friends," Lou Anne said, extending her hand.

"No question," Celeste answered, taking Lou Anne's hand. "Thanks for the raise and for the money for Emily. I sure as hell need it and, most definitely, Emily deserves it. Speaking of Emily, I've got to run. See you at the concert!"

Chapter Seventy-Five
⌘
MILLIE

Emily was standing outside waiting for Celeste.

"Hey," Celeste called out, waving.

"She wouldn't let anyone call you," Emily said, tears welling up in her eyes. "They took her."

"Who took whom?" Celeste said, "Where?"

"The ambulance. To the hospital."

"Oh, my god, the baby! Is Gabriella okay? Where's Franco?"

"The orchestra is backstage getting ready. Millie fell, maybe fainted, not sure. She hit her head. There was blood everywhere. The EMS people said it might have been a small stroke or a heart attack or something horrible like that, I don't know, they wouldn't tell me. I was so scared. I didn't know what to do. I should have called. I'm sorry, I'm really sorry," Emily plopped down on the steps of the auditorium and began to sob.

Celeste put her arms around Emily.

"She was giving orders?" Celeste asked.

"OMG. Yelling, telling me not to call you, that no one was to tell you what happened, that we needed to get things cleaned up before you got here so you wouldn't know. The EMS guys were trying to stop the bleeding on her head, and she kept pushing them away, saying she had to make sure the place was cleaned up before she left. Franco tried to calm her. Danielle grabbed a towel from the EMS guys and started mopping up the blood on the floor. It was crazy, but we got it cleaned up to Millie's satisfaction and she agreed to let them put her on the gurney and into the ambulance."

"Millie can be bossy. Stubborn too. Used to scare me to death when I was a kid whenever she started yelling. Like, if I crossed her, the world would end. If she's giving orders, you can be sure she's going to be fine. But I've got to go to the hospital. There will be paperwork, things like that. Millie needs me. You did fine, just fine. Now, you're going to have to pull yourself together and step on the stage tonight to welcome the crowd. Don't forget to thank them for coming, for supporting us. Tell them there's one more night, that we're all sold out for the last concert, but that we're already planning for next year."

"You're not coming back?" Emily asked.

"You're going to have to stand in for me. You look beautiful tonight, by the way. Just perfect. When you walk to the center of the stage, stop and take a second to look out into the audience. Give your eyes a chance to adjust to the lights. They're bright. It scared me the first time I did it. Thought I was going to do or say something stupid. But I didn't, and you won't either."

"I'm only an intern, no one will listen to me."

"You're my assistant. My first paid employee. The Board gave me the money tonight. It's official now so there's no excuse. I've got to get to the hospital. I don't know how long this will take or what Millie is going to need. I don't think you can count on me coming back this evening to help close up."

"My mom can help," Emily said.

"Get the orchestra out of here and on the way to the hotel as soon as the concert is over. They're exhausted. They've got one more concert, and it's got to be good. Don't let them come out to the lobby to mingle. They can do that tomorrow. Tell them we'll do a fancy champagne thing in the lobby for them to celebrate the last concert."

"Do we have the champagne?"

"Tell Binky to work with Lou Anne and get it organized. It will give them something to do," Celeste added. "Ask your mom to pick up some nice cocktail napkins. She should also rent champagne flutes and order six or seven cases of champagne. The same kind we had for the gala. Tell her to ask Seaboard Wine if they'll make us a deal again. There's a refrigerator in the green room backstage. We can chill the champagne there like we did for the gala. Let Franco and the rest know I've gone to the hospital to take care of Millie. Tell them she's going to be okay. She's tough. She'll be fine, but I need to be at the hospital with her. Text me if you need something, or if Franco and Danielle start fighting during the middle of the concert, or Gabriella pushes Franco off the stage. You never know what might happen with this crowd. I'll keep my phone turned on. It's okay to tell your mom, but if anyone else asks why I'm not here, just say Millie wasn't feeling well and I had to take her home. No need to alarm folks."

"What if I fuck up?"

"I've been holding my breath, waiting for months for you to fuck up. You warned me, but I don't know, I just don't believe it anymore."

Celeste was sitting in the hospital emergency waiting room. A nurse came in and called her name.

"Your mother's MRI was normal. They're stitching her up, right now," the nurse said. "You can go to her room if you like, rather than staying out here in the waiting room. They'll be done shortly. I'm sure she'll be happy to see you."

"I wouldn't count on that. She hates it when people make a fuss over her."

"Talk about a fuss!" the nurse laughed.

"Please tell me she didn't..." Celeste started to say.

"Only if you count calling the EMS team a bunch of pissants for cutting up the sleeve of her dress in order to get her IV started."

"She doesn't get dressed up all that often."

"Any other family?" the nurse asked.

"Just me."

"If you're the only one, I'd say you've got your hands full for sure!"

Celeste found Millie's room. There was a plastic hospital bag on the chair stuffed with Millie's clothes. Celeste pulled out her dress and saw where the EMS team had slit open the sleeve from the wrist to above the elbow. In all fairness, it was Millie's best dress. Celeste was trying to decide if the sleeve could be repaired when she noticed dribbles of dark brown blood all down the front of the pale blue silk dress. She folded the dress and put it back into the bag. She'd throw it away when she took it home.

Celeste heard some commotion in the hallway. They were bringing Millie back. Her head was freshly bandaged, and her hair was stiff with dried blood.

"I'll buy you a new dress," Celeste said, when Millie was wheeled into the room.

The orderly helped Millie get into her bed, then turned and left the room as quickly as possible.

"Cut the bejesus out of the sleeve of my dress, like I was dying or something, and they were going to have to do CPR. I told them it was my best dress, but they just kept cutting. Pissants. Ought to make them pay for it. Gonna have a shiner for sure. Look at my face!"

"I'll buy you a new dress," Celeste said again.

"With what money? That dress was one hundred percent pure silk. Bought it on sale at Thalhimer's before they went out of business. Wore it to your wedding. And for your information, it still fits. Nicely, I might add, and there wasn't any need for them to go cutting the sleeve open like that."

"I've got money," Celeste said. "Charles and the Board gave me a big raise this afternoon along with some kind of bonus. They even said they were going to pay Emily next year."

"How much are they going to pay you? Ought to be plenty. That's a hell of a festival you've built for them. I even liked the music, and I don't much care about that classical stuff. How much?"

Celeste opened her purse and pulled out the envelope from Lou Anne and when she did, she discovered the check David had given her. She had forgotten it was in her purse. In fact, she had never looked at it.

"I got money from David too," Celeste told Millie, waving the check from David in the air.

"What's that?"

"Money from the sale of the big house of bad taste. David gave it to me." Celeste took a quick look at the check, then quickly folded it back up and stuffed it in her purse.

"Enough to buy yourself a house?"

"Enough to buy you ten pure silk dresses. Do you want me to move?" Celeste asked.

Millie eased herself back down onto the narrow hospital bed.

"Up to you," Millie said, turning her head to face the opposite wall.

"I was thinking I'd stay put for now, if that's okay with you. Maybe use the money to take a trip."

"Always wanted to take one of those cruises across the ocean. That's what I think you should do now that you're rich. Buy yourself a couple silk dresses and take a fancy trip on the Queen Mary."

"Only if you'll go with me," Celeste said. "I owe you something for all the work you did catching Charles up to no good."

"I was pretty instrumental in getting him nailed, don't you think?" Millie asked, turning to face Celeste again.

"We couldn't have done it without you," Celeste responded.

"I doubt you would have gotten that bonus and that big raise without me getting the goods on Charles. David probably caught wind of what I'd discovered and decided to come clean. Don't you think?"

"Most likely. In any case, Lou Anne is leaving Charles and has grabbed control of the Board. Looks like she's twisted Charles's arm. As part of her divorce settlement she and Charles are making a rather big donation to, as she says, get the fundraising ball rolling for next year."

"David gave you enough money from the sale of the house for a trip?"

"Pretty much," Celeste answered.

"Didn't you just say you wouldn't go on a trip without me?"

"That's what I said," Celeste answered.

"I'll take that trip with you on one condition," Millie said holding out her hand to Celeste as though they were going to have to shake on it to seal the bargain.

"And that is?" Celeste asked.

"That you buy me not one, but two new silk dresses, and we book passage on the Queen Mary, first class, of course, with a balcony. I'm thinking I'll take my binoculars along and spend the whole voyage sitting on that balcony watching for whales or whatever else swims or flies by on our way from New York to England."

Celeste opened her purse and took a second look at the check David had given her. A smile spread across her face.

"I don't know if I can afford both a trip on the Queen Mary, with a first-class balcony, *and* a new house," Celeste announced.

"I was kind of hoping that might be the case," Millie said.

Chapter Seventy-Six
⌘
THE MONEY

It was ten-thirty p.m. when Celeste finally got away from the hospital. She had wanted to wait until her mother fell asleep before she left, but Millie pushed her out the door.

"Sleep? You'll be sitting here past midnight if you want to watch me sleep, and then only for five minutes or so. Can't a person fall down anymore without doctors crowding around taking your blood pressure every five minutes and acting like you've had a heart attack!"

"Maybe you did," Celeste told her.

"People who have heart attacks feel grateful to be alive and start declaring they love the world. I'm feeling hateful rather than grateful, so that ought to be a clue. I just fell."

When Celeste got to her car, she called Binky.

"How did Emily do?" Celeste asked.

"Emily was nervous, but wonderful," Binky reported. "She took to that stage like she'd been born to be up there running the show. You might have some trouble on your hands trying to reclaim your rightful role as director of ceremonies tomorrow night."

"I had planned to have Emily on stage with me to introduce the final concert."

"How's Millie?" Binky asked.

"Fighting mad that the doctors made her stay overnight. They hooked her up to a heart monitor and told her to quit fussing. She probably had a mild heart attack. I shouldn't have asked her to do so much."

"She loved every minute of it," Binky said.

"How was the music?" Celeste asked.

"Stunning. People stood and applauded until they forced Franco to bring the orchestra back and play an encore. How did you know Raleigh would love them?"

"I didn't," said Celeste.

"Why did you trust Emily?" Binky asked.

"Because no one else had."

"I wish I could say you were wrong," Binky said.

"No one had trusted me either. I think I always knew the trip to Pietrasanta, the job and the festival, had nothing to do with Charles or the Board or anyone really believing I could do this, or that anyone would care whether the Chamber Society existed or not. That it was some kind of trick, or worse, a joke. Emily was like me. We were the same, and one of us had to step up and trust the other, believe that together we wouldn't fuck up."

"You okay?" Binky asked.

"I'm worried about Millie. Tired. Scared," Celeste said.

"Millie is going to be fine."

"David sold the house, the big house of bad taste," Celeste said.

"You should have gotten the house."

"He gave me the money. It's here, in my purse. I had forgotten about it, hadn't looked at it until tonight at the hospital. I was telling Millie about the money the Board had given me for next year. I got a raise. They've also decided to pay Emily."

"What are you scared of?" Binky asked.

"That I can't do it again. That I got lucky with the orchestra, with Emily, you, the list from Jessica, and Charles cheating on Lou Anne. That the whole world will be watching next year: wanting more. Betting that I'm going to fuck up."

"Not a chance," Binky said.

"You're sure?" Celeste asked.

"Sure, pretty sure, sure enough. What are you going to do with the money from the house?" Binky asked.

"Take Millie on a cruise," Celeste answered. "Will you help me with the festival next year?" Celeste asked Binky.

"Thought you'd never ask."

Chapter Seventy-Seven
⌘
THE LAST CONCERT

There were empty champagne bottles, wadded up napkins and discarded champagne flutes strewn all over the lobby. The audience and the orchestra had hung around until the last bottle of champagne was drunk and the last bit of applause had died down.

"All this work, and then it's over," Emily complained.

"How do you feel about washing dishes?" Celeste asked.

"How much does it pay?"

"Not as much as a lot of other things." Celeste handed Emily the rolled up and ribbon-tied check she had written for her graduation.

"What's this?" Emily asked.

"A late graduation present and a thank you."

"For?" Emily asked, unrolling the check.

"Not walking out on me when you discovered that I didn't know how to surf the internet, build a website or tweet."

"Or make a spreadsheet, or create a listserv, or..." Emily added.

"I had planned to give this to you when we had a quiet moment back in our office, but Millie has managed to rearrange my plans for the moment. If you get this mess cleaned up, I can pretty much guarantee you will have a job tomorrow, with pay and a title. It's time to start all over again, planning for next year," Celeste said, laughing.

"And while I'm cleaning up, you'll be?" Emily asked.

"Backstage making sure the orchestra gets packed up and out of here."

Franco had pulled off his black silk tie and stuffed it into his tuxedo pocket. He was picking up folders and odd sheets of music scattered here and there. Danielle and Gabriella were huddled together, talking. The rest of the orchestra members were milling around, chatting and sipping one last glass of champagne. Manuel had managed to nick a couple of bottles from the lobby and was filling glasses.

"To Celeste," Manuel offered as he handed Celeste some champagne.

"Celeste!" the orchestra sang out, raising their glasses.

"Thank you for the magic of your music!" Celeste said, lifting her glass and turning to Franco. He nodded then slipped his arms through the straps of his cello case and left.

The moment felt both heavy and hollow. Celeste followed Franco out of the backstage door to the loading dock.

"Hey," she called.

"It was good, yes? They loved us?" Franco asked, lighting a cigarette.

"They loved all of it. The music was magnificent," she said.

"It was our last concert," Franco offered.

"The last for the festival, but not forever," Celeste said, "there's next year."

"Not for us," he said.

"You won't come back?"

"Danielle is leaving me. Leaving the orchestra. She told me so this afternoon. She's taking auditions. She will find something, someone else. She is the best."

"I'm so sorry," Celeste offered.

"Gabriella is moving back to Avignon to live with her family. They are excited about the baby. It is good," Franco said.

"What about the rest of the musicians?" Celeste asked.

"They will all find other orchestras, other jobs. I will find something as well. That is the way with music. It is beautiful, and then it ends until it begins again."

"Thank you for the music, the festival, for everything."

"Thank you," Franco said, kissing her cheek.

Celeste's phone rang. She checked the caller ID.

"I need to take this."

"Is your mother okay?" Franco asked.

"She's home and probably wondering where I am," Celeste blew Franco a kiss then walked off to answer her phone.

It was David.

"She's resting," he said.

"Thanks for sitting with her," Celeste said.

"I think she had a wonderful time this evening giving me orders. Threw in a lecture or two about the evils of infidelity when she had her fill of asking for more ginger ale and Cheez-it crackers. She told me you two were going to blow all that money from the sale of the big house of bad taste on pure silk dresses and first-class tickets on the Queen Mary. How much are these boat tickets going to cost?" David asked.

"Not as much as the check you gave me, but she doesn't ever need to know that."

Because you're planning to keep living with her," David said.

"It's been a good year. For both of us," Celeste offered.

"Binky called earlier to check on Millie, told me the concert was great. She also said that you and Emily were quite a team on the stage tonight. Sorry I missed it," David said.

"We're back to square one. Franco and Danielle are splitting up, Gabriella is moving home to have her baby and the other members of the orchestra seem to be scattering to wherever they can get a new job. Emily and I will take a few days off to catch up on some sleep, then we're back to work.

"There's quite a bit to do to close out the books on this year's festival, clean up the office and get things filed. When that's done, we can start working on next year."

"I cancelled our dinner reservations."

"Thought I might swing by Five Star on my way home and pick up take-out."

"Get enough for three. Millie made me promise I'd wake her when you got home. She can't wait to hear all about it."

THE CHAMBER SOCIETY

presents

THE TUSCAN CHAMBER ORCHESTRA

The Festival Program

Welcome!

When I accepted the position as the Director of the Chamber Society, I had no idea what I was doing. In fact, you could rightfully say that naming me the Director was about as farfetched of an idea on the Board's part as imaginable. And, accepting the position could be honestly seen as presumptuous on my part.

While I was trying to figure out what an arts director is supposed to do, I discovered the Tuscan Chamber Orchestra in Pietrasanta, Italy and began to dream this festival.

To say their music moved me is an understatement. The Tuscan Chamber Orchestra changed the way I thought about the world. They breathed a wild, free life into the music they played, and, as they did, I began dreaming about creating a summer festival in Raleigh filled with the best of what is happening in classical music today.

I was surprised to discover how much work it took to turn this dream into a reality. I couldn't have done it alone. I can never thank Emily Covington enough for all she did to help me: creating a website; giving the festival an online presence (whatever that is!); creating this beautiful program and the stunning posters hung all over town; and the thousands of other things she did to keep our office going and this festival growing.

The most amazing thing Emily did, however, was awaken in me the belief that the arts are the heart and soul of what makes us human and gives us hope and purpose.

Thank you, Emily.

This festival is not just a dream. It's a big dream, and when you dream big, something magical happens.

This week, because of our big dreams, you will have the privilege of experiencing the magic of the Tuscan Chamber Orchestra.

They work without a conductor, which allows them to talk to one another about how they want to interpret the music. But, they do more than talk; they listen to each other. And, in this talking and listening, they build a wall of sound...the sound of one heartbeat, one stunning burst of musical energy you feel as well as hear.

Welcome to our big dream, and thank you, each and every one of you, who donated time, money and bought tickets in order to make this festival a reality.

Celeste Anderson
Festival Director

THE TUSCAN CHAMBER ORCHESTRA

First Violins

> Danielle Flory, Concertmaster
> Phillipe Anet, Assistant Concertmaster
> Michele Neveu
> Alain Hasson

Second Violins

> Sophie Singelée, Principal
> Ingrid Becker
> Miguel Alvira

Violas

> Manuel Bianchi, Principal
> Carmen Molinelli

Celli

> Franco Dall'Abaco, Principal
> Gabriella Bailly

Bass

> Guido Scontrino, Principal

CONCERT PROGRAM
WEDNESDAY, JULY 10

THE TUSCAN CHAMBER ORCHESTRA

Simple Symphony, Op. 4
B. Britten (1913–1976)

Boisterous bourrée
Playful pizzicato
Sentimental saraband
Frolicsome final

Serenade for Strings in E Major, Op. 22
A. Dvořák (1841–1904)

Moderato
Tempo di Valse
Scherzo (Vivace)
Larghetto
Finale (Allegro Vivace)

— INTERMISSION —

The Four Seasons
A. Vivaldi (1678–1741)

La Primavera (Spring), RV 269
  Allegro
  Largo
  Allegro
L'estate (Summer), RV 315
  Allegro non molto
  Adagio
  Presto
L'autunno (Autumn), RV 293
  Allegro
  Adagio molto
  Allegro
L'inverno (Winter), RV 297
  Allegro non molto
  Largo
  Allegro

Violin Solo: Danielle Flory, Concertmaster

Concert Program
Thursday, July 11

THE TUSCAN CHAMBER ORCHESTRA

Ancient Airs and Dances No. 3, P. 172
O. Respighi (1879–1936)

Italiana
Arie di corte
Siciliana
Passacaglia

Divertimento for String Orchestra
B. Bartók (1881–1945)

Allegro non troppo
Molto adagio
Allegro assai

— INTERMISSION —

String Quartet in d minor, D. 810 "Death and Maiden"
F. Schubert (1797–1828)
(arranged for string orchestra by G. Mahler)

Allegro
Andante con moto
Scherzo allegro molto
Presto

CONCERT PROGRAM
FRIDAY, JULY 12

THE TUSCAN CHAMBER ORCHESTRA

Adagio for Strings, Op. 11
S. Barber (1910–1981)

Divertimento for Strings in D Major, K. 136
W.A. Mozart (1756–1791)

> Allegro
> Andante
> Presto

Holberg Suite for Strings, Op. 40
E. Grieg (1843–1907)

> Praeludium
> Sarabande
> Gavotte
> Air
> Rigadoun

— INTERMISSION —

Goldberg Variations, BWV 988
J.S. Bach (1685–1750)
(transcribed for string orchestra by D. Sitkovestsky)

> Aria
> Variations 1-30
> Aria da capo

CONCERT PROGRAM
SATURDAY, JULY 13

THE TUSCAN CHAMBER ORCHESTRA

Orchestral Suite No. 3 in D Major, BWV 1068
J.S. Bach (1685–1750)

> Overture
> Air
> Gavotte
> Bourrée
> Gigue

La Musica Notturna delle Strade di Madrid, Op. 30, No. 6 (G. 324)
L. Boccherini (1743–1805)

> Le campane dell'Ave Maria
> Il tamburo dei Soldati
> Minuetto dei Ciechi
> Il Rosario (Largo assai, allegro,
>   largo come prima)
> Passa Calle (Allegro vivo)
> Tamburo Ritirata (Maestoso)

Capriccio in e minor, Op. 81, no. 3
F. Mendelssohn (1809--1847)

— INTERMISSION —

Serenade for Strings in C Major, Op. 48
P. Tchaikovsky (1840–1893)

> Pezzo in forma di Sonata
> Valse
> Élégie
> Finale (Tema Russo)

CREATE.
COLLABORATE.
CLASSICALLY.

ECHOCOLLECTIVE.BE

In only a few years, Brussels-based Echo Collective have forged an enviable reputation in the post-classical world: sought out for their instrumental and arranging expertise by icons such as A Winged Victory For The Sullen and the late Jóhann Jóhannsson, or lending their interpretative intuition to genres as diverse as alt.rock, synth-pop and black metal.

Finally, an album of their own material, The See Within, confirms Echo Collective are equally inspired creators, using their past accomplishments as a springboard to a new, illuminating vision. From brief, singular themes to lengthier, shifting and questing episodes, this masterclass in composition, expression and technique bridges intimacy and grandeur in line with the most rewarding of post-classical works.

The See Within is scored for violin, viola, cello, harp and, in its first appearance on an album recording, the magnetic resonator piano (MRP). "All sounds are acoustic, and produced in real time," explain co-founders Margaret Hermant (violin, harp) and Neil Leiter (viola). "No processing or post-production other than reverb. The acoustic element is Echo Collective's identity. A natural sound."

Here's How to Grow the Arts—
give a child the chance to:

Play A Musical Instrument • Sing in a Choir • Dance

Paint A Picture • Throw a Pot • Build a Sculpture

Weave a Rug • Design a Dress • Knit a Hat

Write a Poem • Tell a Story

Put On a Costume and Perform In A Play

Dream

Encourage your child, and the child within you,
to do anything artistic that challenges and delights.

The Arts Matter.
(They Always Have.)

Support
the Arts

Write
a Check

Keep
the Doors
Open

and

The
Dreams
Coming

A Musical Affair is a work of fiction.
The characters are fictional, as are the circumstances.

There are, however, two hard truths in this book:
The arts enrich our lives.
It is difficult to raise money for the arts.

There was no Charles and no black book
to help me raise the money we needed for the
Cross Currents Chamber Music Arts Festival.

There's never a black book.
Nor a Binky who knows the secrets and helps you get the money.
But there are Emilys in the world, and they need the arts to make their lives
whole.
And they also need a Celeste to give them a chance.

Be a Celeste. Help an Emily.
Support the arts.
It matters.

ACKNOWLEDGEMENTS

This book grew out of my experience as the director of the Cross Currents Chamber Music Arts Festival. From 2008-2012, I collaborated with our oldest son, Neil, to build a summer music festival. The festival brought the members of the Brussels Chamber Orchestra, along with some stunning international solo musicians, from Europe to Raleigh, North Carolina.

Build was the operative word. That first year, we presented one concert, an open rehearsal and several master classes for local high school students. The second year, we hosted a gala, held two open rehearsals, four concerts and featured two international soloists, Israeli cellist Gavriel Lipkind and acclaimed Belgian Violinist, Michael Guttman.

During the third year, we hosted additional master classes, a gala, two open rehearsals, five concerts and added jazz to our musical menu with the European based Pierre Anckaert Jazz Quintet and the Will Scruggs Jazz Fellowship from Atlanta.

As part of our concert programming, we played one outdoor concert each year in the Town of Cary at Bond Park during the second and third years of the festival. Then, in 2011, we moved the entire festival to the newly opened Town of Cary Arts Center.

Thanks to the vision and support of Lyman Collins, Town of Cary Cultural Arts Manager, this move allowed us to expand our programming and conduct rehearsals as well as concerts in one location. Lyman's vision of what the festival could mean to the Town of Cary helped us grow and build an even bigger audience.

Because of our partnership with The Town of Cary, we were able to expand our programming to two full weeks and offer area high school musicians the chance to play side-by-side with members of the Brussels Chamber Orchestra for a week of mentoring that culminated in a special concert in which they performed both on their own and with the Brussels Chamber Orchestra during the opening concert of the second week.

During that fourth season, several members of the North Carolina Symphony and the Mallarme Players joined us on stage. Our soloist that year was Lorenzo Gatto, second place winner of the prestigious Queen Elisabeth International Music Competition in 2009.

Our fifth and last year, 2012, was again a two-week festival at the Cary Arts Center with a week of Side-by-Side mentoring of high school students and a return of The Will Scruggs Jazz Fellowship, Gavriel Lipkind and The Lipkind Quartet.

During that last year, students had the amazing opportunity to work with and perform with the Brussels Chamber Orchestra, study jazz composition with the Will Schruggs Jazz Fellowship, and have master classes with Gavriel Lipkind and his quartet.

We continued to feature members of the North Carolina Symphony and the Malarme Players and hosted an evening of opera featuring Rachel Copeland, soprano and the amazing countertenor, Anthony Ross Costanzo.

My son, Neil, is a classically trained violist who, during the five years of the festival, was a member of the Brussels Chamber Orchestra. He has since gone on to create his own group of classically trained musicians, the Echo Collective, and is making a name for himself in the world of neo-classical or ambient music.

Before Neil called to ask if I would help him build the Cross Currents Chamber Arts Festival, I had done many things, but had never created a festival, let alone, an international music festival.

Raising the money was a challenge, as were getting the visas, booking the plane tickets, contracting with soloists, finding housing, meals and transportation for the musicians and their instruments, booking concert halls and rehearsal space, selling tickets, cajoling sponsors, creating posters and programs, and juggling all the what-if things that cropped up along the way.

It was a year-round fulltime job.

We didn't do it alone.

Friends in Boylan Heights, the neighborhood we called home for twenty-seven years, opened their homes and offered to house the musicians. Dozens of local restaurants, as well as some great neighborhood chefs, pitched in and fed them. Volunteers helped with putting up posters, ushering, taking tickets, and providing transportation.

It is no exaggeration to say that the festival was a massive group effort with hundreds of friends, neighbors, local businesses, and restaurants pitching in to help. Thank you to everyone. And a special thanks to Rachel McKay, who was my Emily in the festival. She built websites, designed programs and advertising materials, sold tickets, organized volunteers, kept tabs on the schedule and managed everything with a calm and competence that amazed me.

The festival was more work than I ever dreamed it would be when I first said yes, I'd help.

It was a labor of love. An amazing act of community and kindness. A gift of music everyone who attended the concerts still talks about and I will never forget.

And now, I need to thank one very special person who was there from the first concert to the last and who gave so much not only to the festival, but to the Boylan Heights Neighborhood where she lived with her family, grew a beautiful garden, raised her four children, and pitched in to help whenever help was needed.

She was my friend, my co-conspirator with the Boylan Heights ArtWalk and the Cross Currents Chamber Music Arts Festival.

Elizabeth Vossenberg Dunbar
January 25, 1953- July 19, 2019